The Fake Rembrandt

Alfred Balm

THE FAKE REMBRANDT

Copyright © 2017 Alfred Balm.

All rights reserved. No part of this book may be used or reproduced by any means, graphic, electronic, or mechanical, including photocopying, recording, taping or by any information storage retrieval system without the written permission of the author except in the case of brief quotations embodied in critical articles and reviews.

This is a work of fiction. All of the characters, names, incidents, organizations, and dialogue in this novel are either the products of the author's imagination or are used fictitiously.

iUniverse books may be ordered through booksellers or by contacting:

iUniverse
1663 Liberty Drive
Bloomington, IN 47403
www.iuniverse.com
1-800-Authors (1-800-288-4677)

Because of the dynamic nature of the Internet, any web addresses or links contained in this book may have changed since publication and may no longer be valid. The views expressed in this work are solely those of the author and do not necessarily reflect the views of the publisher, and the publisher hereby disclaims any responsibility for them.

*Any people depicted in stock imagery provided by Thinkstock are models, and such images are being used for illustrative purposes only.
Certain stock imagery © Thinkstock.*

ISBN: 978-1-5320-2099-5 (sc)
ISBN: 978-1-5320-2100-8 (hc)
ISBN: 978-1-5320-2098-8 (e)

Library of Congress Control Number: 2017906784

Print information available on the last page.

iUniverse rev. date: 06/29/2017

"My special thanks go to my son Dr. Mike Balm and my friend Dr. Francis LeBlanc, for their valuable assistance and research."

For Phyllis,
Mike, and Sherri,
and for Roger

Every country has its grand canvas, Sasha—the so-called masterpiece that hangs in a hallowed hall and sums up the national identity for generations to come. For the French it is Delacroix's *Liberty Leading the People*; for the Dutch, Rembrandt's *Night Watch*; for the Americans, *Washington Crossing the Delaware*; and for the Russians? It is a pair of twins: Nikolai Ge's *Peter the Great Interrogating Alexei* and Ilya Repin's *Ivan the Terrible and His Son*.

—Amor Towles, *A Gentleman in Moscow*

1

Suzan and Bob, both resistance fighters, knelt behind the blinded window on the first floor above the haberdashery, where Abraham Rosenbaum, for more than forty years, had made a meager living but a happy life for Ethel and their five children—until the Nazi horror came too close for his liking and they left behind the country they loved and everything they owned.

With his left hand, Bob lifted just a few inches of the bottom of the black paper blind intended to prevent light from escaping from the now dark, empty room. A decree from the German occupier of Holland had forced all citizens to blind their windows to avoid guiding the Allied bombers on their way to Germany. The gap Bob created provided just enough space for Suzan to point her binoculars toward the front of the large villa across the road. Nothing yet.

The room in the empty building was bone-chilling cold. Some windows were broken, the doors smashed in, the furniture stolen, and the walls desecrated with "Jude Schwein" (Jew pig) and a Star of David. The place stank of stale air, dust, urine, and excrement.

It was a moonless night, and what little light penetrated the November clouds reflected silvery white from a thin layer of fresh snow on the cobblestone road between the apartment and the villa across from it. Trees, once lining both sides of the street, had been cut down to provide a free field of fire for the two flak towers' antiaircraft guns, which pointed in four directions, leaving behind the tree stumps as remnants of what used to be lush parasols for prewar springtime strollers.

Suzan was a slender and pretty woman in her midtwenties. She wore her auburn hair tucked under a wool knitted cap and donned dark stockings and a dark blue coat. She held a BA in languages and a black belt in karate. Bob was her senior by some twelve years, tall and not handsome but with a charming smile, perfect white teeth. He wore a black coverall over warm Manchester trousers and a thick wool sweater. Bob was an architect and enthusiastic sportsman, soccer player, swimmer, and skier. He competed in skating the canals in Holland. Both wore sidearms, both were shivering, and both were single.

"What time do you have?" asked Suzan.

"Five minutes to nine. Should be anytime now."

It was dark and quiet outside, which made them talk cautiously in subdued voices. Three hours after curfew, nobody was out and none of the few licensed vehicles passed by.

Then, suddenly, they heard the sound of engines and saw two

narrow triangles of light from the first car as if it were moving snow, pushing it slowly forward in the dark, followed by a second car. The cars made a right turn and stopped in front of the entrance of the villa.

"That's them, exactly nine, just like Wednesday."

The first car, an open, camouflage-colored Kübelwagen, the German equivalent of a jeep, held four soldiers, helmets on, arms at the ready. They did not move but kept their seats as if sitting at attention. The Kübelwagen made way for the second car and kept its engine running. The second car, a black 1938 Mercedes, moved forward, closer to the entrance stairs of the villa. The passenger door opened, and an officer jumped out and gallantly opened the back door. A blonde woman in a cheap fur coat disembarked, door handle in hand. The officer slightly bowed and clicked his heels. The sound reverberated in the quiet night.

"You know her?" asked Bob.

"Don't think so. Not very easy to tell from here." She adjusted her binoculars but could only see the woman's back.

Then, from the other side of the Mercedes, a second woman, resembling the first one in hair color and fur coat, appeared. Holding on to the door handle, she quickly looked over her shoulder and then walked around the car to follow the officer. Her high heels seemed to make walking risky on the slippery pavement. With stiff legs taking small steps, she took the officer's arm.

"They seem to be the same girls, the first one a bit shorter and the second one with that same wiggly walk, as if she is wearing her mother's shoes."

"I think you're right, but for now, who cares? Main thing is to find out if they run the same schedule. I bet they'll be out at eleven sharp."

The large front door of the house opened, and for a moment, four silhouettes became visible, sharply delineated against the backlight of the entrance hall. Music sounded from deep within. Wiener waltzes played on a gramophone.

Both cars disappeared in the same direction they'd come from. The engines could still be heard when the dimmed lights where long out of sight.

"Two hours, Bob. My God, I am cold!" She blew into her fists and pulled her shawl closer around her neck. She sat on the dusty wooden floor, back against the wall, knees pulled up.

"Here. Take a swig. It'll warm your inside." Bob handed her a flask that contained maybe half a glass of Genever, the Dutch gin. He moved closer to her, trying to provide some comfort. She gulped some down and then made a face. She immediately felt the effect and smiled while handing him back the last sip, which he swallowed.

"No point leaving, Suze. You never know what might happen, and as you know, moving around after curfew is damned dangerous. Here—let me put my arm around you and cover you with this side of my coat. My sweater is very thick and warm."

Getting as comfortable as possible, they prepared themselves for a long two-hour wait.

In front of the villa, on the left side of the entrance stairs, hardly visible in the darkness was a guard post. A soldier walked with shouldered rifle from left to right and back again, stamping his nailed boots to keep his feet from freezing, steam clouds escaping his nose or mouth with every exhalation.

"Suzy, wake up!"

The sound of engines signified the return of the cars.

"My God, I actually fell asleep. What time is it?"

"Eight minutes to eleven. Keep your eyes on the door."

At eleven o'clock sharp, the door opened, and the two women stepped down the front stairs, followed by the officer, who took the salute of the guard. Within minutes, the cars turned and disappeared in the distance.

"That's it then, Suzy. Wednesday or Friday night between nine and eleven, we'll have about two hours."

"Okay, let's go. See you tomorrow at the debriefing."

First, Suzan left the apartment, and then Bob followed five minutes later. They went down to the empty shop, where both bicycles were kept, and left through the back door, in opposite directions.

The villa, now occupied by the Germans, had been built around the turn of the century by the local owner of the beer brewery.

With twelve rooms, a theater and ballroom, a large office and a second smaller one, a dining room, and a breakfast room, as well as staff accommodations, it fell immediately into the hands of the German commander Oberst von Gruenfeld. As a Prussian school colonel, he despised the SS fanatics attached to his command but had to live with their interference and tolerate their cruelty to the population and contempt toward his soldiers. The beer baron and his family had left for England. The colonel complained in vain several times to Seyss-Inquart, the German national commander in charge of the occupied Netherlands. Excessive SS cruelty to the local population was, in the colonel's opinion, counterproductive to his efforts to bring Holland within the realm of the great German empire, a mission he believed in. Before the war, von Gruenfeld would enjoy summer trips with his family to the Dutch North Sea coast and its sandy beaches. He had hoped that bringing Holland under the protection of the German Reich would meet with little resistance; after all, were they not kindred souls? During the Great War, so tragically ending for Germany with the draconian Treaty of Versailles, Holland elected to remain neutral. Then, with the strength of the New Germany under Adolph Hitler becoming evident during the late 1930s, the "broken gun" movement in Holland aimed to stay out of the conflict again.

As a strategist, von Gruenfeld agreed with the high command that to conquer France and England, Holland was needed as a base to operate from. The mistake made at the start of the Great War, to attack France through Belgium, the so-called Schlieffen

Plan, would not be repeated. Hitler decided to ignore Holland's neutrality and invaded on May 10, 1940, a strategic move that von Gruenfeld understood. What surprised him—and for that matter, General Kurt Student, commander of the Luftlandekorps, the airborne division—was the fierce resistance the small nation put up. Although it only lasted five days, no less than 50 percent of the available transport planes manned by flight instructors were shot down.

Large numbers of German officers and men lost their lives. Field Marshal Hermann Göring, the fighter pilot ace of the Great War, in charge of the German Luftwaffe, was livid and sent two hundred planes to bombard the city of Rotterdam. It annihilated the entire old center. Von Gruenfeld knew that the heavy losses, kept officially under wraps, would impact the future of German warfare and that Hitler had already emphasized the use of panzer tanks as the backbone of his Blitzkrieg, with the air force in a supporting role.

The destruction of Rotterdam would be a huge barrier in his efforts to win sympathy for a German Europa.

On the south end of Amsterdam, two blocks from the River Amstel was the municipal swimming pool, which authorities were forced to keep open during summer to accommodate the occupying troops. During winter, workers did only basic maintenance to keep the system from freezing and pipes from bursting. Under the Olympic-sized pool was a cellar housing equipment and machinery. The cellar was accessible from both sides. At one end, an underground tunnel connected it to the engine room. The back of the engine room faced an unkept public garden. In the back wall was a window big enough to let a man escape. In this cellar, the local resistance group, under the command of "Roger," a neurosurgeon with five years of military service under his belt, met whenever it was deemed important. At both entrances, a man carrying a Sten MK II gun kept his eyes on the area adjacent to the pool complex. It was 7:45 p.m.

"Each Wednesday and Friday evening, between exactly nine and exactly eleven," Bob answered the question Roger had just asked. "We would have at least an hour and a half. That should be enough."

In the center of the cellar stood a rough wooden table with benches on both sides. A naked light bulb protruding from the low concrete ceiling threw a yellow circle on the blueprints Roger had spread out. Bob and Suzan sat on one side of the table with Roger opposite them. Behind them were half a dozen men of different ages, most of them young, each carrying a weapon of some sort.

"Let's have a look at the surroundings first," said Roger. He unfolded a third drawing, a copy of the city plan with details of the section that included the villa.

His index finger pointed to a small square representing the building.

"There is a large garden behind it and a wide row of shrubs just in front of the back fence. That gives you roughly a soccer-field length of lawn to cross. What if there is a sentry posted behind the building?"

"There is a gravel pathway along the fence in the back. Other than at that meadow, we have not seen any sentries behind the building both days when we checked around before dark," Suzan responded. "We should not have a problem passing and entering through the coal cellar."

"It snowed a bit last Friday. Would it not be all too easy to follow the footsteps after you have done the job and left over the fence?"

"We thought of that," said Bob. "There is nothing prohibiting people from walking or cycling on the pathway. For the night we choose, if it snows, many people will walk around during the day in all directions—we will arrange that—making it virtually impossible to follow particular footsteps."

"Hmm ... is that shed on the left side of that grassland still there?" he asked, pointing at a tiny spot.

"Yes."

"Then that is where your contact will be. The code word is 'Amstel.' They will wait until exactly 11:15 p.m. You will plan for next Friday. If something happens, I will let you know in time. Now let's have a look at the building." He spread out the blueprints, one of each floor and one showing the basement. He took a few puffs from his pipe, spreading a pleasant caramel scent throughout the space, replacing for a moment the stale smell of the subterranean meeting room. "So tell me, how were you planning to enter?"

"There is a coal cellar in the back. It has a door that may be locked, but the chute is open and we'll have to just slide down. The door from the furnace room will be open. Our contact is a lady we know as Janet. She does the cooking. Janet can be trusted."

"Then what?"

"Well," answered Bob, "that depends on what the purpose of this mission is. We think we know how to pull it off. What we do not know is what you expect us to do once we're in. Kill the Oberst?"

"None of that, and, yes, let me brief you. We received a rather urgent request to obtain two SS officer caps, originals, no knockoffs."

Suzan and Bob looked at each other in surprise. "Caps? Two goddamn caps?"

"Shit, Roger. Do you realize we could be killed?"

"I know, guys, but the request came from the highest echelons. I expressed the same concern you have, but the urgency was confirmed through a coded message that Jetje from Radio Oranje in London repeated three times. It must be of great importance."

"Still, jeez ... two fucking Kraut caps."

"Look, you can withdraw, as always, from any mission when you have doubts about it, but let me know soon. I'm running out of time."

Suzan looked at Bob, slightly nodding her head.

"Okay, if it is that important, we're in. Don't worry. We'll do it."

During the same week, a similar meeting took place in Kortrijk, south of the city of Bruges, in Belgium's West Flanders. The resistance organization Witte Brigade (the White Brigade) had received through its channels an urgent request for two original SS officers' long coats. When obtained, the coats were to be taken to the city of Bergen op Zoom in Dutch Brabant, where a courier would take them over for further transport. As with the caps, the vital importance of the request was confirmed from the top, in this case through Marcel Louette himself, head of the Witte Brigade, by Paul-Henri Spaak from London.

2

In Amsterdam, across from the Lido Restaurant on the Leidse Plein, a busy entertainment square before the war, stood a narrow three-story, early eighteenth-century house, safely supported by adjacent buildings on both sides. It was occupied by van Zanten, a violinist of the chamber orchestra. On the second floor, in the cozy living room overlooking the central park, sitting in comfortable leather chairs, appearing as old as the building, were six men. They were smoking pipes and cigars, creating a smoke screen that apparently bothered no one. The three-piece suits, golden chain pocket watches, and clean shaves or trimmed moustaches suggested the meeting was of great importance. There were several other men and women sitting on dining table chairs behind them. Among the six were the president of the municipal museum, David Roell, and his assistant conservator, Willem Sandberg, as well as the director of the Rijksmuseum; the minister of education, culture, and sciences, Gerrit Bolkestein; the president emeritus of the National Bank, Leo Trip; and members of the Rembrandt Society. Behind them were a lawyer, an architect, and two ladies, one of them an art historian. Bolkestein chaired the meeting.

"Ladies, gentlemen, it is clear by now that unless we are able to protect our most precious art objects, our country will be completely robbed of our cultural heritage. As long as Rosenberg and the Katz brothers are able to purchase paintings by the hundreds from Jewish families who have no choice but to sell under duress, with Rosenberg and Katz selling them at a profit but far below value to the Germans, the beast may be satisfied. As soon as those sources dry up, our museums will be plundered."

"I have little respect for those art dealers, Minister, but are we not a bit too concerned? After all, one could hardly argue that there was no art history conscience in Germany," commented a Rembrandt Society member.

"I agree, certainly from a historic perspective; however, since the Nazis gained power, there is not only a difference in determining what art is but also how to acquire it."

Some smiled.

"Let us not forget the book burnings; works from great authors like Walter Benjamin, Bloch, Brecht, Einstein, Engels, and Freud all turned to ashes—self-destruction of a cultural heritage if ever there was one."

"What about the Entartete Kunst exhibitions," added Sandberg. "Degenerate art, according to the Nazis. My God, already in the midthirties they exhibited Chagall, Max Ernst, Kandinsky, Kirchner, Klee, Mondrian, and so many, many more as degenerate artists. By their standards, 70 to 80 percent of our municipal museum, De Stedelijk, would be burned."

"That puts you at greater risk than others, Willem," offered Trip. "What are you doing about it?"

"Rather what *did* we do about it, Mr. Trip?"

"The intentions of the Germans were no secret to me after I witnessed the horrors of the Spanish Civil War. We decided to build a huge bunker in the dunes near Castricum. We are safe for now and even accommodate several colleague museum and private collections—but safe for war damage, not robbery."

"But even this large bunker has its limitations," added Roell. "As far as I know, most collections have been transported to churches, schools, castles, and municipal buildings in the north of Holland, but that is, at best, a temporary solution."

"Not that we were completely unprepared," said Bolkestein. "Immediately after our capitulation, we took initiatives to protect our national art heritage. Castricum is in use, and soon we'll have bunkers in the dunes of Zandvoort and Heemskerk as well."

"A bit late, isn't it?" remarked Trip.

"Yes, it is, but we hoped for the neutrality of our country, as in '14 to '18. The unprovoked aggression was not part of our views of the future, regrettable but true."

"What is—" started one of them, but he was interrupted by a deafening noise, an uninterrupted, high-pitched howling, rising and falling and lasting for a few minutes. It was blaring from sirens on top of the Lido restaurant.

Then they fell silent.

A few pedestrians on the square started running. German soldiers took cover, diving into the bunkers on the corners. A lady threw her bicycle down and ran to the nearest portico for cover.

Silence ... maybe for five or ten minutes.

Then came the ear-splitting salvos from antiaircraft artillery positioned on the four corners of Vondel Park on the other side of the canal, running along the side of the restaurant. A formation of Allied bombers flew over, quite high, but the heavy engines were clearly audible. Unperturbed, they maintained formation and disappeared north in the direction of the central train station and the harbor. Another ten minutes and the sirens howled a long, high-pitched message—all clear.

The group was used to similar scares every time the formations of Lancasters and Flying Fortresses flew over on their way to bomb Germany, so the meeting continued.

"What I meant to say is, what about Rembrandt's *Night Watch*?" one of the society members wanted to know.

"That, ladies and gentlemen," the minister answered, "is why we are here today."

3

Suzan and Bob left their bicycles behind the shed at the edge of the grassy field. They were both dressed in black track suits, black sneakers, and dark balaclavas. They smeared dirt on their faces.

Both carried a sidearm strapped to their right leg and a knife on their left upper arm, haft down, ready to pull.

"Thank God, no snow," whispered Suzan, checking her watch—8:45. The tension of the moment made them forget the cold. Without snow on the ground, the night was even darker than Friday of last week. It had been a heated discussion with Roger to talk him out of sending a few men with them, supposedly for protection. Bob and Suzan both refused. If something went wrong, no number of Sten guns would be able to bail them out. If push came to shove, they would use their handguns and the advantage of surprise and then run like hell while saying a prayer. They would rather rely on their experience, working together in several risky nocturnal operations. It was probably why Roger had picked them anyway.

A horse and carriage appeared from the dark, a farmer slumped half asleep on the box, cap deep over his eyes, the reins loosely in one hand. The horse with its head bent down stepped lazily as if half asleep as well. They passed by without noticing them.

8:55.

"Be ready, Suze, anytime now."

9:00.

"Not a sound."

9:05.

9:10.

They looked at each other, raising eyebrows. *What the hell?*

9:15.

The horse and carriage came back, horse and farmer still half asleep.

"What do we do, Bob? Something is wrong. Something must have happened."

"We'll give it five more minutes; then it's a no-go."

A white balloon slowly floated to the sky on the other side of the villa as if accidentally released by a child, hardly visible in the dark evening and soon out of sight.

"That's it, the sign; let's go."

A spotter from across the villa, positioning herself earlier that night in the same building Bob and Suzan previously had was confirming that the car had arrived and the women were now inside the building. She released the balloon and quickly left.

Agile as a cat, Suzan worked herself over the fence, jumped down, and crouched behind the bushes. Bob followed.

"No sentry," he whispered. "All clear."

"I'll go first and wait behind the building in that dark area. If all is still clear, run."

Bob ran as fast as he could in a straight line and then disappeared in the shaded area behind the house. Suzan was next.

A short staircase, just a few steps down, the brick wall of the coal cellar, a steel door, and the opening of the chute—Bob indicated that he would try the steel door anyway, but as expected, it was locked, so down the chute then.

Suzan slid down, feet first, and landed on a pile of coal. *Just a few bruises*, she thought and climbed over a rough wooden partition, just before Bob landed. They listened. All was quiet. They groped their way to the door, brushing the coal dust off, and very carefully tested the door. It was unlocked. Then they stepped back.

"Let's go over the whole thing again," he whispered.

Sitting across from Roger, less than a week earlier, with the drawings of the villa between them, both Suzan and Bob memorized every detail of each floor of the building.

Roger explained, "The house was built as a large rectangle, a cellar, two floors, and an attic with a square extension at the back, containing the coal cellar, the wine cellar, the kitchen, pantry, laundry, and rumpus room. The front entrance is in the center, with double doors and a large entrance hall with a wardrobe and washrooms. A second set of double doors gives access to a wide corridor. In the center against the back are two staircases, meeting at half level against a landing from which a wide staircase continues to the second floor. On the ground floor are two offices, a large one and a smaller one; a dayroom next to the kitchen for the staff; broom closets under the stairs; a breakfast room; a dining room; a large ballroom; a library; a cigar room; and a sitting room.

"On the second floor are the guest rooms—five on either side—bathrooms, four closets, a second cloakroom, a reading room, a guest sitting room, and two large linen closets. The attic contains sleeping quarters for the staff as well as a storage area. Corridors, stairs, and rooms are thickly carpeted.

"On the right side of the villa, separated from it, stands a four-car garage.

"The owner of the villa, a big man, was an avid art collector and favored monumental art objects and large antique furniture. In the center of the wide corridor, on the left and on the right stand large oak tables covered with Persian rugs. Seventeenth-century Dutch armoires line the walls. Between them are large golden-framed naturalistic oil paintings and Delft blue vases on pedestals.

"The centerpiece is a life-size copy of Rodin's *Burghers of Calais*. Positioned in the middle of the hall, stairs on either side, it is the first thing a visitor notices, a group of six dark bronze figures."

The details, of great importance to Suzan and Bob, were available because of an excellent job done by the woman cooking and cleaning the house for the German squatters.

4

"First this, Suzan, the information provided by the housekeeper, was as seen from the front of the house, so what she mentioned as the right side is our left; seems obvious, but in the tension of the moment, we could make a fatal mistake."

"Agreed."

"I assume that we have little to do on the ground floor, other than getting unseen to the second."

"Let's hope so. I know she said the SS men are on the left side on the second floor and usually take their coats and caps upstairs, but who knows?"

"I'll go first so you keep an eye on me, and if necessary, be ready to shoot. In the panic of the moment, I'll run like hell. Cover me until I catch up with you."

"Okay, head for the kitchen, not the coal cellar. There is a door from the kitchen to the back yard, and it is unlocked. I'll be behind you and keep you in my sight anywhere in the house."

"I know, and thank God for the darkening ordinance. It may

not be what the Germans had in mind, but it sure helps us tonight getting to the fence unseen."

"Check your gun."

"Done."

He hugged Suzan for a brief moment. "Go, girl."

She opened the door just a small gap and listened. Hearing just the faint sound of music from somewhere, she opened the door a bit wider. Nothing. She carefully entered the sparsely lit corridor and began working her way stealthily toward the stairs, back against the wall.

Somewhere in the building, a door slammed shut. It startled her. It felt like an explosion.

Bob moved to a position next to the kitchen entrance, from where he could keep her in sight. She was on the stairs now. He moved to the broom closets on the side of the left stairs.

Fast, with sinuous grace, every nerve in her body tense, Suzan stepped onto the second floor after a quick check if anyone was there. Nobody. They were probably all in the ballroom where the entertainment seemed to be taking place.

Suzan knew that the five rooms on her left side were assigned to SS officers.

The highest rank, an *ObersturmbahnFührer*, a lieutenant colonel, had the room at the far end. Then there were two lieutenants and two sergeants. She would go for the highest rank first.

With no indication that anyone was upstairs, she walked

quickly to the room at the end. Her heart skipped a beat when, gun at the ready, she opened the door. *Thank God, empty.* She quickly closed the door behind her. Bob found a good hiding spot in the cloakroom across from the rooms.

Suzan found the cap on a dresser in the walk-in closet—black with two silver cords, an eagle, and the feared skull-and-bones insignia. She put it under her tracksuit jacket. She carefully opened the door—nothing in the corridor—and then moved to the next room. No cap. And no caps in any of the other rooms either. She panicked.

Walking back to the stairs, ready to shoot and run at an instant, she passed the cloakroom.

"Suze, here," whispered Bob.

She almost screamed.

"Just one cap. What now?"

"Easy, let's think. The Krauts are at the party in the ballroom, so their coats and caps must be somewhere. There is nothing in the cloakroom here."

"There is a large wardrobe downstairs in the hallway across from the stairs behind the double doors. Maybe there?"

"Jeez, so close to the ballroom. What if they—"

"I'll go this time, Suze. You cover me."

"No, I'll go. You watch me from the kitchen. If I find something, I'll join you in a sec. If something's wrong, I'm closer to the escape route anyway. Just don't shoot me."

Bob and then Suzan sneaked down, pussyfooting on the stairs, and went to the kitchen. They quietly opened the door and then closed it except for a tiny crack.

"You may hear something outside when the guard walks his round."

"I know. Stay awake."

On her toes, she walked to the hallway, passed the bronzes in front of the stairs, and opened the right wing of the double doors inch by inch, praying it would not creak. She had handed the first cap to Bob, who, through the crack on the hinge side of the kitchen door, followed her every move, his heart beating almost audibly. There were several long coats and two leather coats in the wardrobe and on a rack above the rail, a hat and three caps. She took one and hid it like the first cap under her jacket.

She was tiptoeing toward the kitchen when suddenly, while she was just beside the bronze statues, the front door opened.

Three officers in gray uniforms entered, talking amicably, a bit drunk.

The guttural voices sounded extra loud in the wide corridor.

Laughing about something one of them had said, they walked in the direction of the ballroom, without noticing that Rodin's *Burghers of Calais* mysteriously consisted of seven instead of six statues, one of them frozen stiff but with a heart beating in her throat, feeling a cold shiver running her spine and an embarrassing arousal taking hold of her body. Subdued total panic. She waited until the ballroom door closed and then ran.

Bob put his gun back in its holster.

They left through the kitchen back door, walked maybe twenty paces, and then ran to the cover of the shrubs and worked themselves over the back fence.

There was nobody behind the shed.

"What the hell? There should be a courier here. We needed less than fifty minutes."

The horse and half-sleeping farmer appeared again, seemingly unaware of their presence but holding his horse in front of them. He appeared suddenly to be wide awake, looking straight at them. Clearly audible, he whispered, "Amstel."

Without a word, they handed him the two caps, which quickly disappeared into the box. The farmer retook his seat and resumed his nap as the horse continued in a slow gait.

5

"Coffee, ladies, gentlemen?"

After politely knocking on the door of his own living room, van Zanten carried a tray with cups and a large steaming coffeepot in and put it on the table at the center of the group. "I am sorry that the only thing I have is this surrogate substitute, but there is still some milk and my own beet sugar." Van Zanten was the kind of a man who would immediately disappear unseen in a crowd. He was of medium height with thinning gray hair encircling the back of his skull and the sickly complexion of a 130-pound body too seldom exposed to the sun. His tie was too old and his collar two sizes too large, and his suit draped around too thin a carcass. But his twinkling eyes and spontaneous smile mirrored his warm heart. He could be fifty or seventy and hated the German occupation with the passion of a twenty-five-year-old man.

"Oh well, very kind of you, van Zanten. That is just fine and thank you," said Roell appreciatively.

They sipped the hot coffee in silence, curious about what the minister would have to tell them.

"Gentlemen, soon we will be joined by Professor Henri Breemer, whom you all know as the most eminent Rembrandt connoisseur our country has." He took a golden pocket watch from his vest, looked at it, and raised his eyebrows. "I assume that the air raid sirens delayed him. Anyway, this is what we will discuss."

"When it became apparent to our government that Europe's art may not be safe from either Nazi looting or destruction, we discussed, of course, as one of the many national treasures we possess, Rembrandt's *Night Watch*, unquestionably our most precious and, as you will all agree, an invaluable painting." All agreed.

"Of course," interrupted Trip. "But one painting? I mean, even this one, should we not concern ourselves with all? I mean, what is to happen with the thousands of paintings, sculptures, everything in our museums and not to forget, private collections?"

"We'll get to that, and yes, that has our attention as well, but we have well-informed reasons to believe that masterpieces from all over Europe will be looted, destroyed when the Nazis consider it degenerate art, or added to Hitler's collection, and Rembrandt's *Night Watch* may be one of the first victims."

"And Professor Breemer is going to make it disappear?" asked Trip again, not without sarcasm, but his old friend knew him well and took no offense.

The Fake Rembrandt

A thick, black smoke bilging locomotive turned on the brakes, and the train came screeching to a halt in the middle of the stretch between Haarlem and Amsterdam. The first-class carriage was occupied by an elderly looking gentleman, distinguished in spite of his worn suit and overcoat, and a woman in her thirties and apparently at ease among the other passengers, all German officers. Sirens could be heard now that the train had stopped, and the officers hurried out to check the sky. Minutes later, heavy bombardments followed, far enough ahead in the direction of the harbor, but it could become a big problem if the station or the rails in front of them were targeted. *Not only that*, thought Professor Breemer, *a stationary train is a sitting duck and an easy target for the Spitfires escorting the heavy Flying Fortresses.* He was relieved when the all-clear siren sounded and the officers climbed on board again. Blowing black clouds of smoke, the locomotive started again, pulling the long chain of wagons slowly back to a safe thirty miles per hour. The central station of Amsterdam was almost empty. On platform 2, a freight train was waiting, loaded with military equipment. Other than that, the large station was unusually quiet.

Professor Breemer disembarked. His hope that a taxi would be waiting was soon shattered, so he started the long walk down the Rokin and the Leidse Straat to the address he had received. Many of the luxurious goods prewar Amsterdam would have had plenty of were no longer to be found. Defaced, emptied, and destroyed Jewish stores, like missing teeth from an otherwise perfect set, contrasted with the rich facades of their neighbors. He reached the square, passed the Stadsschouwburg, the city theater, where *Ins Weiszen Roessell* played, and crossed across from the American Hotel, now accommodating German troops. He avoided the NSB young man collecting for Winterhulp Nederland. NSB, the collaborating National Socialist Movement, were despised and feared by many for their treacherous actions. Breemer turned a left corner and pulled the brass bell of the charming typical Dutch house.

"Gentlemen, may I introduce Professor Breemer."

All stood up and shook hands with the elderly, rather frail professor. They were surprised by his firm handshake.

"Please sit down, Professor, and let me tell you that we are extremely honored and pleased that you were so kind as to join us today. It must have been quite an undertaking."

"Thank you, Your Excellency, and indeed traveling is not what it used to be. I pride myself on arriving on time for whatever appointment; however, the bombing raids on the harbor delayed the train, and there was not a single taxi to be seen. However, here I am, and what pleasure to join such illustrious company."

6

Obersturmbahnführer Richthoff was livid.

"Of course not, Heinrich. I never, ever put my uniform, coat, and cap anywhere else. If my cap is not there, then somebody took it."

"Somebody, Obersturmbahnführer?"

"Of course, somebody from outside, I assume. Two caps don't disappear overnight without, I am afraid, a damn good reason."

"Did you check with the workers here?"

"Nobody was on staff last night, Obersturmbahnführer, and the sentry did not see anything unusual. The two women never left our sight, as is your policy."

"Check all doors and windows. Check around the periphery. If someone had access to our rooms and took our uniforms, or parts of them, we have a problem. And give that sentry a good shake-up. If the asshole slept, I want to know."

Two men, in order not to miss the smallest detail and to avoid the possible assumption that one of them might be involved, checked the entire building while two others scoured the periphery.

"From the coal cellar, Obersturmbahnführer Richthoff, we found small traces of coal dust coming from the cellar toward the stairs. The door was unlocked."

"Unlocked?"

"Definitely, Obersturmbahnführer."

It did not take long before it was obvious how the intruders were able to enter the building and could have had access to the bedrooms while a party in the ballroom was going on.

"Donnerwetter!" (damn it) cursed the Oberst, with a puffed-up face as red as a cooked lobster. "Interrogate every single staff member. Don't spare anyone, and don't let off until I know which one to kill with my own hands."

The twelve members of the staff—three from the kitchen, five housekeepers, and several valets—were lined up in the ballroom against the wall. They were kept standing for over an hour, not knowing the reason for this unusual behavior but increasingly worried and scared the longer they were forced to wait, without being allowed to say a word.

The Oberst walked in, accompanied by two officers.

Looking as if he had just swallowed a porcupine, hands behind his back, in full uniform of riding breeches and boots without cap, he looked different, less impressive but scarier. The staff was terrified.

He walked slowly in front of the line as if inspecting troops.

He turned back, walked the line again, and stopped in front of a young kitchen helper, next to the lady so well connected to the resistance. The boy was terrified and looked down, afraid to meet Richthof's eyes. From where he stood, the German did not move but shifted his gaze to the person next to the boy and noticed her trembling hands. Then he continued to the next one and the next one. Suddenly, he turned around, marched to the spot in front of the woman.

"That one, *raus*!" (out) he shouted, and immediately four strong arms grabbed her and walked her to the exit door.

"To the police quarters. Schnell! Quick! I will be doing the interrogation myself."

One of the few victories over the SS brutes he had to accept in his quarters was that von Gruenfeld, the soldier, forbade any use of the rooms in his building as interrogation cells. It had been a fight that played out at the highest level, but von Gruenfeld's excellent career in the end settled the issue. It dismayed the SS. A local police station was now the place from where they operated, known and feared by the local population as the "slaughterhouse."

In one of the cells, not much bigger than a walk-in closet, with a wooden bunk but no mattress or pillow, a bucket in the corner, and sparse light from a tiny hole high in the wall, Janet was on her knees, praying her heart out. "Lord, give me the strength I need. I am not a hero. Help me to be strong!" she cried.

Why this unbearable waiting? Why did they throw her in this pigsty and then seemingly just forget about her, no food, no water even, and this humiliating stinking pail in the corner? It must have been the third day now. She felt weak, exhausted, dried out, and extremely hungry.

The cell door opened.

"Meekomen" (come).

She followed the policeman, her own countryman for Christ's sake, shunning the light that her red eyes had to adjust to, and was placed in a small office on a chair facing an empty desk.

Then Obersturmbahnführer Richthoff entered.

Sitting down behind the desk, he took a silver cigarette case from his inner pocket and leaned back, all the time observing her. He retrieved a cigarette, closed the case, and tap-tap-tapped his cigarette on it before putting one end between puffy lips. He lit it, deeply inhaled, and then blew the smoke from wide-open nostrils.

Like a mad bull, she thought.

Then he smiled at her like a tiger about to bite into the neck of its prey.

"Aber Fräulein Janet, this is not the way we like to express appreciation for the good work you have done and are still doing for us. Can I get you some tea or coffee? We have some real good coffee, you know. Water maybe?"

"No, thank you. Why am I here?"

"Well, let us say that it was necessary for a few days to allow us to confirm a suspicion we have had for some time."

His smile was gone now.

"Suspicion?"

"Jawohl, yes, exactly. We received several warnings that our Dutch staff had been infiltrated by a group of criminals calling themselves resistance fighters. Cowards, really, that don't do their country a favor and who do not understand how useless their criminal acts are."

"And what has that to do with me? Do I look like a criminal?"

"More like an informer, Frau Janet, a collaborator who opens doors so criminals can enter at night."

"Ridiculous." But her answer did not sound very convincing. She was so tired, so thirsty. Her mouth felt like leather. She had no spittle to wet her tongue, and she wanted to sleep.

"I don't have the slightest interest in you. All I want is the names of those who sent you, and then you can go home." The lie came easily.

Janet said nothing.

Suddenly, from behind her, a man's fist hit her and then delivered another blow and another. She fell to the floor, half conscious, bleeding from her ear and nose, vomiting from an empty stomach. She pulled her knees up against the pulsating gastric pains and then thankfully nothing.

She awoke, lying on the wooden bunk in the same cell, dried blood all over her face, her dress sticking to her painful body; she had wetted herself.

7

At her next interrogation, after Janet had been hardly able to walk, following the policeman, there was no chair in front of the desk this time, she had to remain standing. The niceties were gone. *Just as well*, thought Janet, trying to steady herself.

Richthoff shoved a pencil and paper toward her.

"Names."

Janet did not move.

Something hard hit her in the side. It felt like her kidney had been crushed. She fell.

"Stand up."

First on her hands and knees and then slowly standing up, leaning against the excruciating pain in her side, she straightened, looking Richthof straight in the eyes.

"Names."

She prepared for the next blow, but nothing happened, and then suddenly it did.

She screamed and then fell to the floor when her other kidney was hit. She bit her tongue, and blood filled her dry mouth. She did not faint.

Like a shepherd would carry a lamb over his shoulders, the policeman brought her back to her cell. She fell on her knees beside the bunk and sobbed.

It must have been late at night—she could tell day and night by the light from that small hole high up in the wall—when someone tapped against the bars of her cell. *Please, God*, she thought, *not another interrogation*. Her insides still hurt like hell.

"Pssst," the policeman she feared whispered. "Here, have some water. Not too much though. Your body won't take it."

Not sure if she could trust him, she worked herself toward the bars and gulped the cool water from a flask he held out.

"Thanks," she whispered. "But why?"

"Things are not always the way it looks. I need to be careful. Try to sleep."

He was gone.

Janet wondered if water could heal pain. She felt better but had noticed blood when she urinated. She was afraid that her kidneys were badly damaged.

When she woke up the next morning, after only a few hours of sleep, she found a thick slice of bread next to her head, and she devoured it like a hungry wolf would his kill.

At midday, she was brought to that terrible office and its barbarians again.

This time, however, there were no questions—only one short sentence, but it hurt her more than any physical torture.

"Frau Janet, since you have decided to remain silent, you will be shot within forty-eight hours."

She was lying on her back, staring at the low ceiling, not able to cry, not able to pray, those awful words echoing repeatedly in her brain, "You will be shot. You will be shot."

Not able to sleep, she thought about her life, her parents when she was a child, her wedding to Ernst Jan, the children, her school, her friends, and her younger brother. As in a camera obscura, pictures appeared and disappeared but in no logical order, jumping from memory to moment.

"Pssst."

She looked at the policeman, who apparently waited for the dark to visit her. *My last meal?* she thought. *He can keep it!*

Then he turned a heavy key in the lock and opened her cell door. She froze. *Please, God*, she prayed. *Not that ...*

"Janet, listen, I am here to help you. I have a job to do here, and Roger briefed me. Are you strong enough to hit me? I mean, hit me *really hard*?"

Janet was flabbergasted. "Hit you? But why, for Pete's sake?"

"It's the only way you get out of here alive and I won't be executed. If you walk to the right and then at the end to the left, you'll see a steel door; it is unlocked. A bicycle is parked outside against the wall. Get the hell out of here. Go underground until it is safe to contact Roger. Be careful. Now, hit me!"

She slapped his face.

"Not like that. Come on; I can take it. Our lives depend on it. Pretend I am Richthoff."

Like a hellcat, she jumped at him. Gone were her pains. With tears flowing, she beat his face, scratched his skin, bit him, and punched his nose with both fists. Then she kicked him and kicked him until he fell on the bunk, blood flowing from his nose and swollen lips.

She ran through the corridor, found the door, and jumped on the bicycle. With every turn of the pedals, pain shot through her body, but faster she went, faster, away from that horrible place. "I'm alive!" she wanted to scream. "I'm alive!" Tears wet her face.

8

Janet knew Amsterdam well, so she had no difficulty finding her way through the narrow streets. Sometimes she would cycle or walk her bike behind the houses, careful not to hit anything she could not detect in time. It was pitch-dark. Reaching the Amstel River, she stopped for a moment, hiding under tall oak trees and giving her aching body a rest—but not for long.

About three miles down the river was a small village, Ouderkerk, with a centuries-old Portuguese-Jewish cemetery. Behind it was a small farmhouse with dilapidated stables and a chicken coop. She put her bike against a fencepost and walked around the house to the side, where she knocked three times, waited, knocked two times, and waited. The upper half of the Dutch door opened, and the sleepy, unshaven face of a farmer appeared, looking her over with suspicion.

"Sunflower," whispered Janet.

The entire door opened, and the farmer stepped aside. "Come in, honey! Come in!" He quickly closed the door behind her.

The room was warm and cozy, sparsely lit by copper oil lamps in the corner, which reflected a wood fire burning in the fireplace. A black kettle extended from a chain. The delicious smell of pea soup brought saliva to Janet's dry mouth. A roughly hewn oak door opened, and the corpulent farmer's wife entered, holding a burning candle. Like in a classic painting, she wore a white lace bonnet. Holding the candle high so as to better view the damage done to the pretty face of the late visitor, she exclaimed, "Oh my God, dear child! What happened to you? Please, please sit down. Let me wipe your face and get you a bandage. Krelis, get that chair and put a pillow behind her back. Are you badly hurt, my child?"

Tears welled up in Janet's eyes. She wanted to tell them, wanted to thank them, but no words came out, only sobs, heartbreaking sobs that started somewhere deep in her painful belly and worked their way up to her throat.

"It's okay, honey. It's okay. Don't talk now. Here, drink some water and let me get you some warm soup. You look like you haven't eaten for weeks. You'll feel better soon. Aunt Berta will take care of you." Janet knew very well that Berta was not her aunt, but the care was welcome.

The thick arm of the voluptuous woman around her shoulders felt like a warm blanket. She drank the hot pea soup from a deep bowl, holding it in trembling hands, warmth finding its way to her empty stomach. Wisely, she did not drink too much of it.

"Come, let me take you to bed. You need sleep more than

anything now. I will get you a clean nightgown. It will be too big, but those clothes of yours need a washing badly."

She walked Janet to a low bedroom. The box bed was more like a wall closet. It had two wooden doors with little hearts cut out, but it had a thick mattress that smelled of fresh hay. On the plank wall inside was a small crucifix. In the corner of the room stood a piece of furniture resembling a low writing desk. On it was a large ceramic bowl, an antique washbasin, and a large jug, all decorated with brownish flowers. On both sides of the stand were thin towels. The farmer's wife lit a candle and put it on a low table between two slightly damaged chairs, the seats and backs of which were covered with hand-embroidered animal figures.

"Let me get you some warm water, dear."

Janet was thankful for a woman understanding another woman and her need to get rid of the filth, physically and mentally. She undressed, dropping her soiled clothes on the antique clay-tile floor. She was shocked, seeing the large purple bruises on both sides of her body. She touched her face to find the damage done there, reading it with her fingertips, like Braille.

"Oh my God! Oh sweet Jesus! What have they done to you?" sobbed Aunt Berta, almost dropping the ceramic jug with hot water. Then she quickly emptied it into the large bowl. She returned moments later with cold water, mixed the two, and then tested the temperature with her elbow, like she would be bathing a baby.

The Fake Rembrandt

"Thank you! Oh thank you so much!" there was no feeling of embarrassment to stand naked in front of a stranger.

Spreading a blanket on top of the mattress, Aunt Berta told her to lie down, which she did without protesting. With tender care, she washed Janet, first just with lukewarm water and then with a brownish soft soap that smelled strange but made her feel good. After the woman toweled her dry, extra careful around the large bruises, she massaged the sore spots with a jelly. It turned out that it was udder cream, used on her dairy cows, but it worked. She tiptoed out of the room after closing both doors of the bed closet.

Janet tried to stretch out, but the bed, *bedstee* as the Dutch called it, was rather short. Ancient superstition was that to lie flat on a bed would make you die and closing the bed's side doors would keep bad spirits out. She curled up, pulled the blanket over her shoulders, and fell immediately into a deep sleep. She woke up the farmers, screaming her nightmare in the middle of the night. Aunt Bertha opened the doors and handed her a cup of warm milk.

"Hush, baby, hush, you are safe now. It is all over. Sleep, my dear." She softly closed the door behind her.

9

The policeman who had so heroically saved Janet's life was Derk De Vlaander, better known by his resistance name as Hopman. He was an important member of the resistance group West. As a police officer, he was in a position to obtain important information whenever the SS picked up people, which he then passed on to the resistance—not that the SS trusted the Dutch police blindly. Many colleagues eagerly served the monster, pocketing without remorse the bonus every time they arrested a man or woman from the resistance or brought in a betrayed Jew. It gave Hopman enough room to be very valuable to Roger.

There were strict instructions, though, never to directly interfere in order not to blow a good disguise and endanger a whole organization. Hopman strictly lived by that rule. Until Janet.

He just could not witness the suffering of that brave young woman any longer, knowing that no bullet would be wasted on her but that she would be tortured to death.

Now he stood in front of Richthoff, acting with great talent as if he were hiding the damage a woman did to him but in fact exaggerating the results.

Richthoff showed a humiliating smile when observing how this Dutch policeman was roughed up by a woman, one they had worked on quite a bit already. He did not care much; he was done with her anyway, and she would have been destroyed the next day.

"Tell me."

"I was doing my round, Obersturmbahnführer, and noticed that she was lying on the floor, not on the bunk. She seemed to be dead. Knowing her execution was to be the next morning, I thought maybe she is just unconscious. I went to get a bucket of cold water, opened the cell, and checked if there was still life in that slut.

"Then, suddenly, she jumped up, I was still kneeling to check her out. She kicked me in my face several times in extremely quick succession. She must have been trained. I tried to get up, defend myself, or kill the bitch, and then she swung at me with the bucket. I think she broke my nose. I haven't been able to see a doctor yet."

"Then what?"

"I don't know, Obersturmbahnführer Richthoff. I passed out. I don't know how long. As soon as I was able, I pushed the alarm button, but by then, she was gone."

What an asshole, thought Richthoff, but arresting her had been right. It must have been that whore helping those criminals, and of course, she was trained to fight when necessary.

"You really love that bitch, don't you, De Vlaander?"

"I am deeply ashamed, Obersturmbahnführer, and I can only hope that when she is found, I may have my time with her, maybe in that same cell, and then cut her throat."

"I have a better idea, Hercules. You go find her. What to do with her is in perfect hands with my men, but I promise you may watch. Now go see a doctor."

———

Roger listened with surgical attention to Hopman's detailed clinical report on what happened with Janet. Four men, their weapons at the ready, covered the entrance and the exit.

"We may have a problem now, buddy, but I can't blame you. In fact, I might have done the same, but she really did a job on you, man. You look terrific."

"I know. It looks worse than yesterday. I am off duty for the rest of the week. I'll see a doctor tomorrow, but there is no serious damage. I'll be all right. Is Janet safe?"

"Yes, for the time being, she is, but they will be looking for her, Hopman. That bothers me."

"Well, as long as 'they' is just me, I don't share your concern. How much does Janet know? If she breaks under torture, do we stand to lose a lot?"

"Yes, way too much," said Roger, without giving further details.

"I may have a solution," answered Hopman. "Can I talk to you in private?"

10

After Roger sent the four men out of earshot, he filled his pipe with curly tobacco from a worn leather pouch and lit it while taking small puffs until the fire took hold, replacing stale air again with the sweet scent of caramel.

"The thing is ..." Hopman started to explain his plan, talking in a subdued voice as if someone could still overhear the discussion. "The thing is that Richthoff, his cronies, and everyone else at the station are convinced that I hate the girl's guts. I did my damnedest to convince them."

Roger remained silent, puffing his pipe like it replaced breathing.

"That is the reason why Richthoff told me to find her. He was convinced that I would be on her tail like a bloodhound."

"I agree."

"What we need is a high enough contact in the Elizabeth Gasthuis, the central hospital, someone who is on our side. Do you think that is possible?"

"Probably," answered Roger, holding back until Hopman revealed his plan.

"I would be looking for a recently deceased young woman in size resembling Janet, about 165 to 170 centimeters tall, preferably dark blonde, one without family to mourn her passing."

"Seems difficult but may not be impossible." Roger had an inkling where this was going.

"I assume you will be able to get ahold of the outfit she was wearing when thrown in the cell—I mean all of it, shoes, dress, stockings, even undies?"

"Yes."

"Good. As soon as a suitable corpse can be located and assuming we can transport it to a safe place, we'll dress her in Janet's clothes, and then her face needs to be made unrecognizable, as if the damage were inflicted in a rage by somebody hating her enough." He paused for a moment; the mental picture was not very attractive.

"That is exactly what those animals expect me to do, given what she did to my face."

His still-swollen lips, the scratches, and the half-closed black eye supported his point.

Roger did not say a word; he looked at the pipe in his hand, now resting on the table, as if a genie might appear from it and provide him with an answer.

"Then what? I assume they don't take it lightly when a

policeman decides to murder the person he arrests instead of bringing her in for questioning."

"Normally, yes, but in this case, a cop being attacked and badly damaged by a girl, losing face with his colleagues, the girl already sentenced to death ... They would understand my fury, and I am convinced I can get away with it."

"It is still very risky. If they see through it, it will cost you your life, and it could jeopardize our organization."

"Right, but think of it this way: I will have revenged myself in the eyes of those animals, I can continue my job, and Janet is off the hook. She very much deserves that."

It was all Roger needed to hear.

"All right. Then here's what I'll do. I know a few colleagues I used to work with, and one of them, I'd trust with my life. I will contact him. But as you know, it is a strange request, and nobody knows how long it will take before a suitable body is available—not that people don't lose their lives in these terrible times."

11

There was a familiar knock on the Dutch door. Aunt Bertha opened the upper wing and smiled at the open face of a young girl, carrying an egg basket on her arm, its contents covered with a tea towel. "Hello, sweetheart. Would you like to buy some eggs?"

"No, ma'am, only a sunflower," replied the child.

Aunt Bertha hesitated for a moment. "Come in, darling."

The little Dutch girl left her clogs at the door and followed on thick knitted socks. Once inside, she handed over her basket. In it, Aunt Bertha discovered a complete set of clean clothes—a dress, stockings, shoes, and underwear. Between the neatly folded dress was a typed note that read, "This is in exchange for the soiled clothes. Please put them unwashed or cleaned, repeat unwashed or cleaned, in the basket, all of them." The note was signed R.

Bertha understood.

The Fake Rembrandt

Doctor Mertens went to the morgue after receiving a message that his opinion was needed. He put a scarf around his neck. He hated the cold and smell of the place. On the dissection slab, he found the naked body of a young woman, probably twenty-five to thirty-five, who could have died from malnourishment were it not for the obvious signs of a bad beating and strangulation. The information chart gave few details other than that she was a prostitute without known family, killed by some pervert.

Poor child, thought Doctor Mertens. It happened too often.

Back in his office, he made a phone call. Realizing that every call could be overheard, his message was short: "Found her."

"How did you find her?" asked the SS officer, when De Vlaander reported to the lieutenant on duty that the escaped women who attacked him had been found.

"A tip-off from an NSB informer, Herr Lieutenant. She was seen in a Catholic church in Amstelveen, just outside the city, and later in a park adjacent to it, next to a Dutch mill. I waited for her behind cover, and she appeared exactly the way she escaped, same clothes, easy to recognize.

"I sneaked up on her, but she saw me and she panicked and started to run. I tackled her and worked her on her back, and then something came over me. I hit her and hit her. I wanted to destroy that hated face until she did not move anymore."

"You killed her?"

"I am afraid yes, Herr Lieutenant."

"Where is she now?"

"Under a canvas in a pushcart behind the station, Herr Lieutenant."

"Show me."

The SS officer marched out of the building to the paved area behind it, walked straight to the pushcart, and pulled the tarp from the horribly damaged, unrecognizable dead woman. Bloodstains covered her soiled dress. One arm was folded under at an impossible angle, and the face was smashed in. Caked blood stuck to her hair. He smiled and patted De Vlaander on his shoulder. "Lieber Gott, De Vlaander, did she hurt you that much?"

For an answer, Hopman spat on the canvas.

An unknown prostitute posthumously saved the lives of two brave human beings.

The SS closed the file on Janet.

12

"Maybe, Professor," the minister continued the interrupted conversation, "it would be appropriate if I explain the reason for your presence here."

The professor nodded.

"Friends, I made it clear that our concern is Rembrandt's *Night Watch*. I was able to have a conversation with Professor Breemer, and a very inventive solution to keep our national cultural treasure out of the hands of the Germans was the result. It is not without risk, and it may turn out to be a costly affair, which is why you have been invited to discuss the feasibility of what we are about to present."

"Sorry to interrupt, Your Excellency, but since the professor is here, would he be so kind as to explain the reason why this particular painting, among so many, is worth our exclusive attention. Not all of us are art historians. I mean, if our input is of any value, we need to understand."

"I agree, madam. So, Professor, would you be so kind?"

Professor Breemer remained silent for a moment. He folded his hands in front of his vest, the fingers spread wide and the tips touching. He scratched his throat and nodded several times.

"With great pleasure. However, I will ask for your patience. There is no such thing as a brief explanation about the *Night Watch* and its creator, Rembrandt, so bear with me. To understand the painting, we need to understand the artist first."

13

"Rembrandt, or Rembrandt Harmenszoon van Rijn to be precise, was born in the city of Leiden, in Holland on July 15, 1606. For ease of reference, I will call the Netherlands and in Rembrandt's time, the Seventeen Provinces, Holland. The country was in the middle of the so-called eighty-year war with Spain or rather the occupation of its territory by Spain. Holland came to oppose the draconian oppression of the king of Spain, Phillip II, executed especially through his governor, the Duke of Alva. King Phillip aimed to defend Catholicism as the one and only religion in the Spanish Netherlands, where Luther and especially Calvin found fertile ground. Alva's strategy was to conquer a city and to virtually murder all citizens to send a warning to those cities still resisting. To finance the occupation and pay the soldiers, Alva introduced a system of taxation, among others, the infamous 'Tiende Penning' a 10 percent tax. One should not forget that wars in those days were not like in modern times, with countries fighting countries. Cities often fought each other and were therefore fortress cities.

Invaders had to conquer city by city, only for them to be retaken and conquered again. This is important, because it explains why a city like Amsterdam could prosper while fighting was going on elsewhere. Religion was often the cause, Catholics against Protestants, Protestants against Catholics. Incidentally, it caused one of the largest destructions of our cultural heritage, when in 1566, during the so-called 'iconoclasm,' religious paintings and sculptures in Catholic churches were burned or cut to pieces."

"Excuse me. Is that not a bit exaggerated, Professor?"

Breemer smiled. *After more than four centuries*, he thought. The lady who commented was certainly not a Catholic.

"Madam, on the contrary, during the pre-Renaissance and the Renaissance, commissioning art was practically the prerogative of the Catholic church and of royalty and nobility. By far, the majority produced ended up in Catholic churches. We will never know how many Jan or Hubert van Eycks ended up on the bonfires of iconoclasm," the professor continued.

14

"In these tumultuous times, Rembrandt grew up, went to school, and from 1620 to 1624 or 1625 was trained as an artist. For three years, he remained with Jacob van Swanenburgh in Leiden and after that with Pieter Lastman in Amsterdam. During these years, Rembrandt developed his interest in the effects of light in pictorial applications and in history painting, at the time the highest level of all genres. Then he returned to Leiden and settled himself there as a master painter, only nineteen years old. His early self-portrait shows a young man with curly hair, looking startled at the viewer, meeting our gaze as if he were surprised about his success or the world he lived in. Rembrandt remained in Leiden until 1631, and much of his later style found its origins there. In 1631, he moved to Amsterdam but kept in close contact with Leiden.

"In Amsterdam, Rembrandt joined a business cooperation with an art dealer, Hendrick van Uylenburgh. He would work in his paint shop for nearly four years, painting many portraits, and would marry his patron's cousin Saskia in 1634.

"Amsterdam in the early seventeenth century was a booming city, the center of Holland's Golden Century. Jews persecuted in southern European countries could live free and prosper in Amsterdam, contributing to science, commerce, and trade. Huguenots, Protestants escaping from France, found a safe haven in Amsterdam and brought with them capital and culture, knowledge, and contacts. It was a society where people appreciated art, and many wanted their portrait painted.

"The old and the new collided continuously in this thriving city, hanging on to what was familiar to the people and progressive in its attempt to understand the nature of things. One of the *chirurgijns*, medical doctors, was Claes Pieterszoon, who became well known for his passion to teach anatomy by publicly dissecting the corpses of hanged criminals. He became one of the leading citizens and was somewhat vain. When he wanted a group portrait while operating on a corpse, he turned to Rembrandt. Considering his name too common, he changed it to Tulp. *The Anatomy Lesson of Dr. Nicolaas Tulp*, painted by Rembrandt in 1632, manifested the artist's astonishing ability to create spatial effects on a flat surface." Professor Breemer paused for a moment. "Could I possibly have a glass of water?"

"Of course," answered the minister, "but even better, I have been able to arrange some sandwiches, not easy these days, but sometimes I shamelessly take advantage of my position."

Nobody complained when the large silver plate with rye bread and old cheese circulated.

15

More than one year into the occupation of Holland, the ugly face of Nazism and racism showed itself, and it was only the beginning. Jews were forced to register and received identity papers stamped with a large letter J. Amsterdam became a busy city. The Germans wanted all Jews to relocate to Amsterdam and to declare the whole city a Jewish ghetto to facilitate the ultimate deportation of all Dutch Jews to Germany. There had been *razzias*, raids, indiscriminatingly arresting Jewish families who then were transported to concentration camps. Protesting against the deportation of their Jews, Amsterdam called a general strike, the so-called February Strike. Heroes like Banker Walraven van Hall went way beyond just duties and helped many a Jewish family financially and to find a safe hiding place. Resistance fighters blew up a villa were German officers lived and the telephone switchboard of Schiphol Airport. The Germans hit back hard. On June 11, three hundred young Jewish men were arrested and brought to the concentration camp Mauthausen. Few survived. For many citizens, life continued, however—maybe not the way they were used to, but to most, the disastrous future was still incomprehensible.

It was a marvelous summer day, that sixteenth of July 1941. For Jan and Miep Gies, it felt like heaven approved of their decision to pick that Wednesday to get married. She looked charming in her long black summer coat and hat, carrying a bunch of summer flowers for a bridal bouquet in her gloved hands. The three-piece gray suit with a matching fedora hat and dark glasses made the groom look as sophisticated as he in fact was. They had decided to invite only a few friends to the city hall, where the ceremony would take place. The van Pels, Victor Kugler, Bep Voskuil, and Johannes Kleiman, among others, attended.

The trip from Merwedeplein to the Dam, the center of the city, had been easy by streetcar. Because of the beautiful weather, some invited guests decided to walk to the Oudezijdsvoorburgwal, where they would meet the bride and groom at the city hall. This group of five adults and two children enjoyed the nice walk, dressed in their finest. There was animated talking and laughing, and because the yellow star that later every Jew was forced to wear visibly on their clothing was not introduced in Holland yet, the Jewish father and daughter did not look any different from the others. He looked dapper in his light overcoat, white shirt, and striped tie, wearing his hat a bit cockily to the right on his head.

He held one of his two daughters by the hand, Margot, the older one, being sick and attended by his wife, Edith, at home.

The twelve-year-old girl looked pretty in her light blue coat and matching light blue hat, framing her smiling face and short black hair. Unperturbed by the tumultuous times they lived in, that day, she felt like a movie star, something, she wrote in her *Diary of a Young Girl*, she aspired to one day become. It was one of the last happy moments in Anne Frank's short life.

16

"Ladies, gentlemen, I would like Professor Breemer to conclude his presentation on Rembrandt. We still have lots to discuss before curfew starts. Professor, please?"

"Thank, Your Excellency. Where was I? Oh yes." The professor took a white handkerchief from his pocket and meticulously cleaned his glasses, as if he needed time to think.

"Amsterdam, like other Dutch cities in those times, used the services of militias, companies under the command of wealthy citizens as its officers, civic guards actually involved in ceremonial events but ready to defend the city, watching at night over the city and opening and closing the city gates. The city was divided into numerous sectors, each sector the responsibility of a certain company. The companies would meet in a prestigious building called the Kloveniersdoelen, referring to the guns, *coleveres*, and the target, *doel*. A series of six paintings was ordered for it, *The Night Watch* being one of them.

"Whenever there was a change of command, the members

of the company would commission a painting, like they would order a group's photo today. Many now famous painters painted such group portraits, like Frans Hals, Van der Helst, Govert Flink, and Hendrik Pot. Not all members of a company could afford to be painted because each member had to pay the artist, and the amount depended on the position in the painting. As a result, many of these group paintings were formal and stiff and meticulously delineated to better recognize the paying members.

"Frans Banning Cocq, the leading figure on Rembrandt's *Night Watch*, was a mayor of Amsterdam, lord of a castle, and captain of the company. Next to him is Lieutenant Willem van Ruytenburch an influential spice trader. Everyone else is grouped around them in a way that sprouted from the brain of Rembrandt. Likeness of the individuals was less important to the artist than the overall composition. A revolutionary approach. The colors are subdued, to achieve a maximum effect from the light that beams down on certain spots or appears from nowhere. It is the pinnacle of Rembrandt's use of light effects, varied brushwork, and paint application. He uses different painterly methods, rather rough brushwork and thick paint application closest to the picture plane, and soft brushes further back to create depth. He balanced the light/dark effect masterly. If we want to compare this painting with the work of any other master painter, we may look for example at Velasquez's *Surrender of Breda* from 1634/35, a naturalistic, meticulous, delineated painterly composition. Side by side, though, we'll notice the innovative approach of Rembrandt, the grouping of the soldiers absorbing the entire pictorial space and each one involved in some kind of action. It was common to depict the members of a company seated at their annual dinner, all directing their gaze at the viewer, shoulder to shoulder to fit within the picture frame.

"Rembrandt painted the group in apparent disorder, preparing and lining up for their annual parade through the city. Instead of letting a static coat of arms of the militia or the city, in the first case a rooster's claw on an oval shield, spoil his composition, he paints a girl with a rooster hanging from her side, with the claws very visible, and throws a spotlight on her. He symbolizes heroism by putting oak leaves on the helmet of the young boy. The focus on the richly dressed captain and lieutenant stands for the wealth of Amsterdam. The shadow of the captain's left arm projected on the yellow tunic of his lieutenant seems to protect the coat of arms of Amsterdam embroidered on it. The captain holds a glove very pronounced against the yellow dress of the girl with the rooster, ready to drop it, symbolizing a challenge.

"*The Night Watch* was once cut on four sides, especially the left, which would have moved both central figures more to the right, enhancing its dynamism even more; it was moved to the town hall on Dam square and had to fit between two doors, so they cut it.

"The person commissioning the painting was most probably Banning Cocq, the lord of the manor of Ilpenstein, a castle with corner towers, a moat, and a drawbridge. Already a wealthy man, he inherited a stately, large, double merchant house, De Dolfijn, the dolphin, at the Singel, where he lived when *The Night Watch* was painted. But since it was in fact a commission for the city, *The Night Watch* always belonged to the city and is on loan to the Rijksmuseum.

"Most of the sixteen men portrayed in addition to the captain and his lieutenant paid one hundred guilders each to Rembrandt, but Banning Cocq paid probably significantly more. He wanted his company portrayed but clearly under his command. So instead of lining all men up as was common, he explained to Rembrandt that there should be no question about who was in command. Rembrandt may have made several sketches, which he presented to the captain. Rembrandt's solution—to depict the moment Banning Cocq gives his lieutenant Ruytenburch the command to prepare the troops for the march through Amsterdam, the soldiers in chaotic preparation to obey—resulted in a lively, unique composition, revolutionary at the time but not appreciated by all. The effect of action is amplified by the soldiers loading, firing, and blowing the powder rests from the pan, with others busy gesticulating. The drummer is about to start his drum roll, and the ensign is lifting the company's banner. The lieutenant points his lance in the direction of the march. In the background, the artist is peeping over the melee as if he wants to witness the assembling of the company. In composition, paint application, and brushwork, in the use of color and light/dark effects, nothing in this painting is traditional. It speaks of the highest level of artistry and craftsmanship of daring originality. A master painter doing his own thing.

"So here it is, one of the most important and priceless paintings our cultural world possesses, as important as the *Mona Lisa* or Leonardo's *Last Supper*, and worthy indeed, ladies and gentlemen, of doing whatever it takes to keep it safe for posterity."

Several of them applauded.

17

"Thank you, Professor. May I now ask Mr. Roell to explain what we suggest could be the best option to keep *The Night Watch* out of the hands of the Nazis?"

"Several decennia ago," started Roell, "our country received so many requests from foreign museums to make *The Night Watch* available for important Rembrandt expositions that it presented us with a huge problem. It was against the policy of the Rijksmuseum to ship the painting abroad. Reciprocal exchanges are common and essential, and we were concerned that cooperation from foreign colleague institutions would become extremely difficult. The board decided to have a copy painted as exact as possible to make it available for international exhibitions. It took two years and was frighteningly close to the original. Then wiser men decided that something was wrong with this approach; after all, museums should not exchange copies but originals, and the copy was destroyed. Schmidt Degener told me all this. A pity from our present position, it would have served us well today, but who would have known so many years ago? The artist passed away in 1934.

"We have learned that scouts are sent to occupied territories with pictures of art objects that Adolf Hitler, Hermann Göring, and others want for their collections. We believe that a well-painted copy could mislead these people, while our original will be safely stored away—"

"Sounds like a plan," interrupted Trip, "but how are we, under the present circumstances, going to be able to paint a copy? Where do we find the artist and the material? And we certainly don't have two years."

"These are all questions we aim to address, so let's start with the most important one, where do we find an artist able to paint an almost perfect copy?"

"Any suggestions, Professor?"

"Well, I was able to give that thorough thought. There are a few names that we want to look at." He took a folded sheet of paper from his vest pocket, unfolded it, and readjusted his glasses before reading aloud the first name. "However, our options are very limited because most artists decided to sign up for the Kultuurkamer, which automatically excludes them."

The Kultuurkamer was the Dutch equivalent of the Nazis Reichskulturkammer, an umbrella organization for culture. Only members could publicly practice their profession. Being a member was considered collaboration because the sole purpose was to Nazify all cultural expressions in Nazi Germany and occupied territories. It was an initiative of infamous Hitler lackey and state-propagandist Dr. Goebbels.

"There is Joseph van der Veken in Belgium. He is a highly skilled restaurateur, but it has been brought to the attention of a few that he offered what was supposed to be an original Memling for sale that appeared to be a fake from his own hands. He might have the ability to paint a copy, although his specialty seems to be Flemish primitives. I contacted a colleague of mine in Belgium who convinced me that we should refrain from working with van der Veken.

"Then there is Tom Keating, living in London. It is only very recently that the art world realized that some of the Palmers on the market where not by Palmer at all, as were other oil paintings from European masters. It has been kept out of the press; however, the art world is aware of it. He is reputed to be a great admirer of Rembrandt, but it is very doubtful that he would be willing to cooperate with us."

"Is there no one close to home, Professor? Among the many artists in Holland, there certainly should be someone able to copy even a Rembrandt?" one of the ladies asked.

"Oh yes, it is quite common for artists to copy the work of great masters, to understand how they painted and why—only to learn from it. As a matter of fact, the best examples have passed the scrutiny of Christies or Sotheby and are hanging unknowingly on the walls of private collectors and museums. But although we have a blacklist of names, it is not an advertised profession, and very few will admit to the successful forgery of art."

One of the next names on the list was that of Henricus van Meegeren, known as Han van Meegeren. For some years, there had been a suspicion that several of the Dutch Golden Age paintings suddenly surfacing—Frans Hals, Pieter de Hooch, Terborch, and Vermeer—were by his hands. There was not enough evidence, however, and art experts like Abraham Bredius were convinced of the authenticity of the paintings. Han van Meegeren had moved to France and was certainly not willing to provide proof of his proficiency to forge.

"That does not sound good," commented the lawyer, "and I am surprised. I realize the complexity of producing a believable second *Night Watch*, but I did not think that finding a capable and reliable artist would be nearly impossible."

"It is not," answered the professor.

18

"**H**is name is Salomon Cohen."

Sandberg stood up as if to emphasize the importance of what was to follow.

"Cohen was an acquaintance of Jacques Goudstikker, the most successful and knowledgeable Jewish art dealer in Holland, specializing in Italian and Flemish masters from the fifteenth and seventeenth centuries, especially from the Florentine and Venetian schools. Regrettably, Goudstikker, a great philanthropist and art promotor, died while escaping Holland on the freighter *Bodegraven* in May 1940. During the night of May 15, he went for a stroll and fatally fell into the cargo hold. Incidentally, Reichsmarschall Hermann Göring got his hands on more than 1,100 of Goudstikker's paintings and art objects on behalf of Hitler and for his own collection, but possibly more about that later.

"Salomon Cohen was a gifted restaurateur, painter, and engraver. He admired Albrecht Duerer and especially Rembrandt. He worked exclusively for Goudstikker and restored several Rembrandts at the time in the collection of his patron.

"I met Cohen in 1934 when we organized an exhibition in Het Stedelijk together with Goudstikker. Cohen seemed to me quite sympathetic. I had a conversation with him and asked what made him so focused on restoration while being a great painter himself. His answer was that nothing gave him more satisfaction than working on a Rembrandt, the artist he admired above all others. The more restoration required, as with a large oil of a Dutch merchant and his wife badly water damaged, the more he enjoyed it. His words were, 'When working on an oil painting by his hand, I become him, I think like him—don't laugh, but I dress like him and live on white bread and pickled herring as he did.'"

"Amazing," commented one of the ladies.

"So, friends, this is our man.

"We do have a big problem though. Being a Jew, he and Sarah, his wife, were arrested and deported to Germany earlier this year after a roundup in the south. We do not know as yet where they may be or if they are even alive. The cruelest rumors are published by Het Parool, and I pray that not all I read is true."

"What can we do, Willem? It makes me sick to my stomach to have to witness how these poor people are treated like animals by those damned Krauts." Trip was mad but expressed the feelings of many in the room.

"We are working on something," answered Sandberg without being specific. "I do have good contacts with the resistance, but what we are proposing is risky. It could be expensive, it could cost lives, and there is no guarantee that our operation will be successful."

"Our operation, Willem?" This time, it was a member of the Rembrandt Society.

"Yes, and the reason we have invited you here today, to listen to our proposal and to give us your honest opinion and hopefully your support. What we have in mind is to obtain the assistance of the resistance here and in Germany to first locate Cohen, and then, if he is still alive, somehow kidnap him and bring him back to Amsterdam through wartime Germany and occupied Holland. As I said, I do have good connections with the resistance in our city, and they are in contact with the Rote Kapelle in Berlin and the White Rose in Munich. It will be an enormous feat if we succeed. If we do, then the material he needs will be organized and he'll have access to *The Nigh Watch* in its present location. We will provide him with whatever he requires to paint a copy in record time. Knowing his admiration for Rembrandt and *The Night Watch*, we expect his full cooperation. Hopefully, the copy will end up on the wall of Uncle Adolf and satisfy the beast ... So that's it, friends." Sandberg sat down.

"Holy shit," said one of them.

19

Professor Breemer never told the team so concerned with Rembrandt's painting why he shared their worries and willfully cooperated.

He was inspired by the tragic death of his good friend the well-known Jewish art dealer Jacques Goudstikker, whose collection of more than a thousand masterworks ended up, through conspicuous machinations, in the hands of Hermann Göring, the result of a purchase that amounted to pillage.

Jacques Goudstikker was the descendant of a famous family of art dealers. His grandfather established the Goudstikker Company in 1845. His grandson's original and knowledgeable approach to collecting and selling great art made the company one of the leading art dealers in the world.

Then the Germans invaded Holland.

They were ill prepared, hoping Holland would maintain its neutrality as it had successfully done during the First World War. The lives of the Jewish Goudstikkers was in immediate danger.

Four days after the Germans bombarded Rotterdam, the

The Fake Rembrandt

surrender of Holland was inevitable. Goudstikker, his wife, and their son, Edo, succeeded in boarding a freight ship at IJmuiden harbor, the steamship *Bodegraven.*

Two days before the ship left the harbor, that sunny but rather cool and windy day of Sunday, May 12, 1940, a British sailor enrolled, claiming that he, an experienced deckhand, would work for free to earn passage to his homeland England. The ship could accommodate forty-eight passengers and would have between fifty and sixty crew members on board. Captain Molenaar approved the hiring of the British sailor.

Several days earlier, in one of Amsterdam's harbor cafés in a secluded corner, a well-dressed gentleman was in hushed conversation with the English sailor.

The sailor was flat broke, having spent what little money he had on cheap booze and cheaper whores.

"Listen carefully," whispered Alois Miedl. "Here is a picture of Jacques Goudstikker; he is the man we are talking about."

Miedl was an unscrupulous German art dealer, Nazi banker, and sympathizer since 1932, living in Holland. He was a friend of Hermann Göring and the infamous Aus der Fuenten, the Nazi involved in the deportations of the Dutch Jewish population.

"I know that this man, his wife, and their son are looking for possibilities to leave Holland via ship. The latest we heard is that he may have found passage on board the SS *Bodegraven* departing from IJmuiden on May 14."

The British sailor was a vagabond, always in trouble with

authorities or the law, living from job to job, always short of money, more than once caught stealing from his shipmates. The amount of money this man was offering him was way beyond anything he could ever put his hands on. And for what? Throwing a man overboard in the middle of the night? A man he never saw before and probably nobody would ever find? It was a piece of cake. And the asshole was a Jew for chrissake. He hated Jews. They were the cause of this damn war, so he shook hands with the man and pocketed the thousand guilders he received as an advance.

"A few more things," said Miedl, "you do what you are supposed to do, and somebody in the harbor in England will wait for you and hand you—after one more thing, just delivering a message—the rest of the money. If you have done nothing and spent the money I just paid you, he will kill you.

"Then here is an envelope you will deliver to the border patrol agent who will contact you upon your arrival. Make sure nobody sees you give it to him. That's all. Good luck."

20

It was a busy affair in the harbor of IJmuiden. Crews and guests were arriving and boarding the *Bodegraven*. She was already under steam, pulling at her landlines, eager to escape the country this evening as the last ship to leave Holland after the country had to surrender to the German rape of its territory. She had only just escaped a different fate when the commander of the Dutch forces intended to block the harbor by sinking her. Ultimately, another unlucky vessel would befall that tragic honor.

Jacques Goudstikker, his wife, and Edo, their son, had to share one cabin, which they did without complaining. There were way more passengers, many of them Jewish refugees, than the official forty-eight accommodation specified. Soon they would be in South America after a short stop in England. Crossing the canal during the night seemed to be a good time to get used to a few weeks at sea, although they were lucky it was going to be a rather smooth sea that night.

In the crew quarters, a nervous British deckhand counted what was left of his Judas pay after the previous night in Amsterdam's harbor pubs and brothels.

What a jackass he had been. It must have been that Asian whore he met after first drinking too much at Fat Charley's. Why the hell did he brag about the cash he was carrying. Some asshole must have sneaked into the room while his pants were on the back of a chair.

One hundred fifty fucking guilders was all that was left. If he could not tilt that Jew overboard, he was dead. Jesus what a mess.

How the hell would he get that guy on deck so he could let him swim without anybody seeing or hearing it? Then to make matters worse, he would have the watch on board that night from ten to two.

He started thinking of ways to disguise himself, so he could disembark without being seen, but if you didn't know from whom to hide, it made it extra difficult.

He carried a stiletto and knew how to use it, but it would not do much against a gun.

The cabin was small but, given the circumstances, comfortable enough. Some cabins held more than six people. Nevertheless, it was an enormous step back for the wealthy family, used as they were to the best things in life. Jacques Goudstikker could not sleep; his mind kept spinning around the multitude of problems he was faced with. He had to leave his entire collection of paintings, all by great masters, close to 1,300 or even more, in the hands of his trusted accountant and friend Dr. Sternheim, who unfortunately had passed away on May 10. The last Goudstikker heard was that his employees Ten Broek and Dik Sr. had taken charge of the company.

"Desi, I am a bit restless and need a breath of fresh air," whispered Jacques not to wake up his son. "Try to get some sleep. I'll be back soon." He closed the cabin door behind him, and passing through the small corridor and up the stairs, he went to the top deck.

21

The *Bodegraven* was well on its way. The sea was calm, and a half moon threw a silvery light on the top deck of the ship and the rolling waves around her.

The British deckhand was smoking a cigarette behind the midship deckhouse.

There were two open cargo holds behind it and three in front.

The deckhand noticed that somebody had come up the stairs and started to walk the deck, toward the bow. The light from the deckhouse shone a moment on the man's face, a face well known to the scoundrel from the photograph in his pocket. It was the man he was supposed to throw overboard.

There was momentarily no one else on deck. Without hesitation, on tiptoes, he followed the figure in front of him, who was unaware of being approached.

Halfway to the center cargo bay in the front of the ship, the deckhand caught up with him. When he was only three paces behind him, the man suddenly turned and stepped away from the railing, closer to the hold. On an impulse, the brute pushed the man hard, and he fell backward. Not even a scream, only a loud thud from deep in the hull.

With his heart beating in his throat but shaking with malicious pleasure at what he had just achieved, he hurried to the aft deck, pretending not to have noticed the night stroller on deck.

"Anything to report?" asked the young sailor who took over his watch at 2:00 a.m.

"Nothing, all is well," answered the murderer.

It was early morning, minutes past five, when Mrs. Goudstikker woke up and realized that her husband was not with her.

"Edo, wake up. Dad went for a walk on deck last night and did not return. Something must have happened." She started to panic and cried, "Oh God, please let nothing have happened to my Jacques."

Edo quickly dressed. He was just putting on his sweater when there was a knock on the door. The captain and the first officer were standing there. When Mrs. Goudstikker read their faces, she broke down.

"Madam," said the captain, "I am sorry to have to tell you that there has been a terrible accident. Your husband must have been on deck during the night and misstepped in the dark. He fell into the cargo bay and fractured his skull. Please come with me, Mrs. Goudstikker."

There was a doctor on board, tending to the man on a

stretcher, who was covered with a sheet. He could do nothing for the patient. On the papers that would accompany the body, when the boat moored in Dover, he wrote, "Deceased, the result of cranial hematoma."

In the consternation of the moment, the culprit sneaked off the ship.

In front of the custom building, with his back against a car, stood a man smoking a cigarette, a fedora deep over his forehead, hiding his eyes. When the sailor approached him, he stepped forward and without a word, handed him an envelope.

The sailor felt the thick wad of money and put it quickly away. Suddenly, from nowhere, a border patrol agent appeared.

"You have a message for me, I assume," he said, holding out his hand, indicating that it had been a statement, not a question. The sailor handed over the envelope Miedl had given him. As fast as he could, the sailor left the harbor, not once looking over his shoulder.

Mrs. Goudstikker and her son were not allowed to leave the ship to attend the funeral of her husband and his father. The border official who received Miedl's envelope was adamant; the papers they carried were not sufficient to enter the United Kingdom.

The next morning, in a dark alley of the Dover harbor, the body of a dead sailor was found, apparently drunk and maybe the victim of a bar brawl. There was no identification on his body, and the police only found some change from different countries in his pockets, a nearly empty pack of cigarettes, and a stiletto.

22

Salomon Cohen would wake up several times at night, crying without tears, disoriented at first, reaching next to him for Sarah before he realized with pain that the body next to him was that of a *haeftling*, a prisoner like himself. They were stacked in rows of four men to one bunk bed, a contraption of rough sawn lumber, three layers high, undernourished men almost worked to death—some crying, some snoring, some breaking wind the slop inflated their body with, all sleeping from exhaustion in an unventilated barracks, stinking like a pigsty.

When they reached the gate with "Arbeit Macht Frei" (work sets you free) and the cattle wagon finally opened to disperse the sick and miserable group, having spent days and nights huddled together, because there was no place to lie down, Salomon almost felt relieved. When they counted the dead bodies of those who perished in the rotten atmosphere of the closed cattle car, an overflowing bucket with excrement and urine in the corner, they thought, *How could Sachenhausen be worse than that train ride?*

It was.

Salomon was directed to the left at arrival. In the barracks, they took all the suitcases, rucksacks, and cardboard boxes that people brought, containing their possessions. They had to strip naked and leave their clothes in a large pile.

First their heads were shorn by prisoners like themselves, wordlessly and emotionlessly doing their job. Large piles of hair accumulated around the benches they were made to sit on. Then a number was tattooed on the inside of their underarm, and they were marched to ice-cold showers, without anything to dry their bodies. Prisoners handed them pants, shirts, and a skull cap from a pile of rags all made of rough linen with wide, dark blue and white stripes and a pair of wooden clogs that someone had worn before. Salomon was directed to barrack 13, where many victims like himself were already present. He found an empty spot on a top bunk, taken by three others, not exactly welcoming the new guest but not able to protest with the kapo guards watching.

Salomon was famished. He had not eaten for days, so he lined up with others to receive a thin gray soup with pieces of turnips and potato peels floating in it, which he ate with gusto, licking the dented aluminum bowl that would have to stay with him.

The first night had been the worst.

Where was Sarah?

What would they do to her?

He prayed in silence, asking God to protect her. Whatever happened to him, he would take it. "But please, please, God, protect my Sarah." He cried himself to sleep.

He never really rested. The third night after their arrival at six in the morning, screaming kapos, the German-appointed camp elders, were beating their sticks against the bunks shouting, "Wake up ... Out, you lazy bastards!"

They were lined up at the camp square, all prisoners in rows five deep. Salomon was in the middle row. The linen prisoner suits did nothing against the biting cold. They stood there, frozen stiff, their bodies shaking and teeth chattering, for an hour without talking. An hour and a half and his feet, used to good shoes, began hurting in the clogs. Then the camp commander appeared. Like a better man inspecting his soldiers, he walked in front of the sorrowful troop, beating his shining leather boot with a riding crop held in his gloved left hand. Several officers followed behind him.

One of the men in the front row collapsed, his thin body no longer able to take the torture. The commander did not even look. He continued, every second step beating the shaft of his riding boot with the whip. One of the officers stopped.

"Stand up."

But the man was unable to.

With controlled motions, the officer unbuckled the brown leather holster attached to his belt. He pulled out his Luger pistol and bent slightly down, pushing the barrel against the neck of the prisoner. The man was paralyzed, but the officer waited and then suddenly a shot. The body jerked a few times, and a puddle of blood formed beneath its head.

A man started to cry uncontrollably. The commander stopped and walked back several positions until he confronted the now sobbing prisoner.

The riding crop changed to his right hand.

"Sing," he ordered in a low voice, staring at the face wet with tears.

"*Sing*!" he shouted, and with a swift move based on experience, he hit the face hard, immediately drawing blood. Then he hit again and again, until the man went down like a sack of potatoes, not moving, not crying anymore.

23

Salomon thought it a bad omen that his barrack was number 13, but he was assigned duties that could have been worse. He had to search for anything of value that the large pile of clothing might contain. First, he checked the pockets. Then, if he could feel something, he tore the seams that often contained rings, gold coins, and even diamonds or pearls stitched into them or golden pocket watches. An impressive basket of valuables accumulated under the watchful eyes of the kapo. A not insignificant advantage was that those working on the clothing line could take warm underwear for themselves, condoned by the kapo, who now and then pocketed something from the basket. Corruption was rampant in the camps, where favors were bought with diamonds, gold coins, or jewelry.

On the other side of the barracks, prisoners forced suitcases open, ripped the cardboard boxes, and emptied rucksacks on the floor. The contents were sorted into different piles, soon resembling a flea market.

Salomon was examining a winter coat with one of the pockets

sewn closed when an SS officer he had not seen before entered, and everyone jumped to attention.

"Salomon Cohen!" shouted the German.

His heart skipped a beat. He broke out in a sweat. A thousand thoughts went through his panicking brain. Was he going to be shot? What did he do wrong? And then, in a paralyzing realization, he thought, could it be Sarah? Was she dead?

"Mitkommen" (come with me).

Hardly able to walk, Salomon followed the officer, who brought him to a barracks further down. Inside was a large room, surprisingly warm and well lit. It had several tables with prisoners on each side. But these seemed to be different, better fed obviously, even talking and sometimes laughing. The now-familiar stench was absent. What the hell was this?

"Sit down, Cohen," ordered the officer who had installed himself behind a large desk. He went through some papers until he found what he was looking for.

"Salomon Cohen, born in Amsterdam, July 14, 1898, married to Sarah Rosenblatt, no children, profession etcher, correct?"

That's it, thought Salomon, *caught in a lie*. When he was asked his profession after being arrested, he thought that Nazis might not have a great need for restaurateurs, so the first thing he could come up with was etcher.

"Yes, Officer."

"Tell me—who are your favorite etchers?"

A trap, thought Salomon. What should he answer?

"Rembrandt is one, but my real favorite is Albrecht Dürer."

Can't hurt that he is a German, thought Salomon, *and indeed the greatest etcher of all.*

Without a word, the officer stood up and indicated Salomon should follow him to a table with a bright light above it and what seemed to be a reasonably comfortable desk chair behind it. On it was a copper plate, and next to it a caelum, the sharp metal engraving tool. The officer threw a black-and-white photo of a man Salomon did not know in front of him. The man had a beard, long whiskers, and penetrating eyes in a weathered face.

"Draw it," said the officer. He then turned around and went back to his desk, not once looking at Salomon again.

Salomon Cohen was no etcher but a very talented artist, and in his career, he did experiment with the needle. He went to work.

"Ausgezeichnet," (excellent) said SS Major Bernhard Krueger, checking the engraving with a magnifying glass. "Welcome to barrack 19."

24

Moving to barrack 19 was easy. All he possessed was an aluminum bowl.

He found a sleeping place, still wooden bunks, with fresh straw and sleeping two instead of four. He received a bar of soap and a thin army towel. Salomon's mind went into survival mode; maybe it was possible after all.

He noticed a completely different attitude by Major Krueger, who even addressed the prisoners working in barrack 19 with the polite "Sie" instead of the usual "Du" or more often "Jew pig" or worse insults to which Salomon as a prisoner was subjected.

Salomon's bed buddy was a Russian by the name of Smolianoff with the familiar name of Salamon. He told Cohen that he knew Amsterdam, had been arrested there, and did time for counterfeiting. He then explained what was going on in barrack 19 and why the treatment there was different from in the other barracks. "But don't make a mistake, and don't take Krueger for granted," he warned in his broken English, with now and then a Dutch word he remembered.

As it turned out, barrack 19 was a production studio for counterfeit money, specifically British pounds and US dollars. There was speculation among the prisoners, all of them one way or another in their previous life craftsmen involved in the process of designing and printing complicated contracts like currencies or official documents. Maybe the money produced would be used to purchase goods needed for the war machine from countries willing to supply. Maybe it could be used to interfere with the British economy; nobody knew. What they did know, however, was that as long as they could work under Major Krueger without screwing up, their life would be saved. They would receive better food and did not need to attend the hated morning head counts; contact with other prisoners was strictly forbidden. Major Krueger seemed to be on a mission from the highest authority to succeed in his endeavor and treated his workers almost with respect, but he was no *maecenas*, on the contrary.

When he suspected a Belgian engraver of sabotaging the process and making intentional mistakes, he had him shot right away.

Soon, Major Krueger realized that with Salomon Cohen, he had an above-average, talented, intelligent worker, and he put him in charge of a unit.

That gave Salomon new responsibilities; besides his own work, he now was charged with quality control of a group of men whose task it was to work on the Britannia medallion on the pound note, an extremely complicated task.

The Fake Rembrandt

To his surprise, Major Krueger would confide in him from time to time, and although Salomon never let his guard down, he realized that in this crazy world of inhumanity, atrocities, and murder, SS Major Krueger seemed to need a normal contact. From one of the talks, Salomon understood that Krueger was quite content with the project he was responsible for, because it kept him away from worse assignments. If Salomon Cohen could stay involved in the production of counterfeit foreign currency, if he could delay the project without being detected, he might avoid being murdered.

25

"That is a bit beyond my abilities, Mr. Sandberg," Roger said in answer to the question that his fellow member in the resistance had just posed. "It is not that I think your plan is not feasible, on the contrary, but it requires contacts of different and very senior levels. I also believe that an amount of money in whatever form will be required that is way beyond anything I could ever get my hands on."

Jonkheer (Squire) Willem Sandberg, assistant conservator of the Municipal Museum of Amsterdam was a respected leading member of the Dutch resistance. Very few of his colleagues were aware of it. "And besides, who would handle the logistics?"

"To be honest, that is one of the first issues we addressed," answered Sandberg, "and we believe we have that covered. Your successful operation with the caps is part of a coordinated effort to have complete and original SS uniforms available for the operation we are planning. We obtained the parts—boots, full uniforms, coats, and caps—from different locations in Holland, Belgium, and France. No officer is going to complain about missing his pants. His colleagues will laugh at him and joke that he probably left them in a brothel. No officer will complain about his boots gone walking; they will just think it's petty theft, and that is only the beginning. We will need German-registered cars—a Mercedes or Kubelwagens, the German jeep—the necessary paraphernalia, weapons, documents, and yes, a large amount of money. Plus, of course, a team of highly capable, trustworthy, and brave people, fluent in German."

"People may not be the biggest problem. As you know, we have good contacts with resistance groups in Germany, especially in Berlin. Sometimes we forget that Hitler never received majority support in Berlin and that his dreams about a new capital called Germania is based on his grudge.

"You mentioned Salomon Cohen. We have the details of his arrest together with his wife, Sarah. By the way, she ran a successful sewing shop, making uniforms for the police. It did not protect her though. It was a Dutch policeman who betrayed them."

"Will you be able to find out where they went, where he is?"

"Yes, to find out where they ended up upon arrival in Germany or Poland is not too difficult. If they are moved to other camps, it may become extremely problematic."

"But not impossible?"

"No, the system within the camps is thankfully very corrupt, which allows us to sometimes succeed in obtaining information, but not always."

"Then the first thing now, Roger, is finding out where they

are, where he is, and if they are still alive. Is that something you can handle? And if so, what would it take?"

"Money, maybe some gold or diamonds as part of a fortune you may have to find to cover the cost of the whole operation."

"Then I know just the right man to talk to," said Mr. Sandberg.

26

The Zeedijk is one of the oldest streets in the center of Amsterdam. Centuries ago, sailors returning from faraway places in the East Indies, Ceylon, or exotic islands used to stay in a charming wooden building, an inn oddly named In't Aepjen, old Dutch for "in the monkey." It is the oldest still existing tavern in Amsterdam, its history going back to the sixteen hundreds. Money never stayed long in the pockets of sailors, returning to Amsterdam and its harbor pubs and brothels. Often, they would bring a monkey with them, which they then used to settle their bill. It gave the pub its name.

It was one of the places in wartime Amsterdam where a surrogate coffee could be ordered but where insiders known to the innkeeper could still have a beer or a *genever*. It was not the kind of place Germans were interested in; they would rather go to Schiller on Rembrandt Square.

It was early in the afternoon when Sandberg opened the door and entered a dark room with empty tables and chairs. The innkeeper was behind the bar, cleaning cups. He paid no attention to the visitor. At a table in the back of the room sat a young man, reading a paper with an untouched cup of surrogate coffee in front of him.

"Good afternoon. Does Richard still work here?" asked Sandberg.

Understanding the code, the man indicated with a head movement to the back of the room where the young man was now paying attention. When Sandberg approach him, he stood up and smiled.

"Mister van Tuyl?" asked Sandberg.

"Yes, and you are Willem Sandberg. I know of you, but I am very pleased to meet you in person. Do sit down please."

Mr. van Tuyl, also known as Oilman, was a handsome young man, about thirty-five years old. His personality radiated energy, confidence, and irresistible sympathy.

He was neither van Tuyl nor Oilman, but the banker Walraven van Hall, a heroic, unselfish leader of the resistance. "How can I help you, Mr. Sandberg?"

"Please call me Willem, and I sure hope you can."

It took almost an hour to explain why Sandberg had come to see van Hall, who listened patiently, never interrupting. At the end, he asked a few pointed questions that Sandberg had no difficulty answering.

"Coffee, gentlemen?" the innkeeper put two deliciously fragrant cups of real coffee in front of them and then discreetly withdrew.

"He is a member. Don't worry."

Willem was not worried because he had made sure that their conversation could not be overheard.

"How much do you think?"

"Don't know. Maybe fifty thousand, could be double that," answered Sandberg, hesitating. "Even more—some in cash, some in gold or diamonds. Cash does not work for us in Germany."

"How much time do you have?"

"Weeks. We have no news of Cohen yet, but if they locate him, we must move before he is put on transport or worse."

"Consider it done. I'll send a courier who will offer you pencils for sale. Then you know the goods will be ready for pickup. Same place on any Friday at four. Your man should ask if George is home. The innkeeper will understand, and within fifteen minutes, someone will show up."

A very relieved Sandberg thanked van Hall, who smiled and lifted his shoulders as if to say, "Hey, no problem."

27

"What is the next step, Willem, now that the funds have apparently been secured?"

The person who asked the question was Gerrit Van der Veen, a leader of the Dutch resistance. With him was Willem Arondeas. The three of them went over the entire plan of operation, one of them playing the devil's advocate. Van der Veen, a forty-year-old sculptor, was a heroic opposer of the Nazis, helping Jews and sabotaging the German efforts to register all Jews living in Holland. Arondeas was an early openly gay painter, illustrator, and author. He was about forty-five years old, and, like Van der Veen, was heroically fighting the persecution of Jews and the rape of his beloved country. Both would pay with their lives.

The meeting took place in one of the stately merchant houses on the Prinsengracht, the outer canal of the canal ring and close to the Amstel River. They went through the logistics, filling in names of candidates with the required abilities—fluent in German for example and possessing an enormous dose of guts.

The Fake Rembrandt

"We need contacts in Germany to find out if Cohen is still alive and where he is before we can fill in the details."

"That should not be too difficult," commented Arondeas. "We can check with our contacts in the National Railway, which transports the poor devils in cattle cars to Germany. We'll have a bone to pick with some big shots there when this nightmare is over."

"Great, but if we know the camp he was sent to, are we then able to find out more specifics, like if he is alive and where and how we can locate him?"

"Yes," answered Van der Veen. "I know that Harro is able to obtain information, but he will need some gold or diamonds to first receive details and to make sure that Cohen survives long enough."

Harro was Harro Schulze-Boysen, a German Luftwaffe (air force) staff officer who used his position to fight the Nazi system. He was secretly the initiator of the Schulze-Boysen/Harnack, a resistance organization. Harnack was Mildred Harnack, his American wife. The group provided important intelligence to the United States through Donald Heath, the attaché at the American embassy.

"Okay, I will make sure that you have the gold or diamonds, but how do we get that in the hands of this Harro?"

Van der Veen thought for a moment. "That may be a bigger problem than receiving Harro's cooperation. What we need is some damned good couriers from here to travel to Berlin. Arranging the contact there is something I can take care of."

"Then," Sandberg suggested, "I know just the perfect couple for that mission."

28

"What exactly do they mean as husband and wife, and wipe that smile off your face."

Suzan and Bob were posing for passport pictures needed for the false identity papers they were going to have. "Well, my dear wife, you know what papas and mamas do when little girls are sleeping don't you?" the smile on his face grew even bigger.

"Forget about it, Manti."

"Manti?"

"Yes, you know about the praying mantis, don't you?"

"You mean that ungrateful female grasshopper that beheads the man after mating?"

"That's the one buddy, and that female is me!"

"Well, at least there are worse ways for a man to lose his head, but seriously, I agree with them that it would be awkward for a man and a woman to travel these days to Berlin, other than a couple who outwardly sympathizes with the bastards and may hope to see the führer in person at some big event."

"I understand, and of course I'll play the part. Don't get big headed now, but I could think of a worse husband."

"And I could imagine being in love with you." And this time, there was no smile.

Both had been invited earlier to come to the practice of Doctor Brouwer for a medical checkup. Both were in excellent condition. The checkup was in fact a briefing about the request from top brass to travel to Berlin on an important mission.

"You realize that our cap adventure was kids' play compared to what is expected from us now, don't you, Suzy?"

"Of course I do, and it was about time for some excitement again. I was getting bored anyway."

The couple was going to become Mr. and Mrs. Keizer, a good Germanic-sounding family name. His profession would be listed as bookkeeper, and she was the owner of a flower shop in Amsterdam. They were married two months before, and this was going to be a honeymoon trip. They hoped to be in the audience when Adolf Hitler appeared at some event. In their possession were books and pamphlets that proved their sympathy for Nazi Germany. If gold and diamonds were found in their possession, that was how they hoped to settle bills if, for whatever reason, they had to stay longer than planned and they ran out of reichsmarks. Mrs. Keizer even carried her bridal veil and some dried flowers in her suitcase.

Arondeas, who supervised a team that produced thousands of false identity papers for Jews in hiding or resistance fighters, did an excellent job on the documents Suzan and Bob required. With the necessary stamps and signatures, it would pass close-scrutiny. The trip would be by train, first class, as might be expected of a couple on their honeymoon.

Roger supplied the wedding rings with the date engraved inside and handed them a leather pouch with four big diamonds and a large quantity of golden ten-guilder coins.

Then Mr. and Mrs. Keizer went to different homes to pack their suitcases.

29

On the third platform of the central station in Amsterdam, the train for Berlin was ready for boarding. Red-capped porters were carrying luggage, people were saying their goodbyes—everything seemed as normal as before the war, except for the large number of German soldiers in a variety of uniforms, laughing and talking loudly, excited to go to their Heimat, their fatherland. A conductor blew his whistle and shouted, "All aboard, train to Berlin! All aboard!"

There were only two first-class wagons and then several second- and third-class cars, typically for officers, subalterns, and then soldiers, respectively.

Suzan and Bob settled down in the comfortable red velvet chairs. He took the aisle seat. The car was not full, and the places in front of them remained empty. There were only a few civilians—all men—the other passengers were all officers. Bob winked at Suzan when they noticed the large number of military caps in the overheads.

Until Hilversum, everything went smoothly. There was coffee

and a kind of cake sold by a young woman, and then three men, two in uniform, entered the car. Without being asked, the military handed over their IDs, which after a quick inspection and a polite "Danke schön" (thanks kindly) were returned. When they came to Bob and Suzan, one of them said roughly, "Ausweis" (identity papers). Neither of them moved. Bob said in quite a loud voice and in perfect German, "What happened to identity please?"

The men were clearly taken aback by his attitude. No Dutchman would ever talk to them like that, unless this was some important man on his way to Berlin, traveling first class.

"Ausweis bitte" (identity please).

Both handed over the fake papers. The man in civilian clothing looked at each of them very carefully, taking his time, and then he handed them back with a nod to one of the military men. "In ordnung" (okay). Outwardly very calm, they pocketed the papers and continued their discussion, Suzan cuddling up to Bob like a newlywed would.

Between Amersfoort in the center of the country and Apeldoorn, it was an uneventful ride, and then suddenly, they heard loud screeching as the emergency brakes had been activated. Luggage and coffee cups were rolling over the floor, and several napping officers were unceremoniously thrown out of their seats. The shock reverberated through the train. It took surprisingly long before it came to a complete stop only a car length in front of a large pile of junk, concrete, scrap metal, and trees on the rail section, evidently intended to derail the train. Bob and Suzan understood immediately that the resistance had been active.

The officers jumped out, shouting orders to the soldiers now pouring out of the cars at the back. Bob and Suzan jumped out too, making sure they were close to the highest-ranking officers. Suzan shouted, "Goddamn saboteurs! They could have killed us all."

"Fucking Communists," added Bob furiously.

Suddenly, distant shots were fired from the woods on high ground alongside the tracks. One officer went down, blood flowing from his upper leg and coloring his riding breeches dark red. Soldiers returned fire while the officers took cover behind the train. A sergeant led a unit of men up the embankment, running to the source of the shots, but came back soon when nobody could be found.

It took the soldiers more than an hour to clean the tracks so the train could continue.

A medic took care of the wounded officer, who seemed to be in a lot of pain before the morphine shot he received started to work. When they reached Hengelo, close to the German border, the colonel gallantly offered both Bob and Suzan a glass of wine, which they thankfully accepted. Clearly that nice newlywed couple could be trusted.

30

Crossing the border was easier than Bob and Suzan had anticipated. The papers they presented were accepted without comment. They passed Bad Bentheim, Osnabrück, and Bad Oeyenhausen. The signs of war were all over the country, and Bob made mental notes of what he observed. It might be of value later.

Most of the passengers were sound asleep by then, and Suzan rested her head against his shoulder, tired of the long ride and from looking out of the window, purring like a kitten. Bob smiled.

One of the civilians left his seat and stealthily walked to the front where the colonel was snoring. In the man's right hand, Bob noticed with shock, was a revolver. In a flash, disaster went through Bob's head. This could be big trouble. If the idiot thought he would get away with murdering a colonel for whatever reason, he was nuts. No civilian in the compartment would survive.

He was on his feet in a split second. Before the man could pull the trigger, Bob's left arm held his neck in a stranglehold. His right

The Fake Rembrandt

hand clasped the butt of the man's revolver and pushed it up. A shot fired ...

The man cursed, screamed, and cried like a being possessed. Then panic broke out at first when all woke up, not immediately grasping what had just happened.

One quick-acting young officer close to the scramble grasped the man's arms, the revolver now on the floor, worked him down, and forced both arms behind his back. Another officer held a pistol against the man's head.

"Don't shoot!" shouted the colonel, who, startled at first, quickly took control of the situation. "This is a case for the Gestapo."

The culprit was handcuffed, arms behind his back, his feet bound with rope and pulled up high against his bottom. His mouth taped, he was on the ground now on his belly between four officers in the back of the compartment. Bob felt awful but had to play the game. Besides the man was apparently suicidal and would have been shot on the spot. What tragedy was behind his desperation? What the hell was he thinking?

The colonel turned to Bob. "Tell me please what happened, Herr ...?"

"Keizer," answered Bob. "My name is Bob Keizer." Bob explained what had happened.

"I owe you a great thank-you, Mister Keizer. It is my good fortune that at least one person was awake and alert. We will find out what this criminal's motives are and who may be behind this.

Would you and Mrs. Keizer be kind enough to join me at my table for the balance of the trip? I believe a dinner will be served soon."

Mr. and Mrs. Keizer were quite willing.

"Honeymoon," explained Mrs. Keizer when she was asked. "And my hope is to be able to see the führer in person if he appears in Berlin while we are there."

"Well, I do hope you may, Mrs. Keizer."

The colonel seemed to be quite a nice person. He presented his card to Bob. Oberst Weinberg turned out to be, as the discussion revealed, Doctor Baron Weinberg zu Falkenhause, a colonel in the Luftwaffe. He had been in Holland to inspect the airfields. His gray hair and weathered face suggested that most of his years in active service might soon be behind him if the war permitted.

"I am most grateful to you, Mr. Keizer." He shook Bob's hand when the train finally stopped at the Lehrter Bahnhof, the central station in Berlin, and made a gallant bow toward Suzan.

"You have my card. If ever I can be of service to you while you are in Berlin, do not hesitate to contact me."

He stepped down from the train, answering the many raised right arms and "Heil Hitlers," the Nazi salute, on the platform with a traditional military response.

31

Suzan was in awe at the palatial central station of Berlin. It was her first visit to the city, and she was surprised about the grandeur. The taxi ride from the station to Unter den Linden, where they would check in to the famous Hotel Adlon, was short, but the driver, apparently proud of his city, pointed to the Reichstag building, the German parliament, which still showed damage from a fire years ago, and the impressive Brandenburger Tor, before stopping in front of the majestic old Hotel Adlon.

Another surprise was how normal life seemed to be in wartime Berlin. Everything functioned as if the world were not on fire, except for the omnipresence of the military and the numerous swastika flags flying from buildings. Gallantly dressed people were strolling on Boulevard Unter den Linden or arriving, as did Bob and Suzan, in limousines and taxis to check in to the hotel.

Suzan always thought that the Amstel Hotel in Amsterdam must be the optimum of luxury, but the Adlon was beyond anything she could have imagined. The moment the taxi stopped, two doormen in very neat uniforms took the luggage while a piccolo opened the doors and Mr. and Mrs. Keizer entered the posh entrance hall with its magnificent chandeliers, fabulous art pieces, red carpets, marble, and palms, the tangible atmosphere of luxury and the immediately obvious presence of the belle monde, war or no war. The moment the entrance doors closed behind them, Bob and Suzan felt like the belle époque of Europe had never left this establishment.

Suzan realized that she quickly needed to change into something more in line with what she noticed the ladies were wearing and was thankful that she had packed like a young bride on her honeymoon.

While Mr. Keizer registered, showing the documents and marriage certificate, Suzan checked the massive guestbook and noticed that she was in the illustrious company of guests like opera singer Caruso, Albert Einstein, Charlie Chaplin, Marlene Dietrich, Roosevelt, Herbert Hoover, scandalous topless dancer Josephine Baker, and royalty from all over the world. *If only*, she thought, *all missions would come with perks like this, the resistance would not be so bad after all.*

The suite was magnificent, almost overdone in rococo style with thick carpets, real art on the walls, and a deliciously chic bathroom with fluffy towels, a large bathtub, and warm and cold water. A bottle of champagne, a fruit basket, a silver plate with delicacies, and a handwritten welcome on embossed hotel stationary with a large bouquet of red roses were on the coffee table.

But there was not a couch big enough to sleep on and only a king-size bed.

32

Bob and Suzan decided to go for drinks in the cocktail lounge at 5:00 p.m. to mingle with the crowd and to allow whomever would contact the newlyweds to be able to find them.

Dressed in appropriate black tie, Mr. Keizer seemed to be one of the regulars, moving around with ease, chatting here and there, enjoying his whiskey sour.

Mrs. Keizer drew appreciating eyes from both the ladies and the gentlemen. With her rich auburn hair fashionably coiffed and an ivory-colored long silk cocktail dress with just the right jewelry, she looked like the young bride she was supposed to be with even a slight blush. She moved among the crowd, charmingly accepting the gentlemen's half bows and even the hand kiss of what appeared to be an old Adlon patron.

What an advantage that both were fluent in German, because of the curriculum in the Dutch educational system, which included English, German, and French as obligatory.

There was lively conversation among the more than one

hundred guests, while scores of waiters and footmen in livery carried silver serving plates with crystal glasses of champagne, caviar, foie gras, lobster hors d'oeuvres, and so much more. An ensemble playing on an elevated platform in the center was hardly audible above the crowd. Popular singer Zarah Leander sang in her heavy, sultry voice, "Ich weiss, es wird einmal ein Wunder geschehen" ("I know that someday a miracle will happen"), which yielded her suppressed applause.

Bob noticed the number of senior officers in mess kits with decorations, being different, not the types he was used to seeing in Holland, no SS either. These seemed to be members of the Prussian aristocracy in uniform because that was family tradition for generations. How had it been possible for a lowly Austrian corporal to scream his way to the top and make these military men subordinate to him?

"Do I detect a Dutch accent, sir?" asked an officer in a friendly way from behind Bob, almost startling him.

Bob turned around, smiling. "Is it that obvious? My German teacher would box my ears."

"The name is Schulze-Boysen." He shook hands, a bit unusual for a German officer in uniform, albeit the cocktail variety. Bob noticed he did not mention his rank either, but he was clearly a staff officer.

"Bob Keizer, and this is my wife, Suzan. I still need to get used to that. This is our honeymoon."

The Fake Rembrandt

"Angenehm," (pleased to meet you) he said, "and welcome to Berlin then."

"I used to spend my holidays in Delft," continued the officer. "Great city and great university. Are you by any chance familiar with it?"

They understood the code; this was their contact.

"I sure am," answered Bob. "I studied engineering there but had to give up after two years when my presence was required in my father's company, which went through difficult times."

The confirmation.

A waiter patiently stood aside with a plate of delicacies in case they would be interested. He seemed to be Italian, with dark black hair and an olive tan, not common among the employees in Adlon.

The officer waved him away. "No, thank you."

"In that case, Mr. Keizer, would you and Mrs. Keizer be interested in joining me and my wife for an after-dinner drink? I am very interested to hear how things are in Holland today. My suite is 422. Would nine be convenient?"

"Most kind of you, Officer, and yes, we would love to."

33

The dinner was sumptuous, and the hotel had been considerate enough to provide a table for two for the honeymooners.

"Are you ready, darling? It is almost nine," said Bob.

"Yes, dear, but you need to excuse me for a moment. I would like to redo my hair and freshen my lipstick. Be with you in a sec."

Both stood up. When Suzan left, Bob sat down again and waited.

She was back soon, now carrying a purse that was large enough to hold more than a lipstick.

"Ready, love."

Suite 422 was large. It had an entrance with a crystal chandelier and a large, well-furnished grand room, separated from the bedroom, which seemed to be behind the double doors, thought Suzan. A serious-looking lady, between thirty-five and forty opened the door and invited Mr. and Mrs. Keizer to follow her to the salon, where Schulze-Boysen stood with a glass of cognac in his hand.

"May I introduce Mrs. and Mr. Keizer, gentlemen," said the lady in perfect English with a thick American accent. It was Mildred Harnack, the American wife of Harro Schulze-Boysen and, like him, an active member of the Rote Kapelle, the Red Orchestra, Berlin's main resistance group.

An elderly gentleman in a military uniform stood with his back to the group, hands behind his back, looking out of the window, and then he turned around.

Bob's and Suzan's hearts stood still. Was this a trap?

"How good to see you again and so soon!" said Oberst Weinberg. He smiled, while walking toward Bob and Suzan with an outstretched right hand. "Unexpected, I suppose, but please sit down and let me explain. By the way, this room has been swept."

Oberst Weinberg explained how not everything in Berlin was the way it appeared. Many opposed in secret the vulgarity of the Nazi regime. A country that used to be in many respects ahead of the world—in science, technology, philosophy, medicine, and the arts—was now a war machine, annihilating intellectuals, gentry, Jews, and anybody with different views on the Nazi version of society, guided by a psychopath whose power was based on unfathomable cruelty, who dreamed of a thousand-year German Reich, and who demanded oaths of unquestionable loyalty to his egocentric person, who built concentration camps instead of educational facilities, burned books, and soon would burn whole populations.

Some, like the people present in the room, were willing to risk their lives in the hope that one day the country would be normal again and decency and civility the victors.

"I have received the request from contacts in your country to listen to you, Mr. Keizer, so please go ahead. I am listening."

Bob explained why it was essential to find out the whereabouts of Salomon Cohen. He provided information about the train transport that included Mr. and Mrs. Cohen and its times of departure and arrival in Germany and possibly its arrival at Sachsenhausen.

"If it is possible at all," Suzan added, "it would be advantageous to know where Sarah Cohen is. After all, Salomon may not be very motivated with his wife still in a concentration camp."

Mildred smiled. "You are so right, dear, and it takes a woman to think about that."

Then Suzan opened her purse and handed over the leather pouch containing the gold coins and diamonds. "I was supposed to give this to you for obvious purposes," she said.

After a French cognac served in a tumbler, the ladies preferring a vintage port wine, it was time to call it a night. Mr. and Mrs. Keizer thanked the hosts for their friendly hospitality.

"Your room, by the way, is checked and safe," commented the Oberst with a wink.

When Bob and Suzan left the room, they noticed a servant bending down and picking up a tray with used cups and saucers from the floor at the door adjacent to the suite they had just left.

It was that Italian waiter.

34

"What do you think?" Suzan asked.

"Well, it was certainly a surprise to meet Baron Oberst Weinberg again, but I have a feeling that they are well organized and probably able to do more than we ever hoped for."

"Eerie, this thing about sweeping the rooms, but I guess that necessity comes with compliments of a totalitarian regime. I don't think I could stay here very long. I can't help thinking what the situation in Holland is now. Living as if this is the golden age of Germany makes me sick to my stomach."

"Talking about being sick to your stomach, Suzy, if for whatever reason someone questions why a couple on their honeymoon would be leaving after only two nights, it is because you are pregnant, feel very sick, and want to see your own physician in Holland, okay?"

"Oh my, I knew already as a young girl that you could get pregnant from a kiss. Why did I not listen to my mommy?" she said, and they both laughed.

"Now let's get practical, dear wife. You take the bathroom

first. Girls are known to take long showers or almost fall asleep in a tub ... I've learned from friends," Bob explained, reacting to Suzan's questioning look.

He was wrong. Less than twenty minutes later, a freshly showered Suzan reappeared, drying her wet hair with a towel and dressed in pajamas that would easily have fit Bob.

"Chastity?" he asked and smiled.

"Pregnancy," she answered. "Your turn, Daddy."

When they were finally in bed, side by side with a wide neutral zone separating them, Bob was very conscious of her presence. It aroused him. His heart had skipped a beat earlier that evening when he noticed her self-assured presence among the high brows. It was as if he saw for the first time what a natural beauty she was.

Suzan thought, *How come I feel comfortable in bed with a man who is not my lover or husband at all? How come I don't resent his musky scent? How come I like his clean smell of shaving cream and soap? How come I am noticing his charm, his guts as a resistance fighter, and his muscular body just now?*

They both kept looking at the ceiling.

"Suzy, mind if I move a bit closer?"

"I'll meet you halfway, Don Juan, but no monkey business."

She realized he probably was entitled to a somewhat more intelligent explanation. She moved a bit closer to him and rested her head on his shoulder without their bodies touching. He inhaled the scent of her hair.

"Look, Bob, I feel protected with you, comfortable and secure.

The Fake Rembrandt

I like you very much, and under different circumstances, in different times, it could be much more than that. But not now, Bob, not in this crazy world we live in, where each one of us could be killed, where we both could die. I could never do what needs to be done, worrying about the man I love. If they ever caught me and told me they were torturing you, I would spill the beans on the whole organization."

He did not move and did not say a single word.

"Besides, I am rather conservative. I did not get the greatest of examples in my family, but love for me, real love, is happiness, a large pink balloon that I keep for the man with whom I want to spend the rest of my life. There were boyfriends in high school. We danced, sometimes kissed, but never more than that. I have a lot of love to give, Bob, and with all my heart, I hope that I will live to give it to the man I feel can make me happy. But not now, Bob, not now.

"I pray that we will see the end of this disaster, and tomorrow would not be soon enough for me. Until then, I will put my love on ice, but if this nightmare is over and the sun shines again, it will melt the ice in a second, and I pray to God that you will still be around."

She gave him a quick kiss and then rolled over on her side and said, "Good night, Bob."

"Sleep well, Suzy."

But it took a long time before he fell asleep and could steady his fast-beating heart. Her words kept resounding in his mind over and over.

He never saw the tears on Suzan's pillow.

35

"Sachsenhausen Oberst," the man talking to Oberst Weinberg was a typical Westphalian farmer, maybe in his late fifties, a farm accident as a boy had cost him his right hand, which he had learned to compensate for by mainly using his left hand, supported when necessary by what was left of his right. He wore a soiled checkered cap, which he respectfully held against his chest when talking to Oberst Weinberg. His handicap had kept him out of the army. He smelled bad, was missing three of his front teeth, and was slightly cross-eyed, and the first impression of him was that he was probably a bit featherbrained, but one would misjudge his cunning character. Nobody thought of him as anything other than that gullible farmer, bringing his stuff to the camp, which gave him unprecedented freedom of movement.

"He works in the group of a Major Krueger, which is a very secretive group of prisoners who are separated from the others in a special *lager*, no. 19. Nobody I talked to knows what they are up to, but they are treated better than other prisoners. I may be able to get a message to him through my contacts, Obersturmbahnführer Richthoff, but it will cost money."

Twice every week, the man known as Bauer Berent (Farmer Berent) would drive his horse-pulled wagon through the gate with "Arbeit Macht Frei" at Sachsenhausen, delivering beets and potatoes. It allowed him to organize contacts inside, which for substantial financial benefits, he used to provide information to the man he knew before the war as Baron Weinberg.

The Rote Kapelle maintained a network of similar contacts in several concentration camps, which was how Salomon Cohen could be located, in just a couple of days.

Oberst Weinberg handed the farmer his usual fee of one thousand reichsmark, a substantial amount for the information provided, but it kept the informer hungry, and more details would be required before the planned operation.

Farmer Berent seemed to be a weak shackle in the chain of underground operations, but he would die before he ever revealed his contacts in the resistance. Berent had been married to a buxom farmer's daughter, who passed away three years after their wedding. It left him with a son, whom he loved above anything in his world, a Down syndrome child the Nazi system considered unwanted. As with so many mentally handicapped Germans, he should have been euthanized under Hitler's decree Aktion T4, which would cost the lives of 70,273 people. Farmer Berent, who for many years had worked on land owned by Baron Weinberg, pleaded tearfully for help. The baron helped and in what appeared to him as divine interference, the life of his Karlchen was saved and the boy kept safely hidden in the country. Berent would not talk, but to keep his child safe, he needed money—hence his undercover operations within the camp.

"Thank you, Berent. That is very helpful for now. No message needs to be sent to Salomon Cohen. I will contact you, as always, if I might need you again."

Both men left the freshly plowed field of the Weinberg estate on the edge of which the meeting took place, each in a different direction.

36

When Bob checked out, the receptionist expressed his surprise. "Was everything to your liking, Mr. and Mrs. Keizer?"

"Oh yes, certainly," responded Bob. "However, unfortunately, my wife does not feel well at all and prefers a thorough checkup from her personal physician, so we will have to postpone our honeymoon."

"I understand, sir. May I wish you and Mrs. Keizer a good trip home and may everything turn out for the better, Mrs. Keizer. We hope we will have the pleasure of your return."

The taxi ride to the station was much shorter this time without the tourist route and explanations. It was a busy day. Cars and taxis were dropping off hundreds of people with their luggage. Military men in a variety of uniforms, accompanied by their wives and children, girlfriends, and sometimes parents, crowded the area in front of the station.

The taxi driver was thanking them politely for the tip he had received and offering to carry the suitcases to the entrance, when two men, dressed in long black leather coats, approached them.

"Mr. and Mrs. Keizer, we would like you to follow us please." It did not sound like a request.

"Why? And to where? We have a train to catch, and my wife does not feel very well. May I ask who you are?"

Both men showed their identity cards, Gestapo, the feared secret state police.

Bob and Suzan realized that refusal was no option. Since the occupation of Holland, there was no official representation of the Netherlands in Nazi Germany anymore, so they were on their own.

They were loaded into the back of a car with one of the Gestapo men sitting next to the driver. No one said a word. Bob held Suzan's hand very tightly, but her response was a quick nod of her head, indicating she was okay.

The car stopped in front of a large building that resembled a museum. The only sign in front of it indicated that this was Prinz-Albrect-Strasse No. 8, the headquarters of the Gestapo. Swastika flags decorated the front.

Suzan and Bob were marched into the building and immediately taken to different cells in the basement where they spent two days with little food or water. On the third day, Bob was brought to an office on the ground floor and was unceremoniously planted in a chair, facing an empty desk from behind which a man in civilian clothes, bald and with fishy eyes behind steel-rimmed glasses, stared at him without saying a word.

Then, finally, in a voice hardly audible and very slow but menacing the more, he asked, "So, Mr. Keizer, tell me, why did you come to Germany?"

"I object against this treatment and especially against this arrest of my wife and me. We came to Germany with the best of intentions, to enjoy our honeymoon in one of Europe's finest hotels and to hopefully attend an event in the presence of the führer."

"Is that so? Then tell me, why did you have a meeting with Oberst Weinberg?"

"What meeting? The gentleman was so friendly as to have my wife and me invited for drinks, as he recognized us among the guests at Adlon. After all, I happened to save his life during the trip by train from Holland."

"I am aware of your heroic intervention and am even willing to believe in unbelievable coincidence, but let me repeat myself, Mr. Keizer, why did you come to Germany?"

"Then let me repeat myself also, I came to Germany to spend my honeymoon in Adlon."

"Very well, we have ways of improving your memory. As soon as you tell me what the purpose of your meeting with Oberst Weinberg was, you may be returning to Holland. Until that time, you will be our guest here instead of the Adlon," and to the armed guard standing at the door all the time, he said, "Take him to his cell."

Suzan received a similar treatment but gave such a credible

performance of a very sick, probably pregnant young bride that she was taken back to her cell without a very extensive interrogation.

Not being able to communicate, neither of them slept that night, terrified of what the future might be and if they would even have one.

Then, suddenly, at midmorning the next day, both could leave without any explanation.

An urgent message from Reichsmarschall Hermann Göring himself to the head of the Gestapo that under no circumstances should the Dutch couple be harmed and that they should be released immediately probably saved Bob and Suzan from torture or even death.

Oberst Weinberg appeared to be one of Göring's confidants, and the story of how his life was saved by the brave Dutchman was enough for the field marshal to take immediate action.

A taxi waited for them at the front of the building, and much to their surprise, their luggage was in it. Dirty and hungry as they were, they decided to immediately go to the station and take the first available train to Holland, which luckily happened to leave in less than an hour.

They freshened up a bit in the washroom, and after a coffee and rye bread with ham, which they hungrily devoured, they settled in the plush seats of the first-class compartment, very tired but very relieved.

"What made this happen?" wondered Suzan. "You think the room was bugged anyway?"

"No, they were apparently fishing. If the room had been bugged, we would have been in much deeper trouble. My guess is that Italian waiter must be the Gestapo's spy in the hotel."

"But what about the certain release? That did not make much sense."

"We may never know, but someone seems to have interfered. Anyway, let's be happy we're on our way home. That building, those monstrous people, they gave me the creeps."

"Is our honeymoon over now?" Suzan smiled and moved a bit closer to Bob.

"No, Mrs. Keizer, just indefinitely postponed and relocated to a tropical island."

They leaned back and, totally exhausted, closed their eyes.

37

In the basement of the Lido Hotel in Amsterdam, Sandberg, Roger, and a third person, an impressive giant of a man in his midthirties only known as "Vincit," which was a play on his real name, Vincent, were discussing their options.

The Latin word *vincit* was taken from Virgil's text *Labor Omnia Vincit* (work overcomes everything), and the man adopting the pseudonym certainly looked like he could conquer adversity.

"You have to take over from here, Vincit. I will do whatever I can, but the overall coordination requires your influence and your connections." Sandberg was convinced that with Vincit in charge of the operation, the possibility of success would increase significantly.

Vincent was born in Balik Papan on Borneo, one of the islands in the Dutch Indies, which in postcolonial times would become the independent republic Indonesia. His father was a petroleum engineer with the BPM, a Dutch oil company, and his mother a colorful mixture of cultures with an intellect matching her beauty. She insisted that Vincent should attend the HBS in Bandoeng, the excellent Dutch high school. He passed all exams with ease, was a star tennis player, and won the national amateur boxing championship several times. He was sent to Holland to study at the Technical University in Delft, his father's alma mater. He had to cope with a bout of homesickness at first, but his impressive personality and sympathetic character soon made him popular among fellow students.

Then Holland was invaded.

With other students who resented the rape of their country, he became active in the resistance. His natural leadership ability soon put him in charge of a regional unit, and subsequently, he became the leader of the intelligence organization. Vincent became Vincit, the conqueror.

"What is it exactly that you would like me to do, Willem?"

He quickly explained the goal of the operation to keep Rembrandt's masterpiece *The Night Watch* out of German hands, but what "taking over" would entail was something Vincit needed to completely understand.

Sandberg filled him in on what they had achieved thus far.

"We sent a couple to Berlin to contact the Rote Kapelle and find out to which concentration camp Salomon Cohen, the artist we believe is able to paint a credible copy, had been transported. We now know he is in Sachsenhausen and may not be in immediate danger of being murdered. But he is a Jew, and we all know what that means these days."

"Who is that couple?" asked Vincit.

Roger explained, "Two of my best, gone through several successful operations together, both highly motivated, intelligent, brave, and fluent in German."

"They returned after an eventful trip that included several nights in Albrechtstrasze," added Sandberg, "but with the information on Cohen and without giving a sliver of information to the Gestapo."

"What we would ask you to do, Vincit, is organize the kidnapping of Salomon Cohen from the concentration camp and bring him to Amsterdam. We'll take it from there."

"Is that all?" Vincit said and smiled with a slight undertone of cynicism, but the spark in his dark eyes revealed that he liked the challenge. "Okay, I'll do it. I will coordinate from the city of Amersfoort, where I can avail myself of some of the assistance required. I will let you know where to send the uniforms that you assembled. I will personally call on you for the funds we will need."

The men shook hands, and at ten-minute intervals left the building through a back door.

Vincit was now in charge of Operation Night Watch.

38

The city of Amersfoort is situated in the center of the country. Its history goes back more than a thousand years. The heart of it is called De Muurhuizen, the wall houses, for the dwellings that were erected in the fourteenth century on the remnants of a previous city wall. The houses are well preserved, and some formed ideal hiding places for the resistance, who operated from several locations. Amersfoort also housed the regional resistance weapon depot, existing of a variety of guns, handguns, Sten guns, hand grenades, and explosives. The arsenal was hidden outside the city center in the space under the basin of the Sportfondsenbad, the municipal indoor swimming pool. The pool was often enjoyed by German soldiers.

Across from Vincit sat Huub Fremouw, the pool manager and an early member of the resistance before it became an organization. There was a small space where parts and tools were kept, and in the back, well hidden from view, was an area that functioned as office space. In one of the closets was the communication equipment that kept Vincit in touch with other units.

It was also the place where the miscellaneous parts of SS officer's uniforms stolen from different locations were stored, neatly folded trousers, jackets, and coats with belts and boots and on top of it the caps Bob and Suzan delivered. An additional number of complete soldier uniforms and helmets, which were easier to obtain and used several times in operations, were in a closet. From the supply of Fremouw, a large selection of miscellaneous things that an officer or soldier might carry—photos, a billfold, German money, and cigarettes—all from articles left over time in the changing cubicles by swimmers were stored in a wooden crate.

"What about the papers?" asked Huub, who had been briefed by Vincit and pleaded enthusiastic support.

"The selection of the men comes first," responded Vincit. "We will receive assistance from our contacts in Berlin, but they insisted that beyond equipment, that is to say cars, they would only supply two drivers; the officers and soldiers need to come from us."

"I see. Do you have some in mind? How many do you need?"

"Two senior officers in the back of an open Mercedes staff car and a sergeant to sit next to the driver. In a Kübelwagen, next to the driver, we need a sergeant and two soldiers in the back, all four heavily armed. What would you have available?"

"I could supply three Luger PO8, a sidearm of most Waffen SS, and three Mauser HST, also a Waffen SS favorite, but the Maschinenpistole thirty-eight, the automatic weapon you would need for the Kübelwagen guys is somewhat more complicated. We have two; you would need four."

"Any other weapon we could use?"

"Not without drawing attention from a smart observer, no you need four of the same. Very unlikely that the four guys would be from different units. "Give me a couple of days. I'll check around."

The Nazi Germans considered themselves the Herrenvolk, the master race, and visits to brothels in occupied territory were not something the system promoted.

Nevertheless, soldiers, often drunk, did visit, and losing part of their uniform or, more important a weapon there was something difficult to explain to a commander.

It became a valuable source of supply to the resistance. Within a couple of days, Huub would have the two additional guns Vincit needed.

39

On the outskirts of Berlin, in the back room of the local grocery store, Simon van Amersfoort presented verbally his coded credentials to the German air force staff officer known as Harro within close circles of the resistance. Simon was a confidant of Vincit and was sent to Berlin to discuss the plan of operation and to obtain details on the assistance Rote Kapelle would be able to give. One of Simon's greatest assets was his brilliant brain and fabulous memory. No matter how complicated a plan of action, he would be able to memorize it and days later pass it on verbatim. No incriminating documents would ever be found on Simon.

"The men need to be fluent in German, without accent, especially the one doing most of the talking," commented Harro, when Simon told him that the officers and soldiers needed could be found in Holland.

"That will not be a problem," answered Simon. "All will be fluent and the one doing the talking will be from German parents immigrated to Holland long before the war."

The Fake Rembrandt

"What about equipment, weapons, uniforms?"

"We have it all, including the personal items, identifications, photos, German cigarettes, and some Dutch money as well, but the cars with Berlin license plates and the SS standard need to come from here."

"I know. We are aware of it, and that won't be the biggest problem. What we still have to do is decide on the spot from where the operation starts."

"The closer the better, I assume, sir."

"Agreed, and please call me Harro, but it is an additional risk at the same time. The area around Sachsenhausen is closely watched, but we have a suggestion."

Harro produced a map of the northern part of Germany and spread it out on the table. He placed a finger on the province of Brandenburg, "Look," he said, "how the men will arrive in Berlin and where they will stay, we'll address later, they will need to stay undercover, the Gestapo is very interested in any foreigner coming to Berlin these days."

"I understand, and none of the uniforms or weapons will be traveling with them. We have alternative solutions for that," answered Simon.

"Then let me show you what we are proposing. Here we have Germendorf, a small hamlet, part of Oranienburg." Harro pointed to a spot on the map.

"From there, it is only 8.5 kilometers to Sachsenhausen. That should only take twenty minutes by car. We have a safe house there beneath the old brick church in the center. The problem is that to the south of it, some six to eight thousand prisoners from Sachsenhausen are forced to work at the Heinkel Airplane Works. The appearance of some SS big shots from Berlin would not raise eyebrows there, but as with every other route, there may be thorough inspections. Serious bluffing might solve that problem. Besides, better being scrutinized outside the camp than once within it. We could bring the cars to Germendorf without too many questions asked."

"But what about the men? How do we get them in the safe house?"

"Let me explain," answered Harro.

40

"The brick church in Germendorf, built in 1739, has a square tower without a spire. High in the tower, above the clock, on each side, are three openings, twelve in total. An excellent location to keep watch over the whole 360 degrees of the area. We could send a van with technical equipment to be installed in the tower. With it should be a team of technical experts, your guys. Most likely one or two sentries will be assigned to watch over the installation. If so, they will need to be silenced by your men."

It sounded like a matter-of-fact statement made by an officer used to making wartime decisions.

Simon kept looking at the spot on the map, as if answers could miraculously come from there.

"Our second alternative is operating from Oranienburg, which is even closer to Sachsenhausen, only some 2.5 kilometers and less than a ten-minute drive."

"That sounds like a better option. What is the problem?"

"A big one. Some activities there are so secret that I don't know much about them, but it possibly has to do with some form of energy that could provide Hitler with a super bomb."

As it turned out, after the war, Nazi Germany's nuclear-energy project was based in Oranienburg.

"Because of it, security in Oranienburg is so tight that it may be extremely dangerous to operate from there. Nevertheless, we have two safe locations there, one the house of a widow, the other a car repair shop with a junkyard behind it. The Kübelwagen will be obtained from there, assembled from crashed wrecks. The extreme security might work in favor of the operation. Nobody would expect something to be wrong with high-ranking SS officials coming to visit from Berlin. Nor would they suspect your *technicians* apparently involved in secret research. We can provide them with appropriate IDs and paperwork."

"Any third option?"

"I don't think so. I would not recommend starting the operation from Berlin, too many curious eyes; besides, the longer drive increases the risk."

"What about the return trip? After all, that is the purpose of the mission. I assume we can't just let them take a train or a taxi to Holland."

"No, that wouldn't work but compared to the first part of the mission, that is not the most difficult part."

"Do you have any suggestions?"

"Yes, we do. As a matter of fact, it may be easier than you think."

Simon raised his eyebrows. "Now you're making me curious."

41

"I know you Dutch people are proud of one of your aircraft pioneers Anthony Fokker, but very few know that his career started in Germany. In 1912, Fokker had already established in Johannisthal, close to Berlin, his first company, Aeroplanbau. When the First World War started, he built the Fokker Eindecker, a monoplane, and the advanced Fokker Dr.I the triplane made famous by the Red Baron, Manfred von Richthofen, who shot down eighty enemy planes and reputedly circled to salute them on their way down. Anthony delivered many of those planes to the military and became extremely rich. At the end of the 1920s, Fokker was the largest aircraft builder in the world. Not less than fifty-four airlines operated with the popular Fokker F VII. He left for America where he started the Atlantic Aircraft Corporation, which later became the Fokker Aircraft Corporation of America, but went back to Holland after General Motors took over his company. He made the international press again when, on December 30, 1933, with a crew of four, a record return flight to Batavia in Indie was made with the three-engine Fokker plane De

Pelikaan. However, ultimately, technological developments from competitors overtook his traditional approach to plane building. But with new enthusiasm, Anthony Fokker developed the D.XXI. The Netherlands government bought thirty-six of them, of which twenty-nine were still in the air when our troops invaded Holland.

"Then, in 1936, Fokker presented his very advanced Fokker GI fighter plane. It was unique in many respects, a twin-engine double-fuselage plane, with eight machine guns in the nose. It was too late, however, to have a significant production available to Holland when Germany rearmed itself."

"Very interesting, Harro, and indeed some of the details are new to me; however, how could this be of any importance to our operation?"

"I will get to that in a minute. When the fighting was over in Holland, our troops confiscated the Fokker factories to use them to produce parts for our Junker JU 52 transport planes.

"It was much later that through information obtained from prisoners who worked at Fokker before the war, we learned that a secret team within the company was well ahead of the latest developments and worked on a fighter plane superior to anything we know of today." Harro stopped to let the importance of that information sink in.

"Your men will travel back to Holland together by train, in comfort and first class, in possession of the most excellent forged papers, which even the Gestapo will respect, signed by Göring himself. Their task will supposedly be to find the drawings and documents produced by that secret team. It was an oversight of those who started the production of the Junker parts not to immediately surge for documented advanced technology. They could have assumed a company that, even before the First World War, invented a method to shoot a machine gun through a turning propeller without touching the blades, should have hidden secrets somewhere."

"But papers signed by Hermann Göring? Is that not a bit far-fetched? The second in command? Only Hitler outranks him."

"Well, here is the great secret. Hermann's younger brother Albert despises Nazism. We have a contact with him through the highest level of the resistance. He has been arrested many times for his subversive activities, but every time, his big brother has interfered. He does whatever Albert advises."

"Wow, that is brilliant, Harro! The return was one of our main concerns. There is no way that we could have come up with a better plan."

"I know. Just make sure you pick the right guys, brave and intelligent enough to quickly read up on some aeronautical technology. I am sure you can get your hands on something."

42

Vincit listened patiently to the long debriefing from Simon, without interrupting him once. The trip to Berlin had obviously been a risky necessity, but the information received was of great value. When Simon was finished talking, Vincit smiled.

"My God, that solves some of our most serious problems. We can draft the logistics now from start to finish, and I would appreciate your help."

"Of course, Vincit."

"Let's draw the profiles of the men we need. I was already aware that we need men who are fluent in German and with an admirable portion of guts. This information completes the requirements."

"First, the two senior SS officers sitting in the back of the Mercedes. I would say between thirty-five and forty-five years old, authoritative characters, of average height so the uniforms we have will fit. Both fluent in German and preferably with a technical education, but at least some technical background. Both should have fighting experience, to be able to at least have a chance if found out."

"That seems to cover it."

"Then the sergeant sitting next to the driver, he could be younger, also with technical experience or know-how, but his German must be flawless without any foreign accent. The driver is no problem since he is German and supplied with the car by the Rote Kapelle."

"Correct."

"What do you think of the guys in the Kübelwagen that escorts the big shots, Simon?"

"Those could be younger men, typical soldiers ready to shoot it out if that would be necessary. But because of the technical tasks the group is assigned to, both at the church in Germendorf and when returning to Holland, it probably is better that they are also around thirty-five to forty years old to be credible as technicians or scientists. And of course they should also speak credible German."

"I will send messages to all units in the country. I am convinced there will be more suitable candidates than we need. What do you think of sending a reserve in case something unexpected happens to one of them?"

"That would be a good idea, but I advise against it. Having someone with the knowledge but not participating in the operation may be an extra risk. No, I think we have to rely on the group we select."

"Okay, then this is what I'll do. First, I will draft the outlines of the whole operation. Don't worry; I have hiding places safer than the Central Bank. Then I want some of you—Roger, Willem, Gerrit, yourself—to go to a farmhouse in Bunschoten, not far from here. I don't want that meeting in Amersfoort. We will go over the plan as often as necessary until we are all satisfied."

"Yes, I can see the need for that. The lives of some of our bravest are at stake."

"Then, Simon, I want all six men—the two officers, the sergeant, and the three soldiers—here. They will be informed they will be isolated until back from this mission. We will brief them, assign their tasks, have a uniform fitting, and adjust where necessary. They will be made familiar with the weapons. I have a location on the outskirts where we will dry-run the operation, with some of my men acting as aggressive, suspicious Germans under different scenarios. In the meantime, and there will be ample time, all identification papers will be made and CVs drafted for each person."

43

"You want me to do *what*?" Bob wanted to be sure that he fully understood what Roger had just proposed.

They were walking along the River Amstel. The weather was great, and they were not the only people enjoying the sunny afternoon. There was nothing suspicious about two men leaving the city to enjoy a walk in the countryside.

"Not so loud. Yes, and I am sure you understood me, that is exactly what we are asking you to do, but again, it is up to you. We have alternatives, but we need to know fast."

Roger had done what he was authorized to do. He explained the plan to one of the trusted members of the resistance whose profile matched the details provided by Vincit, as required for one of the senior officers.

"But why me?"

"For many reasons, not in the least because you can be trusted. You also happen to match the profile sketched by Vincit, the right age, fluent in German, technical background, lots of experience, and gutsy enough to pull it off."

"Thanks for the compliment, but this requires great team work. Where the hell do you think you can find six men suicidal enough and all fitting the profile to pull off an operation like that?"

"The answer is among the members of all units, and as a matter of fact, six have been selected, including you. By the way, there were more suitable candidates than you might think, suicidal or not."

"That makes six suitable individuals, Roger. I was talking about a team. You know darn well that eleven players don't make a soccer team. Look at the miserable results we have against Belgium. By the way, who are the other guys?"

"In the first place, this is hardly a game, Bob, and you will meet the other members soon enough if you accept. You will then work, isolated from the world, to get to know each other, to work on team building and to practice, ad infinitum, the whole operation."

"Who is in charge?"

"Of the logistics, Vincit himself. Leading the operation in Germany, that will be decided during training by two sergeant majors who went underground after they had to lay the weapons down against their principal. They will do the training. They have a quarter century of experience forming an odd group of civilians, all young men, into efficient fighting units. In addition, there is an aircraft engineer who used to work at the Fokker plant; you will later understand why."

"I see, but what about timing?"

"We won't have much time. That is why we need your decision pronto. You must be aware of some conditions. The first one is, no talking about what we discussed, not a word and not even to Suzan. Then from the moment you accept, you will be taken to Amersfoort, where you will meet everybody and receive training. You can still bail out then, if something or someone concerns you. But in that case, you will be kept there, isolated from the world until the return of the group."

"What about the arrangements in Germany? I was quite impressed with those whom Suzan and I met there, but don't forget; we were also the guests of the Gestapo. By some miracle, we were released from custody but could have easily been killed. I realize there is never a full guarantee, but what can you tell me about it?"

"Only this, the Rote Kapelle is giving us full support. They have offered a brilliant solution for safe return that we ourselves never could have come up with. The operation is obviously extremely risky. That is why we prepare and train the team extensively. Every single person in the team is thoroughly checked out again, even though none is a stranger to the resistance—in fact they are all committed members. What will it be, Bob?"

The two men were sitting on a concrete bench on the side of the river, staring over the water in contemplation. The windmill on the other side slowly lost its colors and became a dark silhouette against the orange of the setting sun. A young fisherman in front of it reeled in his line; the strollers had gone home. All was quiet.

Finally, Roger spoke. "What do you think, Bob?"

"Well, what *did* you think? You know me. Count me in."

44

In the center of the city of Amersfoort, known as De Muurhuizen, are the characteristic dwellings of different designs but all centuries old. Having monument status, they are well maintained under protective city by-laws to conserve their historic value for posterity. Among them stand two brick houses, built as twins in 1585. Leaning against the one on the right is a charming white step-gabled house, appearing smaller than its rather roomy interior. What few people know is that these three structures, like several others within De Muurhuizen, were interconnected through underground tunnels, dating back to the sixteenth century, when violent faith disputes pitted citizens against each other. The ability to hide and safely escape from these houses served the inhabitants well during the Spanish occupation in the sixteenth and seventeenth centuries and the French occupation of Holland at the end of the eighteenth century. This time, they would serve the Dutch resistance as a safe place from which to operate.

Sitting at a long table in the sparsely lit room under the saddle roof of the house on the right, the small dormer windows covered with blackout curtains, were a dozen very different men.

At the head of the table was the impressive figure of Vincit, his expression foreshadowing the importance of the meeting. At his right side were Huub and Simon, and next to them were the two sergeant majors. The oldest one was straight-backed with a protruding belly, steel-rimmed glasses, and a pointed moustache. Named Wilhelm, he seemed to be a living remnant of the First World War. The younger one, introduced as Robert, was of medium height with a short, military-style haircut. There was not an ounce of fat on his lean, muscular body. A sympathetic smile compensated for a weathered face, an outdoorsman.

Then, in contrast, there was a middle-aged man with an unhealthy complexion, too thin for the gray three-piece suit he was wearing, his thin hands nervously resting on a pile of books in front of him, the Fokker engineer known as Davelaar.

On the other side of the table, across from Vincit, sat Bob. To his right was Paul, who was about his age. Paul had curly brown hair that needed to be cut short, like the hair of the others, to look identical to the German SS haircuts. He was about four inches shorter than Bob. His demeanor was attentive, like he wanted to absorb every small detail. He would be the second officer in the Mercedes, together with Bob. The rest of the group could have been members of the same regiment. They were the same size and age and all fit and appearing able to stand their ground when necessary.

Vincit welcomed all.

"Again, gentlemen, welcome. You have been introduced to each other, and you are to use the names given and nothing else the whole time. Until departure, you will stay in the present houses. Meetings will take place in this room, whenever called by me. This house, the one next door, and the low white one adjacent to it are interconnected in two ways. Aboveground, on the main floors, a door behind the wall tapestries provides access to the adjacent house. You will all sleep in the large room on the second floor, next door. Two toilets and one bathroom will have to do for you all.

"In the back of that house on the ground floor is a large open kitchen where we will have our meals. We will need to be very quiet at meals or anywhere else here for the next number of days.

"Below ground, thanks to the tenants or house owners centuries ago, are tunnels that connect and provide access to the garden behind the third house. It is our escape route. These tunnels will only be used in emergencies. There is also, for some reason, below this house a cellar with a heavy oak door and an air inlet that suggests it has been used as a cell. Let's hope we won't need it, but if we do, it is because German patrols will walk the Muurhuizen, usually in pairs.

"If they come too close for our liking and want access to these buildings, Huub will open the door. When they are inside, we will take them down, tie them up, and keep them in that cell until we decide what to do with them.

"That is all for today, gentlemen. We will have a uniform fitting tomorrow morning and a first dry run. The sergeant majors, Huub, Simon, the engineer, and I will stay in this building; you go find your improvised quarters next door. We'll have dinner at seven. Any questions?"

There were many questions in the heads of each attendant, but they all thought it better to wait until the next day.

45

The room next door was unexpectedly large but gloomy because of the small glass-in-lead windows. Entering through a door behind a wall tapestry was a bit theatrical at first, like in a movie, but easy to get used to.

There were two rows of field beds with a pillow and a sleeping bag and a towel on the foot, plus a chair and a small table each. A wide carpeted area separated the rows. Bob decided to take the one nearest to the back wall. Paul selected the bed on the opposite wall, closest to the door.

Paul was a bit talkative. It irritated Bob slightly, but he thought it must be the anticipation of a great operation.

"When do you think we will go, and what about that strange Fokker character? How does he fit in this operation? What do you think?"

"What I think is that questions should be asked at the meetings. I know as much as you do."

"Okay, I guess you're right. I think I may be just a bit too excited. I love playing the role. In high school, I once played Creon in *Antigone*. This one should be much easier but more exciting."

"It will hardly be a Greek tragedy, Paul. Nobody knows exactly what we will be facing, and the less text the better. What will be of vital importance is secrecy and team play. I am going to freshen up a bit, and to be honest, I am famished. I could eat a horse. I'll see you in the kitchen."

The open kitchen provided ample space for the whole team, six men each at two tables. The surprise was that Vincit appeared to be an excellent cook, and the dinner of tasty pork chops with thick gravy, endives, and potatoes was a better meal than many of them had had for a long time. There was also plenty of it. They even had a real cup of coffee with sugar and cream after dinner. The resistance must consider the planned operation of great importance. In an amicable atmosphere, in low voices, the men wisely held only small talk. Everybody was tired, and they all went to bed early.

Bob could not get any sleep; he was exhausted and yet wide awake.

Something bothered him, but he could not put his finger on it.

For hours, he just rested on his back, arms folded behind his head, staring at the ceiling while the five others were fast asleep, breathing heavily or snoring loudly.

He thought about Suzan.

All he could tell her was that he would be away for an uncertain period and that she could not call on him. She had just looked into his eyes, but asked no questions. When they said goodbye, he noticed her moist eyes and felt the swift kiss on his cheek, and then for a moment longer than the kiss necessitated, she hugged him.

"Please be careful, Bob."

He would be, more than ever now.

It must have been midnight or even later when Bob sensed more than he could observe movement at the end of the opposite row. He wanted to whisper, "Is that you, Paul?" thinking maybe the guy had gone to the washroom. But something stopped Bob from doing it. Instead, he pretended to be asleep. Never having slept yet, his eyes were adjusted to the dark room and he noticed that Paul was fully dressed. He had been undressed when he went to bed earlier. Bob's heart started to beat faster. Why would a guy get dressed to go for a pee?

46

Bob waited until Paul, after listening if everybody was asleep, sneaked out of the room. Breathing heavily, Bob pretended to be asleep. He waited until Paul left, quickly dressed without making noise, and then followed him, realizing with a shock that he had gone to the basement and entered the tunnel to the white house next door. He followed.

It was pitch-dark, and Bob could not see if Paul had left the tunnel, but he assumed he did, so he felt his way to the exit.

There was just enough moonlight to see a shadow walking fast to the back of the garden and then tiptoeing through a narrow pathway to the street in front of the houses.

Bob followed at a safe distance.

Paul walked fast, pussyfooting close to the front of the buildings to stay in the shadows of the dimly lit streets. Around the corner was a narrow footbridge built as an arc across the ten-yard-wide canal. Paul stopped there, leaning his back against the forged-iron railings, looking around him as if expecting someone. Bob waited at the corner, just outside his view.

Suddenly from the shadows on the other side of the bridge, a man approached and shook hands with Paul, who handed him something. They then whispered a few words.

Bob tried to get a good look at the face of the man through his pocket binoculars, but he wore a hat deep over his eyes. What he did see was the black/red triangle on the lapel of the man's jacket.

NSB, the infamous Dutch collaborators.

Bob's heart skipped a beat; Paul was a traitor.

The men shook hands again and then each went in a different direction.

Bob stayed where he was, hidden from view.

What was he going to do? If he went back fast and stealthily, he might be in bed before Paul returned; however, he could not let that collaborator leave.

He might have been handed valuable information on the operation, and letting him go could be a disaster.

Paul's eyes would be used to the sparse moonlight. He might see very little entering the room and would most probably not notice that one bed was empty.

Bob followed the NSB stranger, who moved slowly, afraid maybe to be seen or heard.

Just before the second bridge across the same canal, Bob caught up with him and had him in a headlock before the man even noticed he was being followed.

Bob tightened his grip. The men's legs gave away, and a subdued gurgling escaped his throat. He gripped Bob's arms in vain, and then there were a few spasms and he moved no more.

Bob put him on the ground and quickly went through his pockets; he found a note, an NSB identity card, and some change.

He shoved the body over the railings of the bridge. If the body was found, one might assume that he had lost his way in the dark and fallen into the canal where he drowned. This was wartime with very few pathologists interested in checking the corpse of a drowned NSB figure.

Bob never went back to bed, but the next morning, he was the first in the shower, and with most of the men still asleep, he entered the room and quite loudly woke them up. "Good morning, beauties. Time to wake up. Who is next in the shower?"

One of them was quick, but Paul acted like he was still half asleep, and yawning loudly, he stretched his body.

"Morning, Bob. God, I must have been tired; I was out like a light the moment I hit the sack."

"Great. Take your time. I am going to see if I can give Vincit a hand with breakfast."

When Bob told Vincit what had happened that night and handed him the piece of paper with information on the group and the planned operation with the NSB identity card, he clenched his fist, his dark eyes spitting fire.

"Great job, Bob. Leave it to me. Act normal, and don't say anything to anybody. We'll deal with it at the meeting."

47

It was eight o'clock sharp. Everyone sat in his assigned seat at the table in great anticipation.

Vincit stood behind his chair, a thin folder in his left hand.

"First thing today," he started the meeting, "is taking pictures to take care of the documents, and then after that, I expect delivery of the uniforms from their present location. If adjustments need to be made, we need a bit of time. That's why it is on my list as one of the first items."

He paused, and then while talking, he started to walk around the room. He walked around the table and stopped behind the chair to the right of Paul.

"Because we'll have some time before the photographer gets here, we will have a role play."

"It is understandable that we focus on Germany, but let us not forget, gentlemen, that we are and still will be in Holland until we cross the border. We run the risk of being stopped by the Gruene Polizei, by the Landwacht or Dutch policemen collaborating with the enemy; even the NSB might ask us questions. Therefore, Paul,

I want you to be one of them. Bob, you are stopped by him. He'll ask you for your papers and whereabouts. Start."

Paul stood up from his chair, a tiny smile on his face, but a keen observer would have noticed a slight twist at the corner of his mouth.

"*Halt*!" he shouted at Bob, who had taken position in front of him. "Where are you going? Papers!"

"I am on my way home. I wanted to see my brother, who fell ill."

"Papers."

"I am afraid I don't have papers," answered Bob.

A triumphant smile appeared on Paul's face. He felt that he was going to be the star of the role play.

"Could it be this paper?" interrupted Vincit. In his right hand, very visible to Paul, was the paper with the information he had treacherously handed over to the NSB during the night.

Paul changed color and started shaking and sweating, knowing what was to follow.

"Gentlemen, we have a traitor in our midst." Vincit threw the paper and the NSB identification card on the table. The group was speechless. They could hardly comprehend what they had just witnessed, still half into the role play.

"This piece of shit—excuse my French—left the building in the middle of the night to snitch on our operation and to hand the details over to our enemy. I don't know, nor am I interested what his motives are for putting the lives of all of us at stake. His mistake was that he did not understand that we have eyes and ears everywhere, even at night." *It did not hurt,* Vincit thought, *to let them all think no move would be made without him knowing about it.*

Addressing the sergeant majors, he continued, "Gentlemen, please take this asshole to the cell downstairs, tie him up thoroughly, and tape his mouth. The National Resistance Council will deal with him. May God have his rotten soul."

Robert was on his feet like a tiger jumping his prey. He grabbed Paul's arm and turned it behind his back. He then used his own right hand to grab Paul's curly hair and pulled the man's head back. The elderly soldier was surprisingly quick behind the traitor. He grabbed the back of his pants and almost lifted him off the floor. While they marched the culprit out of the room, the traitor cried like a baby, leaving a wet trace behind; he had wetted himself.

48

"How did he pass the scrutiny of our interrogators?" wondered Huub. "He came with perfect credentials, and what the hell were his motives?"

"I don't care a rodent's rectum about his motives," answered Vincit. "How he fooled our people is something we will work on."

"For now, we have a problem, guys," offered Simon. "We can't have just one officer in the Mercedes. Vincit, do we have a reserve?"

"I must remind you that you were the one who advised against it, Simon. No, we don't. Give me some time to think of an alternative."

"Excuse me, sir." It was Robert, who had returned from securing the traitor. "I volunteer, if you would have me, sir."

It was quiet for a moment. No one in the room had thought of these military men other than as drill sergeants, certainly not as active participants in underground activities.

"Well," said Vincit finally, "that is much appreciated, and you would certainly look the type in the right uniform and accoutrements. However, all these men are fluent in German, which is a necessity for this operation."

"That won't be a problem, sir. My parents used to have a maid from Germany, a spinster who took a liking to me. She encouraged me to speak German to her at an early age. I became fluent in it—actually picked up quite a bit of her Bavarian accent, sir."

Vincit turned to Huub and Simon. "What do you think?"

"Great," commented Simon. "It looks like a perfect fit, and nothing better than practicing what you teach, so I say let's take a vote on it."

They all were in favor.

"Right then. Welcome to the club, Robert."

The doorbell rang, Huub went downstairs, and after looking through the peephole, opened the door for an elderly man. He wore a black coat, an oversized bow tie, long white hair, and a moustache, and he carried some equipment—the photographer.

When he entered the room, Vincit stood up immediately, took a few steps toward the old man, and with a big smile, gave him a bear hug.

"Gentlemen, this is my oldest and most reliable friend and master photographer, who, thanks to his appearance, you may call Einstein."

They all laughed. The photographer comically bobbed a curtsy.

Einstein installed a tripod in front of the wall. After taking down a golden-framed painting of a herd of sheep in a purple heather landscape and using the nail to hang a white screen, he attached a camera on top of the tripod. It had a large black cloth, under which his Einstein head disappeared. After he was satisfied and moved the tripod a foot back, the first picture could be taken. Vincit made sure that the windows were covered tightly so no light from the flash could escape the room. Hidden under the cloth, his right arm extended high, holding a large flashlight, he shouted, "No moves," and flashed the first of several pictures.

When he was done with all and after a large coffee, which he seemed to greatly enjoy, Vincit bear-hugged him and showed him out.

"Bob, could you please take two men and go down to the tunnel. If all went well, close to the exit, you should find two cases. Please bring them to your sleeping quarters. We'll see you there."

The two large, heavy crates contained complete uniforms, accoutrements, weapons, and miscellaneous items. The men looked at each other; it felt eerie, as if the Nazi uniforms radiated evil. It had been a wise decision to let them get used to wearing them.

This time, the dry run was an extremely serious matter.

Vincit explained that his original plan to practice in a location on the outskirts of the city was no longer possible, since the Germans were in the process of building a flak tower across from it. They would dry run the entire program in the room, after first temporarily removing the folding beds to create space.

"Gentlemen, do not take these exercises lightly; your life may depend on them later. You will all act like you are the persons you will pretend to be. No words are to be spoken unless in German. I will be either at the gate in Sachsenhausen, the camp commandant, or the Gestapo asking who you are, what you are doing, and so on. Sergeant Major Wilhelm will assist me. The one thing that will be different is the level of your voice. Keep it down. I don't want anybody outside to hear us scream. Now change into your uniforms. Check each other, and check your weapons. If you have questions about your outfit, ask me."

Bob felt odd wearing the hated uniform. It did fit perfectly, but after he put on his boots, tightened his belt, and put on the cap, with which he was familiar, he experienced a bout of nausea when he looked at himself in the mirror. After the short lunch of white bread and cheese, each of them had a haircut and shaved close to the skull above the ears. What then appeared below the high Nazi cap in the mirror was a Kraut face. On his tight-fitting black collar were SS insignia on the right side and a stripe and four stars of the Obersturmbannführer on the left. Around his neck was an iron cross. On his shoulders were the braided shoulder boards of his rank, lieutenant colonel. His belt held a brown leather case, containing a Luger revolver. Bob checked to make sure that it was empty. He worked his left hand into a tight-fitting black leather glove and then his right. He was ready.

The other members of the group looked the part as well after a few corrections here and there, but no adjustments to the size of any uniforms were necessary. Robert added to his rank a natural military posture, which almost made it appear that in this outfit was the real SS officer and the one who had just shed his civilian clothes was an actor.

Chairs were placed in a row in the center of the room like kids playing train ride.

But the stern commands with no room for questions from the senior military instructor soon made it clear that this was no game. His German was surprisingly good, and he gave his orders with the guttural sounds required, even clicking his heels, as if he were a German, an SS Hauptscharführer.

He approached Bob, who was sitting in one of the front chairs, and clicking his heels and raising his right arm, he commanded shortly, "Heil Hitler. Papieren bitte, Obersturmbahnführer" (papers please, Colonel).

"Heil Hitler," answered Bob, raising his arm just a bit and then slowly with controlled disdain because he far outranked the subaltern, handed him a piece of paper. "Mach schnell, und Ich wohl unmittelbar Ihr Commandant sprechen" (Hurry up, and I want to speak to your commander immediately).

"Stop," interrupted Vincit. "You are an SS senior officer. Why did you not raise your arm when the guard did?"

"Auf zwei Gründen," answered Bob, so much in his role that he automatically continued in German. "For two reasons, I far outrank him; second, I am sitting down in the back of my car, raising an arm is not common then, especially not to answer the salute of a subordinate. Just raising my hand to about head level is what a senior officer would do."

"Excellent, continue."

The training went on until dinnertime. Vincit insisted that they continue to wear their uniforms to practice where they would put helmets, caps, and weapons and how to eat and talk. There would be no small talk or inconsequential conversation, especially among the officers. A different vocabulary was required for the soldiers.

When they finally finished their coffee, they all rearranged the bedroom and went to bed. They folded their uniforms neatly on the chair next to their cot, helmet or caps on top, the shiny boots together under the chair. With one leg, they were already in Nazi Germany.

49

In what was now called the meeting room, on Tuesday evening at nine o'clock, six men sat at the table—Vincit, Simon, Huub, Gerrit, Roger, and Willem at the invitation of the man now in charge of the project.

In answer to Willem's question about how things went, Vincit, who had a trick up his sleeve, just said that things went well without giving further details.

"What still concerns me, gentlemen, is although I believe we have an ingenious plan to bring all back into our country, we still have to get them to Berlin."

It was a statement presented as a question, but nobody had any suggestions. At last, Roger proposed hiding them in groups of two in the railroad cars that took the forcibly decommissioned Dutch factories to Germany, but the proposal was considered unfeasible.

Suddenly, Simon started to laugh. The others looked at each other. What was wrong with him?

"It was right in front of our eyes all the time, gentlemen."

"Then would you be so kind to explain to us dumbos what we missed?" suggested Huub.

"Fokker, the technology the team is sent to Holland to find, all we have to do is turn the sequence."

"Turn the sequence?"

"Exactly, we will send the whole team first to Berlin by train, with information that Fokker was onto something so advanced that the Reich wants to have their hands on it. It may take some creative writing, but I think I could come up with something that Harro could present to Weinberg, so seductive to Göring that he'll sign the documents we need. I will draft an agreement that works both ways—something like, 'The bearer of these documents is on a top-secret mission by my order concerning the development of our aircraft production technology. Under no circumstances should bearer be hindered in the execution of his duties; neither should access to the documents he is carrying be demanded or attempts be made to receive verbal access to this classified information. Any action contrary to my orders will result in severe punishment.'"

It was quiet for a moment.

"Brilliant."

"That may work."

"I like it."

"It seems almost too obvious, Simon, but yes, a brilliant thought indeed," commented Willem. "I see one problem though, the position of Weinberg. If it turns out that nothing shows up,

The Fake Rembrandt

I mean, that after some time no new technology exists, then his position and probably his life will be in danger."

"A hypothetical problem, that is why we have the ingenious engineer Davelaar here. Those who met him already in our meeting must have noticed his nervousness. He has good reasons. Davelaar was one of the members of a close team of technicians working with Anthony Fokker, who realized that against the aeronautical developments in mighty America, his technology would soon be obsolete. The team worked on theories so advanced that it aimed to regain its predominant position in airplane production. Davelaar is in possession of the documents, drawings, mathematics, and descriptions, some of it encrypted.

"Fokker was very close to building a prototype, but the war interfered. We approached Davelaar; he was adamant not to comply, so we needed to put some pressure on him to cooperate, but we offered him no alternative. What we agreed to, however, is that he would work on the documents and mathematics untraceably so that the technology just could not work, but that would only be found out if ever the Nazis would build a prototype."

"Weinberg does not run any risk this way. Each of our members will carry copies of part of the technology, an additional security, so each is individually protected. Besides …"

But Vincit did not continue, loud knocking on the door downstairs startled them, and then they heard the sound of heavy boots running up the stairs. Someone kicked open the door, and two soldiers rushed in, pointing their guns at the group.

"Hände hoch! Schnell, gegen die Wand!" (Hands up! Quick, against the wall!)

They all obeyed instantly.

An officer entered the room. Hands on his back, he walked slowly along the line of frightened men, their hands high against the wall.

"Wer ist Willem Sandberg?" (Who is Willem Sandberg?)

There was no answer from the group. Out of the corner of his eye, Vincit noticed Willem's face, white as a sheet and he was perspiring.

"Okay, guys, that is enough. Thank you. Good job."

It took a while for Willem to let sink in what had just happened.

"Goddamn it, Vincit! Was that necessary?"

Then to the still shaking Sandberg, Vincit responded, "Oh yes, Willem, very much so. If you can be fooled by men you know, then I think they are ready to risk their lives for the job you consider so important and you asked me to organize."

"Coffee, gentlemen?"

50

In the room on the second floor of the white house, six students, officers, and soldiers alike were sweating over the books Davelaar had given them. He was available to answer questions, but none of them had formulated one yet. Vincit had been very persuasive; they all needed to learn enough basic aeronautical technology and technical expressions to fool Nazi interrogators.

After a couple of hours, having gone through material of which he understood very little, one of the soldiers asked, "Mr. Davelaar, I think I finally understand why a plane actually stays in the air and how smart Orville and Wilbur Wright were to fly that *Kitty Hawk*. I think I also understand that Fokker built on it and came up with innovative new technologies. What I don't understand is how many disciplines, I mean different skills or professions, it takes to work on new developments. Are we all to be engineers?"

Vincit explained earlier what was expected of them and how they would travel to Berlin and—they hoped—return.

A smile warmed the face of the otherwise solemn scientist.

"Well, that is a good question indeed; ostensibly, all it would take is engineers and people knowing how to fly. However, in aeronautical engineering, we are dealing with many disciplines, such as aerodynamics, propulsion, avionics, materials science, structural analyses, manufacturing processes, fluid mechanics, electrotechnology, mathematics, and more. And because the purpose, in principle, is to go higher, further, faster, and safer, the impact on the human body needs to be closely monitored as well. Yes, most if not all of you will be purported to be engineers, each, however, with a special expertise, and the documents each one will carry will reflect that.

"Without bothering you gentlemen with too many details, what we were working on and what I personally would love to have seen proven, is based on an observation pilot designer Anthony Fokker made; it had to do with the air particle compression, the Venturi effect, as explained in the law of Bernoulli.

"If," he wondered, "there is a possibility to use that principle for propulsion, we might avoid the theoretical problems of the propeller at super-high speed. It was an interesting assumption, and we were close to proving that the theory would work, but it required a completely new principle of airplane and engine design and construction. Most, but not all, of our findings are specified in the documents you will be carrying. It is my understanding that, at the conclusion of our sessions in the coming week, I intend to find out, based on the answers I receive from each one of you, what your particular discipline should be."

"Excuse me," said Bob. "Is that not a bit late? I don't think that any one of us is able in this short time to absorb enough of this material to be even a bit believable. Why don't we determine right now who is going to be what; then we can spend the time more focused rather than going all over the map."

"You may have a point there. Let me talk to Vincit. I'll let you know tomorrow."

And that is what happened, each one of them received the book most applicable to his adopted profession. Bob's technical education came in handy; his focus was on structural analyses; it was not the same as in construction, but the principle was the same. Throughout the engineering design process, from the conceptual layout of the different elements of the structure of all the components of the plane, the purpose was to determine manufacturing methods based on the strength and dynamic analyses of assemblies. It would not be difficult, unless the person asking the questions was an aeronautical specialist, to give a credible performance.

Not everybody was so lucky. One of the soldiers, who decided early in high school that his curriculum should not contain mathematics above the level of a ten-year-old's, was complaining loudly.

"How am I going to sleep with this fucking Fokker flying his biplane around in my head?" he lamented.

"If you don't stop complaining, I'll use my boot to make him do a crash landing," commented his buddy.

None of them slept early. They were all involuntarily repeating in their brains, again and again, the stuff they had read that day.

51

Salomon Cohen realized that compared to other prisoners his life in the camp was bearable. Although there was no contact with others beyond barrack 19, rumors of the bestialities, the cruelty of the Ukrainian guards, the way people were worked to death, died of malnutrition or diseases, or were murdered circulated among his colleagues. The contact with Krueger was certainly quite normal, and sometimes discussions lasted for an hour, with the major doing the talking, but Salomon never let down his guard. He was aware that he was still a Jew in a Nazi concentration camp and thus expendable.

The food was basic but enough, and as long as Krueger was satisfied with the work that his group delivered, Salomon felt that there was no immediate danger. But he worried day and night about Sarah.

One day, during a discussion initiated by Krueger that seemed to be more relaxed than ever, Salomon tried very carefully, if it was possible, to obtain information about where she was and if she was still alive, but Krueger just looked at him and stopped the conversation.

When one day he wondered if it would be possible for him and his colleagues to receive some books, much to his surprise, several books in different languages, probably taken from arrivals, appeared.

"What do you think, Smolianoff," he asked his buddy one day, "are we going to survive?"

"Probably, Jew." It was not used derogatorily; it was Salaman's way to address Salomon. "If what we are doing here is important to the Nazi pigs, then our chances are good; if it ceases to be so, we're toast."

Salomon did not like the mental picture.

Then one day, to the exaltation of all, Red Cross parcels arrived and were distributed. What caused this deed of unusual generosity was unclear and irrelevant. It felt like contact with the other world, the land of the living, and more important than the knitted socks, the stale cookies, or sweaters was that feeling of not having ceased to exist.

In Salomon's box were socks, a shawl, woolen gloves, some chocolate bars, a pair of slippers, and a bar of soap. There was also a book.

The book was apparently not new; it had a jacket of paper, shiny on the outside, the inside covered with printed numbers. The book was in Dutch with the title *Basics of Aeronautical Engineering*. Salomon smiled. Some joker maybe thought he could build a plane here and fly home. But then something hit him like a hammer.

On the first page was a handwritten message:

Dear Salomon, I hope you are well. I am sending you through the Red Cross some things you might need. I also send you the book you liked so much because of your interest in planes. Take care of yourself, Little Brother.

Your sister Havah

Salomon did not have a sister.

He did not have any interest at all in planes.

The box was clearly addressed to him.

What the hell was this supposed to mean?

He decided not to discuss the book with anyone and just pretend to be enthusiastic about it. But when he had time to read that week, he could not find anything in the text that made him any wiser. He read it again the week after and then again. When he was about to give up, assuming the book must have been for a namesake, he thought of the jacket.

The page was filled with random numbers, grouped in segments of three, neatly stacked in long rows, readable row by row from top to bottom or sideways. It did not make sense. It was just a piece of print someone cut to fold a jacket. But did it really make no sense? There was absolutely nothing in the book. Was there a message in the numbers? He did not have a clue.

Then, almost asleep one night, lightning hit him. He grabbed the book from under his pillow and began trying to read, but it was too dark. He had to wait until the next evening, when his work was done.

The moment he was free, he opened the book and checked the numbers on the inside of the jacket.

2 3 5

He quickly went to page 2, then the third sentence, the fifth word. "You."

His heart started to beat faster.

3 4 3 "Must."

4 5 7 "Read."

5 5 3 "This."

5 6 4 "Book."

6 3 6 "Carefully."

Salomon could hardly breathe. A message and no misunderstanding, this was for him. Would it be from Sarah? His hands trembled when he continued.

The message read, "You must read this book carefully, become familiar with the technology and technical terms. Sarah is alive. You will hear from us."

Sarah was alive! Salomon wanted to cry, to scream. Spasms welled up in his stomach like he was going to vomit. He tried to suppress it, but heavy sobs, starting somewhere deep in his belly, welled up. His face hidden in his pillow smoldering the sounds, he cried his heart out.

Sarah was alive.

52

In the back office of Kleidung Werkstatt Gunter Schneider GMBH, outside Berlin, Harro was in conversation with Kurt Schmidt, the senior staff member in charge of logistics. The company was very busy. Its owner, Gunter Schneider, had inherited the company from his father, who had died during the Great War. He was a fanatic member of the Nazi Party, which explained the large contracts his company secured from the government. Unbeknown to his employer, however, Kurt was a fervent opposer of the Nazi Party and all it stood for. He was an active member of the Rote Kapelle.

"Yes," replied Harro, to Kurt's question, "we are sure Sarah Cohen is in Ravensbrück. Weinberg received confirmation that she is there and still alive."

The concentration camp Ravensbrück was built in 1938 by Sachsenhausen prisoners and would house specifically women. The camp was situated about eighty-five kilometers north of Berlin. Twelve feet high walls topped with barbed wire encircled the compound. The women suffered from endemic extreme cruelty.

Almost a hundred thousand perished from starvation, sickness, medical experiments, or by random execution. In the framework of murder action "14f13," Jewish women especially were murdered by a bullet, a lethal injection, or hanging, or they were transported to Majdanek or Auschwitz to be gassed.

Sarah was one of the few exceptions, but for how long?

The women were used as forced laborers to work for companies like Siemens, who built twenty factories around Ravensbrück and owned nine barracks with prisoners. Other prisoners worked in weapon factories or in agriculture, made shoes and uniforms, or were maintaining the camp.

Uniforms, of which large quantities were required, was why Sarah was still among the living. Her past experience as the owner of a workshop in Holland, making uniforms for the police, got her put in charge of the large section responsible for cutting and sewing uniform parts and sewing them together. The increasing demand put enormous pressure on the section, as virtually unattainable quotas were set each week and then increased again the next. Fortunately, Sarah was responsible for quality control and not for production numbers. Three women with that responsibility were already shot when the immense quota was not delivered, even after fourteen hours of continued slavery.

The brutal female supervisor, Else Ehrich, who later became commandant of Majdanek, known among the women as Die Teufelin, the devil, introduced her own specific incentive. If a quota was missed the first time, one woman would be hanged; if a second time, two women; and so on. Almost daily women just perished from exhaustion on the floor.

The contract that Gunter Schneider received so dishonorably was to collect from the different camps the uniforms, sort them to size, bundle them, and transport them to different consignees within and outside Germany, mostly by train but also by truck.

"Presently there is a truck twice a week in Ravensbrück that may become three times," Kurt told Harro. "The goods arrive here in the warehouse and are inspected, sorted, and bundled, and then either loaded onto trucks or directly into the rail cars at the back of our building. We presently receive goods from twenty-three production sites. Occasionally we have a transport to Holland by truck, to Enschede just across the border, usually in combination with other goods—towels, underwear, blankets, and so on."

"That's great, Kurt, but what about inspection at the gate when the loaded truck leaves the camp."

"That becomes routine. Yes, they stop the truck, have a quick look at the load, but that's all they can do. Besides we always send the same trucks with the same drivers, so the guards know them well and often even just wave them through. We keep track of that, and usually on a Friday, there are two sentries who just don't seem to give a damn. Thank God for our German Punktlichkeit, punctuality, always the same men at any given day."

What the Rote Kapelle planned after Suzan's pleading to Weinberg to try to bring Sarah home if possible, not in the least to have the full cooperation of Salomon, was to have her hide in a truckload of uniforms, bring her to the warehouse, and then ship her the same way to Holland.

"What about your people in the warehouse here?"

"No problem. The truck arrives at the end of the day on Friday. It stays inside overnight. I will retrieve her from the load and hide her here in this office until the large truck for Enschede is loaded. I will make sure that she boards the vessel undetected."

"What about the weight though? Is she not going to suffocate under the load?"

"It will be tough but bearable from the camp to here; as for air, some of the material delivered to the camp arrives rolled on carton tubes. The driver, one of us, of course, will tape several of them together and as soon as he is out of sight of the camp will arrange a duct for her to breath.

"When loading the large truck, we will create room with pallets to carry the load and to let her be a little bit more comfortable with the same tube providing air to breathe."

"That sounds great, and thanks a million. Let us know when you think you are ready, and we'll take care of things in Enschede. By the way, what if she has to pee?"

"On German uniforms? Is that not exactly what you guys want?"

53

On an industrial lot, just outside the city of Oranienburg, north of Berlin, was a large junkyard. A sign above the wide gate read, "Autoverwertung Blum" (Scrapyard Blum). A chained mongrel dog of undefined racial mixture protected the place, a true graveyard of German car manufacturing—Opels, Mercedes, DKWs, BMWs, and the badly damaged remains of some military vehicles. Among them were a few hardly recognizable Kübelwagen. Blum made a sober living; there just were no takers for the car wrecks he fixed up, it seemed.

In a shed at the end of the terrain, two men were welding, hammering, cutting, and drilling on a carcass that was supposed to become an operational Kübelwagen again. Blum walked around nervously in his soiled coveralls, trying to clean some grease from his hands with cotton wool, his welding glasses high on his sweaty forehead.

Only two days to finish the job and deliver the vehicle to the man who would pick it up. *Must be a rich guy thus far exempt from service for some reason, who nevertheless gets a kick out of playing soldier.* Or if there was another reason why someone would pay 5,000 reichsmark for a fixed-up Kubel, Blum did not give a damn. It was more dough than he saw in months these days.

If they had to work the entire night, they would. Day after tomorrow, the car would be ready, looking fine, the requested Berlin license plates and all. He had asked for cash, and without a moment of hesitation, the guy forked over two grand in advance.

When someone arrived to pick up the car, to Blum's surprise, it was not the same man but a soldier in uniform. *What the f...*

But when one of his mechanics drove the Kubel out, the engine running smoothly and no trace of any crash visible, the soldier handed over the remaining 3,000 plus 300 extra for the mechanics. He warned them not to talk about the transaction and there might be more. Blum thanked him profusely and gladly complied.

The driver was Hans Weber, one of the two drivers the Rote Kapelle made available to the Dutch group. In his military uniform, nobody paid any attention to the Kübelwagen he was driving to the estate of Oberst Weinberg. The car was parked there, in the equipment shed next to the baron's large, open black Mercedes.

A small hole was drilled in the fender of the Mercedes, where later the mount and pole for the SS car flag would be attached.

The next day, the same buyer, not the soldier this time, came back. Blum thought, *My God, something's wrong with the Kübel.* But it was not so. On the contrary, this time, the man came shopping for a van, and Blum just happened to have a few of them.

One, a white van with some still visible damage but most of it well repaired, was ready to drive. Three thousand reichsmark later, the man left a flabbergasted but brightly smiling Blum behind, wondering how his luck had suddenly changed.

There was room for several more cars if needed in the large equipment shed.

In prewar times, a mechanic was on staff at the estate to keep all rolling material running. There was a large workbench, welding equipment, hand- and electrical tools, and cans of paint and brushes, garage jacks, and worn tires. Cobweb-covered lamps, extended from the ceiling on an electric wire, were spreading a faint yellow light on the white van. A man was busy painting black letters on one side of the van, the left side was done. It read, "REICHS ELEKTRONISCHES INGENIEURWESEN" (Government Electronic Engineering Institute), without any address or contact information. This was the van that would take the first group to the brick church in Germendorf. On the large workbench, a man was welding parts together—four rods looking like antennas, tubes, and insulated wiring all connected to four receptacles. On the bench stood a sealed thick black metal box the size of a small suitcase. The man welded several pieces of scrap together to give the box some content. Four thick cables with electrical outlets, to be later attached to the receptacles of the antennas, protruded from the box and were rolled into a coil. On top of the black box was the following text: "Warning, this equipment is the property of the German government and remotely operated. Under no circumstances should attempts be made to access this box before or after installation. Any action contravening this instruction will be punished by death."

After they had finished topping off the tanks, replacing needed license plates, and adding hand tools and coveralls, the van with the equipment for the *technicians* operating from the church in Germendorf was ready. The open Mercedes would wear its SS identification flag; the Kübelwagen was dirtied up a bit to hide its recent restoration. The Rote Kapelle was ready.

54

Outside Amsterdam, halfway to the village of Ouderkerk, on the left bank of the River Amstel stands a well-kept Dutch mill, its vanes slowly turning in the morning breeze. Under its reed roof, among the hand-chiseled oak rafters, the wooden driveshaft, and the sprocket wheels, the resistance would meet from time to time. The miller and his wife were beyond suspicion and posed at times in their traditional Dutch costumes for German soldiers, keen to take a picture as if they were on a holiday instead of committing country rape.

The couple was of great importance to the resistance. From their elevated position, they received and sent messages to London.

When the vanes were turning, the resistance knew it was safe to come to the mill. When in horizontal position, the vanes forming a cross, it meant, "Come now; we have a message from London." When the vanes were in fixed diagonal position, it signaled emergency, extreme danger.

Talking louder than normal to understand each other among the noisy, screeching mechanism of the old mill, seated on wooden crates were David Roell, Willem Sandberg, Gerrit Bolkestein, and Leo Trip.

"I just came back from Amersfoort, gentlemen, and all I can say—probably all I should say—is that the plan of operation is sound, the men almost ready to start," said Sandberg.

"How many days do you think, Willem?"

"That I don't know, but I am sure we will be briefed the moment they leave."

"So if you prefer not to provide details, which I fully understand," offered practical Leo Trip, "why then are we here?"

"If indeed the group is leaving any day now, they could be back before you know it if everything works out the way it is planned. We should give Salomon a bit of time to get used to his return. Then we need shelter for him and hopefully his wife, Sarah, and a place where he can work. Not a small order.

"But he should be able to start rather sooner than later; we don't have a clue at the moment how long he will take. Then we need people to find somewhere in this crazy world, the material, the frame, the paint, the brushes, old nails, and whatever he deems essential to paint a *Night Watch*.

"So, gentlemen, why we are here is to assign these tasks. If each one of you is focusing on a certain need, we may get it done."

"Okay, I see. Sorry I asked. You are right. And by the way, let me take responsibility for the shelter. I have some ideas."

"I will handle the brushes, paint, and canvas," offered Roell.

"However, I don't have a clue where to find a seventeenth-century frame."

"That leaves me then with trying to take care of that, but it may not be too easy."

"Is that really necessary?" asked Bolkestein. "Do you really think the persons selecting which art should be sent to Germany to become part of Hitler's or Göring's collection will focus on a frame?"

"Oh, most definitely, and the less educated in art history, the quicker they will focus on the frame. No, canvas, paint, and frame should be old or very professionally made to look old, and whether restaurateur Cohen will have the time and means to do that is a big question."

"How do we give Cohen access to *The Night Watch*?" asked Trip. "The way I understand it, that may be virtually impossible since it is rolled up in a carpet and presently in a large safe in Heemskerk."

"We thought about that too, of course, Leo. Let me tell you what we are organizing. Cohen will need to work from photographs. Not just a few pictures, as you can imagine. David took the initiative a few years ago to produce very detailed files containing photographs of *The Night Watch*, realizing that in case of any damage restorers would benefit from them."

The project required a very special professional photographer with the most modern equipment. After ample consideration of multiple names, the project was assigned to Eva Marianna

Besnyoe, who was a Jew of Hungarian descent and presently living in hiding in Holland after she escaped Nazi Germany. What she produced was beyond the Rijksmuseum's expectations. She made numerous black-and-white pictures and then the same number in color.

She designed a fine grid with squares of ten by ten centimeters. Then she photographed every square in detail and brought it into a flawless system.

"We have access to those files. The color photographs will naturally not be suitable for reproduction in paint on canvas. However, let us remember that Cohen is a Rembrandt fanatic; he worked on many of Goudstikker's paintings. Besides, although there is no access to *The Night Watch*, we may be able to provide Salomon with one or two Rembrandts from the same period, depending of course on the safety of the place where he will paint."

Bolkestein closed the meeting; it had been a very productive one.

One by one, at intervals, they left the mill, two on bicycle and two on foot.

Next to Willem's bicycle behind the mill, he noticed a pile of thick, weathered, hand-chiseled oak beams that were too old and here and there had spots of woodworm. They would not still be considered reliable, so they were replaced by the miller. A pile of firewood next to it indicated what the future of those beams would be. Willem smiled; one of them would be cut into a century-old frame. The *poldermolen*, or polder mill, he had just left was built in 1632. Rembrandt might have painted it.

The water in front of the mill was known as a good spot for fishing.

When the men left, in canvas holders, they carried three sections of a fishing pole and some lines and floats. Nobody would find it suspicious that they came from the mill.

Sandberg peddled across the Berlage Bridge, his fishing gear strapped to the frame, a large pike, compliments of the miller, dangling from his handlebar.

There were two German sentries on the bridge; one of them probably an enthusiastic sports fisherman back in Germany, smiled and gave him a thumbs-up.

Willem Sandberg, senior member of the Dutch resistance, waved back and continued his way.

55

It was a Friday afternoon when Franz and Willie drove their truck through the gate of Ravensbrück. Franz, a somewhat porky sort of a man, was the driver.

Whatever he was wearing, somehow it always seemed to be the wrong size. He had a friendly, freckled, boyish face and uncontrollable curly red hair. Women usually liked him with motherly feelings.

Willie, however, was a charmer.

Tall and handsome with the complexion of a ski instructor, pearly white teeth, thick dark hair, and a perpetual twinkle in his blue eyes, he had women falling for him like ripe apples from the tree.

The guards just waved them through, never bothering to ask questions of the men they saw two times a week.

The truck stopped in front of the barrack where the bundles of uniforms were to be loaded. Both men jumped from the truck and walked into the building, where piles of uniforms with a rope around each twenty-four were ready.

Waiting for them, her hair curled as was the case only when she knew the truck and with it Willie would arrive, her uniform blouse a size too small to better show off her breasts, was Johanna.

"Guten Tach, Liebchen," (Good day, darling) Willie said and smiled, conjuring a slight blush on the otherwise devilish face of Oberaufseherin Johanna Langefeld, the brutal female head inspector of the uniform production.

"Guten Tach, Willie. Wie geht es Ihnen heute?" (How are you doing today?)

"It could be better, hon. There will be a Bierfest und Tanz a beer party with a dance tonight, and I don't have a girl to dance with. How about you, Liebchen, darling—can you not take one evening off?"

She laughed, knowing very well that he knew that was impossible, but she was flattered anyhow.

"What about a little drink here then, hey?"

Willie produced a half bottle of schnapps from under his jacket, unscrewed the cap, took a sip, and seductively licked the tip of the bottleneck, and then, with a wide smile, he offered the bottle to Johanna.

She accepted it with both hands and then, with her lips encircling the glass, slowly pushed the bottleneck up into her mouth, all the while locking eyes with Willie. Then she closed her eyes and took a big gulp. Licking her lips, she passed the bottle back to Willie, who repeated the performance.

"Oh Goddamn it!" shouted Franz on the other side of the

truck. "Look what happened to my sleeve! I got stuck to the damned door lock. Hey, Johanna, how about one of your wenches stitching me up, hey?"

Johanna was not interested in stitching something up or in wenches. Her seductive little game with the handsome Willie hardened her nipples. Pointing to the woman in charge of controlling the loading, Sarah, she shouted, "Hey, you! Do what that man is asking and get out of my sight."

She took the bottle with both hands again, now licking the top and pouring some of the liquid over her half-opened mouth. There was not much of it left.

With her hands trembling a bit, out of sight of the lascivious overseer, Sarah started to sew the driver's sleeve.

"Listen good," whispered Franz. "Read this paper. Remember everything well, and then eat it." He put something in her hand, a piece of paper folded to the size of a matchbox. Almost paralyzed, Sarah quickly hid the paper in the canvas apron she always wore when loading the truck. With hands trembling more than before, she closed the tear and cut the thread. Franz went back to the truck.

The schnapps was gone, and a lock of hair was in front of Johanna's hot face.

"Ready, Willie? Let's go. You can make love next time."

All three laughed.

Singing horribly out of tune, the amorous Oberaufseherin, the head inspector, started to imitate Sarah Leander, while looking at

Willie. "Es wirt einmal ins Leben ein Wunder geschehen ..." Then came a loud hiccup. "Once in our life a miracle will happen."

"Auf Wiedersehen, mein Pupchen," (See you later, my doll) he said. Softly to Franz so the woman couldn't hear, he added, "What a horrible slut."

But when he just wanted to step into the truck, he noticed something in the corner of the building, a pile of cardboard tubes.

"Mind if I take a few, and have someone throw a couple in next time we come? Sleep well, darling."

The truck, loaded with uniforms now by Sarah and other prisoners, left through the gate without being checked, the guards just waving a hand.

"Did she get it?" asked Willie.

"Yes, and I told her to read it and then eat it. If it is found on her, she'll die a horrible death."

"Let's take this load home; then you contact Harro, okay?"

56

Sarah could not breathe.

Her body was shaking; she felt warm and then cold as if in a fever.

At first, she thought that it must have been a trick to compromise her or something after she had unwillingly witnessed the vulgarities of that monster.

But then she realized that what was hidden in her apron, feeling like a lump of burning coal, was indeed a message from the outside. Could it be from Salomon? Every minute she still had to work that Friday felt like an eternity.

At ten o'clock, they could finally stop the sixteen-hour workday. One of the women, ostensibly weaker than the others but worked to death daily, fainted and fell backward off the wooden bench. The half-drunk horny overseer discharged her frustration by beating the poor woman to death with the bludgeon she was wearing and then kicking the dead body now on the ground several times hard in the stomach. Sarah had known Rachel, the young woman well. She came from Belgium, and every so often, the two had a whispered discussion whenever possible while working to give each other hope and strength to hang on.

Rachel had been seven months pregnant.

After hungrily eating the slob she was served in her bowl, Sarah hurried to the latrine.

She removed the piece of paper that was hidden earlier, undetected, in the heavy apron from her underwear.

On the far corner of the latrine, one could catch just enough light from one of the floodlights shining at the high wall surrounding the compound. Most women were shunning that spot, ashamed of their sorrowful state and avoiding the light that would shine on them.

Sitting on the pole above the disgusting ditch, pretending, Sarah nervously unfolded the thin piece of paper that turned out to be quite a page. She read,

Sarah your husband is alive and will hopefully soon be back in Holland.

You will soon join him if you do what we say. Act normal when the truck arrives next Friday. There will be a diversion. The driver will help you to get in the back of the truck. Hide among the bales. You will be breathing through the cardboard tubes you will throw between the bales when loading. Keep your eyes on the driver. When he drops his glasses to the floor next to the truck, act like you are going to pick them up. He will help you in the back and cover you. When home, ask for Suzan. Mazel tov. Eat this paper.

For a moment, Sarah could not.

She wanted to hang on to the paper, to cover it with kisses. Tears flowing freely now, she made a small prop and then swallowed it, feeling it sit in her belly as something divinely special.

She went back to her cot and lay down next to the other three women who were asleep already, drained from the sixteen-hour working day.

She kept staring at the dark bottom of the cot just three feet above her.

Salomon was alive. Salomon would be in Holland; she would leave this stinking hellhole and be with him. She prayed, "Baruch atah Adonai, rofeh kol basar, u'mafli la'asot" (Blessed art thou Adonai, Healer of all flesh who acts wondrously).

She finally fell asleep.

57

Dr. Kurt Holman visited the hospital, which was more of a sick bay, in Sachsenhausen twice a week. It was hardly the concern of the commandant to provide care to the prisoners; rather the visits were to have Dr. Holman find out if a prisoner was simulating, in which case, he would be shot.

Kurt had been a star student at the Christian Albrecht Universitaet in Kiel.

Knowing how difficult it was for his parents to make a living from the small farm and how his father missed the helping hands of a son, he was adamant he would become a doctor, so he could make their hard life a bit easier. He became a successful one, very popular with the elderly, for whom he always had time and encouraging words.

Concerned, he followed the increasing influence and brown shirt brutality of the Nazi regime, especially the persecution of the Jews. It culminated in the Kristallnacht, a night of riots and murder, when the windows of Jewish stores were smashed in. One of his favorite professors, Dr. Perlbaum, had been among the victims, a great scientist murdered for no reason at all.

Then the war started, and like so many young men, he had no choice. Against everything he believed in, he was forced to wear the uniform of a captain in the medical section. He was sent to Sachsenhausen as a medic. At first, he seriously considered ending his life when he was confronted with so much suffering and cruel barbarism. Then he realized that there was an alternative. If he now and then could save a human being doomed to die, there might still be a mission in life for him. The man in charge of the sick bay when Kurt was not there was a *sanitaeter*, a paramedic with enough respect for Dr. Kurt not to question his decisions.

The sick bay was always short of everything.

In a different building, designed as a proper small hospital, was the clinic where Dr. Holman inspected and treated the German officers, guards, and soldiers. It held an abundance of medical equipment, medicine, serums, and bandages. From time to time, Kurt "borrowed" some, in spite of the risk, to help a patient on the other side.

One of the things Kurt enjoyed during his sparse pastime before the war was playing contract bridge, which he did meritoriously. One of the partners he enjoyed playing with and who became his partner in tournaments was Baron Weinberg. He was a sympathetic man he had befriended, who played well and hated quarrels afterward.

Baron Weinberg opened up to Kurt, and as a result, Dr. Holman had been, for some time now, an active member of the Rote Kapelle.

That day, they met in a Konditorei, sitting at a corner table, enjoying Kaffee und Kuchen, coffee and cakes.

"How are you, Kurt?" asked Weinberg.

"Could be better. What happened to our world, our country? Where did decency and civility go? Where and how is this going to end? I try to do what I can, but the suffering is beyond mediation. If there is a God, somebody better wake him up."

Weinberg sipped from his coffee. Over the rim of the cup, he noticed the young doctor was looking ten years older than only last year.

"The one thing we should not give up on is hope. Every now and then, we succeed in what we are trying to achieve, baby steps maybe, but significant nevertheless."

"Right, my friend, and sorry that I aired it all out; you must have enough troubles yourself. What can I do for you this time?"

"In the very near future, which day I will let you know in time, a Major Krueger will come to your hospital with complaints. Keep him there for at least three days; it is very important."

"That does not seem to be too difficult. How does he get sick?"

"Something in his coffee, compliments of one of the prisoners."

58

The funeral cortege on its way to the train station in Amersfoort was short; there were no following vehicles or carriages.

The black hearse was drawn by four horses respectfully covered in shrouds and with feather plumes on their drooping heads. In front of them and behind the hearse were two men wearing top hats and long black coats, showing the professional grieving expressions expected of them.

The procession stopped in front of the station, the coachman never leaving his box, holding the reins in his gloved hands, as if the horses could gallop away at any moment instead of falling asleep as they did, dropping lunch for the twittering sparrows.

The four men carried the heavy coffin to the train, walking slowly and reverently passing the travelers—German soldiers mostly and civilians, some of whom stopped for a moment facing the coffin. One of them made the sign of the cross.

Frau von Muenster was on her way to the land where she had lived her life and wanted to be buried. The train had only a dozen compartments, most of them holding equipment taken from Dutch manufacturing plants. Four were loaded with miscellaneous food products—cheese, eggs, flour, and so on. There were only two coaches for passengers, mostly military. The coffin was placed in the last compartment.

According to the papers accompanying the coffin, Frau von Muenster, the elderly mother of a German lieutenant, had been able to obtain a license to visit her son, stationed in Soesterberg, the airport close to Amersfoort.

The extraordinary approval from high authority was given out of compassion; the old lady was terminally ill, and the lieutenant could not leave the project they were working on, so no pass could be given to him.

Because traveling to and from Germany was strictly regulated, whether the passenger was dead or alive, documents explaining the situation, stamped and signed by the respective authorities in Germany and in occupied Holland, were required. They were taped to the top of the coffin.

At the border, if inspection was considered necessary, all they needed to do was read the papers. It would tell them that the poor lady passed away days after she saw her son. Her last will to be buried in her Nazi Germany instead of in a foreign country was understood, respected, and therefore approved.

There was no inspection at the border.

When the train arrived at the central station in Berlin, a large black Mercedes funeral car was waiting. The coffin was carried to the car and driven straight to the shed behind the main house of Baron Weinberg.

Tightly wrapped in uniforms, the weapons, caps, helmets, boots, and accoutrements the team would need and, in a separate satchel, all the documents they would have to carry on them when wearing the uniforms had safely arrived.

59

The daily exercises and the conversations in German, along with the hours of studying aeronautical engineering, took a toll on the group. Living in a limited confinement, they started to show signs of cabin fever.

Their uniforms and weapons gone, back in their own clothes, they were eager to start and fired questions at Vincit almost every breakfast.

Then, one morning, Bob was asked to check the tunnel again for a suitcase that should have arrived that night. It had.

When Vincit opened it at the meeting later, it contained six identical brown leather briefcases, with heavy locks, the keys attached with a string to the handle. One of them contained a pile of papers, six *laissez passer* letters from Field Marshal Hermann Göring and identification papers with pictures showing personal details and listing the profession, related to aeronautical science and technology, of each one of them.

Vincit distributed the papers and the briefcases.

After opening the briefcases, everyone found a bundle of documents applicable to the knowledge of the bearer and part of the Fokker secret advanced technology research team. The documents were in a yellow folder with the logo of Fokker printed on the front and below it in bold letters the Dutch words "ZEER GEHEIM" (top secret).

They were all sitting at the table. Vincit stood. It was suddenly very quiet in the room. Obviously Vincit had something important up his sleeve.

"Gentlemen, you will notice that you all received your ID that you are to carry on you at all times, together with Göring's letter. In the identical briefcases, done on purpose to suggest you are a special team, are the documents that Mr. Davelaar reworked and are applicable to your given specialty. Study those documents carefully so you are familiar with the content.

"The letter signed by Hermann Göring may be enough for border patrol or Gestapo not to bother you, but it is no guarantee. The more you know about the material in your briefcase, the better the chances that you will be believed. When traveling and when in the train, you will hang on to your briefcase for dear life. Don't put it in the overhead. Keep it on your lap the whole trip."

"Bob, you will take the lead. In cases of emergency, you decide the response of the team. Team, you are to obey his instructions unquestioningly. If the mission fails due to the disobedience of any team member, he will be held responsible afterward.

"Gentlemen, use the rest of this day to familiarize yourself with the material in your briefcase. Try to have a good rest tonight. You are leaving tomorrow."

60

In the entrance hall of the train station, the curious eyes of fellow travelers watched the strange group of men. All of them were dressed in civilian clothing. They could have been military or maybe police on a special mission—maybe even Gestapo.

They all carried the same briefcase and held on to it like it contained treasure.

When they boarded the train, they went straight to the first-class coach, the only civilians among German officers.

The six men took their seats in the back, the briefcases on their laps, hardly talking to each other. They all seemed to be given to introspection and apparently did not have a need for small talk.

Bob was experiencing a quietly meditative moment, feeling a tight constriction of his chest; he was filled with a consuming sense of urgency. He started to have unspoken doubts about this operation, seeming to be nothing short of foolhardy. He weighed the many consequences of the operation.

He felt the weight of the unasked for responsibility Vincit had handed to him. His mind roved freely, and carping skepticism crept in, but it was quickly overtaken by a spirit for the unpredictable. They would succeed; they had to.

Having slept very little the night before, Bob dozed off now and then, all the while subconsciously hanging on to his briefcase.

In good German military tradition, the most senior officers were sitting in front of the compartment, two of them, a colonel and a captain, occupying four seats.

On the table between them were some papers the colonel was studying and two cups of coffee. The captain was reading a book.

Bob was suddenly wide awake.

A young lieutenant sitting on the other side of the aisle, in the back of the car, obviously already a bit drunk this early in the day, maybe because he was excited to go back home, ostensibly wanted to impress his comrades.

Focusing for some reason on Robert, he started to make funny faces at him and then vulgar, suggestive signs. Robert ignored him.

"Hey, Kaesekopf, cheesehead, going to Germany to fuck little Jew boys?"

Kaesekopf was an often used derogatory term the Germans had for Dutchmen.

Robert's face turned red, but he did not move.

The drunk came out of his seat, turned to Robert, and with his mouth close to Robert's ear, he hissed, "I am talking to you, pervert."

Bob realized this could turn into a disaster.

He got out of his seat and walked straight to the colonel. In his outstretched right hand, he held Göring's letter. In fluent German, he said for all to hear, "Sir, I take offense against the uncalled for insults of one of your officers against one of my men."

The colonel noticed the signature and quickly read the letter; then he uttered some words to his captain, who called the lieutenant.

The young man turned pale and sobered up quickly when he walked to the front of the cabin.

"Stehe stramm!" shouted the captain (at attention).

The colonel gave the unlucky lieutenant a roasting he would never forget.

Much less drunk than he had pretended to be just moments earlier, he went timidly back to his seat, but first, he faced the civilians, stood to attention, clicking his heels, bent his upper body in Robert's direction, and said loud enough for all to hear, "Entschuldigung" (my apologies).

The first test of the validity of our documents passed successfully, thought Bob. This time, he closed his eyes, convinced he would not be disturbed again.

61

The control at the border passed without any problems. Two border patrol officers looked at first with suspicion at this odd group of Dutchmen on their way to Germany. When Bob presented his papers, they appeared surprised at the high authority having signed the documents, but when one of them looked in the direction of the colonel in front of the compartment, the officer slightly nodded. Apparently, he had been informed about this secret mission; after that, checking the papers of the whole group was a matter of routine.

It was a long, uneventful trip. The steam locomotive had to stop several times to take in water and once coal. There was no food or coffee available, and since the team members had slept very little the night before, they were all very tired and very hungry. When they finally arrived at the central station of Berlin, they were still filled with anticipation but longing very much to reach their destination.

Three black cars waited at the entrance.

Porters brought their suitcases to the cars, and after the drivers stowed them in the trunks, they were on their way to the Weinberg estate.

The main house of the Weinberg estate could boast of a long history.

Its owners over the years had a significant impact on the small villages surrounding it, most of them, in one way or another, depending for their livelihood on the barons of the manor. Although, through the ages, the forebears of the present baron had been rather popular, it was still a feudal relationship.

On the far end of its vast farming fields were four houses, built at the end of the eighteenth century, housing the domestic hands of the manor. With the present baron in the service, the houses had been empty for over a year and locked, the window shutters closed. This night, three of them were opened by an elderly man who did not say a single word. Each would provide shelter to two members of the team.

Although there were no other houses in the immediate vicinity, to be safe, the shutters remained closed. There were antique forged-iron beds with mattresses of fresh hay, which made the bedroom smell like a clean horse stable.

On a table in the small kitchen of each house, they found an assortment of German bread, sausage, ham, butter, and milk, which they hungrily gobbled up. There was no electricity and only a few candles, but soon, no light was needed.

Dressed as they were, they went to bed, not even taking their shoes off, ready for immediate action if something went wrong, curious what the next day would bring but too exhausted to care. In the air high above, formations of heavy bombers could be heard flying over.

Soon it was completely quiet.

62

It was still half dark when a soft tap on the shutter of his bedroom window woke Bob up; then, he heard it again, three soft but insistent knocks. He immediately understood that this was just to wake them up; otherwise, it would be a different knocking. He went to the window and answered with three knocks, signaling "I am awake."

He went to the only door of the house, the kitchen door in the back, and opened it.

A man of around forty, dressed in coveralls, an open, friendly smile on his face, said, "Good morning. My name is Werner. I have a message from Copenhagen."

It was the code. "Please come in," answered Bob, not realizing that with the shutters closed and no candle burning, it was a dark invitation. "My name is Bob. I am pleased to meet you." They shook hands.

"No, thank you. I won't come in. We have quite a program for today. Please wake the other guys and come to the large shed at the other side of the field. Shall we say in thirty minutes? The large doors are closed. Knock three times, then once, then three times again. We'll have your breakfast ready."

He turned and left.

The other side of the field turned out to be a twelve-minute walk.

When they knocked, the large doors opened and quickly closed behind them.

There were several men inside the reasonably lit large building, sitting on benches at a long wooden table. They all stood up and introduced themselves.

The leader of the group, all members of the Rote Kapelle, was the man Bob had already met and who called himself Werner. None of the names, everybody knew, would be their real names.

Bob looked in awe at the vehicles—the Mercedes, a Kübelwagen, a white van, and a variety of farm equipment that appeared a bit dusty. He felt a quick, cold shudder when he realized, *This is it. That is the equipment we'll be using.*

"Fruestueck Maenner?" (Breakfast, guys?) asked Werner, and he invitingly pointed at the empty places at the table. There was an improvised kitchen in the shed, but improvised or not, someone produced six delicious breakfasts, with bacon, eggs, and piping-hot real coffee.

"Well, friends, we better show you what we have here," Werner said when breakfast was finished.

"First, you'll be pleased to know that Frau von Muenster has safely arrived. We took the liberty of opening the coffin to make sure that everything was okay. We oiled the weapons, and we have enough bullets available for each type. As you can see over there, on that line, we are hanging out the uniforms. Nothing is badly wrinkled. You also see six coveralls with text on the back, 'Reichs Elektronisches Ingenieurwesen.' Those are the coveralls you'll wear when this van takes you to Germendorf. That box over there, with the wires sticking out, is the black box that you are going to install in the church tower. As you can read from the text on the top, nobody will mess with it. You will take your time to install the four antennas on each side of the tower and connect them to the box. Your uniforms and weapons will be in a locked metal case in the van. When the installation is done, the driver of the van will take you to the ruins of a building outside of Oranienburg. Your Mercedes and Kübelwagen will wait for you there. Get into your uniforms in the van. From there to the concentration camp is about four kilometers."

"How will we know when it is time to leave the church tower?" Bob wanted to know.

"There will be a supervisor in a black jacket with 'REI Supervisor' on the front; exactly thirty minutes after the time of his arrival, the van should leave."

"The supervisor, of course, is one of ours, and he will be on his way before you guys depart."

"Now come with me to the workbench, and I'll show you how to fix the antennas to the tower and connect them to the black box."

63

Salomon Cohen read the book so many times that he could have quoted the content verbatim if he had been asked. It was only after he had removed the cover that he found a small sachet containing a few grams of white powder.

He was familiar with the number code, so it did not take long to decipher the back page.

"Hide this sachet. The same man who brought this book will deliver a letter. That morning, put powder in the drink of Krueger. Be ready."

Be ready for what? thought Salomon, quickly hiding the small, mysterious package. He understood that strong influences must be involved in something he did not completely understand but that he hoped might lead to his liberation from this horrible place. But why?

Who would care for a single, unimportant Jew when so many where killed for no other reason than being Jewish? Whom did he know who cared enough for him to risk so much and challenge a regime that knew no scruples? Goudstikker maybe? But he was a

Jew himself and probably in just as much trouble as Salomon, and if not, then it was inconceivable that his influences would reach all the way within the Nazi Reich.

No, there must be something mysteriously important behind this, thought Salomon. Just the production of this book with the messages must have been an enormous job and then to have it delivered to him by a camp guard, who without doubt risked his life? It was difficult to concentrate on his job and not to arouse the scorn of Krueger. As nice as he sometimes appeared, he could be very unpredictable and very dangerous.

Could I kill him? thought Salomon with a shock.

What was this powder supposed to do?

What if it contained a deadly poison, could I do it?

Then he thought of Sarah and the message that she was alive. The things he knew that were happening in the camps were too horrible to think of in relation to her.

Yes, he would do it.

He would do it to all of them. All these unscrupulous, murderous Nazi self-acclaimed *Übermenschen*, super human beings, who thought they could play God and claim the world for themselves, euthanizing those they did not consider worthy of life. The daily executions and hangings, yes, for Sarah's sake, for all the kids, the fathers, mothers, whole families the rotten system would destroy. If he could kill just one of them, he would.

"Adonai," he prayed, "please let me live, let me see my Sarah again, let me live to tell the unimaginable really did happen."

64

It was silent at breakfast that early morning; there was a tension in the air, a feeling of unpredictability—not uncertainty though. The team felt ready after so many days of preparation. But as much as they tried to suppress the reality of the day, nobody knew if they would see the end of this campaign alive.

Werner and his men were loading the van, first the large metal container with the uniforms and weapons and then the antennas, the black box, and the necessary hand tools.

Bob and his men worked in the coveralls and then dirtied them just enough that they did not appear to be brand new. They got into the van, and the team of the Reichs Elektronisches Ingenieurwesen was on its way.

Hans, the German driver of the van, knew his way and explained that the drive to Germendorf would take just over an hour. "So relax."

There was little relaxation though. At Tegel, about twenty minutes from Berlin, there was a checkpoint, and the van was made to stop. A heavily armed SS patrolman approached the van.

"Papers," he demanded. Very controlled, Hans handed him what he was asking for, his ID, and a document on Reichs Elektronisches Ingenieurwesen stationery that explained the mission and its secret character. "Weiter fahren," (continue) said the SS man, after throwing a quick look at the van and the *engineers* in the back.

At Stolpe, about fifteen minutes from Germendorf, there was another checkpoint. Maybe they had received a phone call from the first roadblock, because the guard waved them through without stopping them.

When they arrived at Germendorf and parked the van in front of the church, they were immediately approached by two SS guards. The sergeant asked what they thought they were doing. Robert explained that they were there to install equipment and that no further details would be available about the nature of the installation.

After meticulously checking the paper that Paul handed him, the guard was still suspicious.

"I have not received any message to expect you here," he said, holding on to the paper.

"I understand. Please call this number." Paul gave him a business card with a phone number. The man walked to a booth in front of the church and dialed a number. It was too far from the van to overhear him, but after first asking a question, then holding for some minutes, he suddenly jumped to attention. Now it was not difficult to understand him. "Jawohl, Obersturmbahnführer, zum befehl" (Yes, Colonel, at your orders).

Werner apparently sounded convincing as the colonel, because when the guard returned to the van, his demeanor had changed noticeably. "In Ordnung," (everything okay) he said. "Please let me know if we can be of service to you gentlemen."

When the team unloaded the equipment, he offered to help, which Robert said was not necessary, but Bob made sure that the guard had a chance to read the text on the black box.

They worked their way up to the top of the tower. "Damn," complained one of them. "Could he not have made that black box a little lighter? I am breaking my back." In his lament, he did not forget to speak German.

When they reached the top, a cold wind met them, blowing unhindered through the four openings on each side. The view was frightfully spectacular. In the distance, they could see the Heinkel Flugzeugwerke, the Nazi German airplane manufacturing plant, where they knew thousands of the Sachsenhausen concentration camp prisoners were exploited as forced labor and many perished.

65

Attaching the antennas was not as easy as it was supposed to be.

Chiseling holes in the bricks with hand tools took time; then inserting the wooden plugs and screwing the base plates in place at each of the four sides took more time and effort than anticipated.

But near noon, all four were secured in place. The cables only needed to be attached to the black box, when an SS officer suddenly appeared.

"What is going on here?" he demanded in a tone he used when addressing his subordinates. The men looked up but continued their work, as if he were not there.

"May I ask who you are?" responded Robert fearlessly, almost intimidatingly addressing the officer, who immediately changed his attitude.

"You may, and I am Lieutenant Zimmermann. This church and its tower are part of the area I am responsible for."

"I am Chief Engineer Erlmann," Robert lied, "and my men

are, as you can see, installing a top-secret system, controlled directly from Berlin." He handed the document that confirmed the mission to the lieutenant. "This area, under your supervision, is one of the first around Berlin where this top-secret system is being installed. It is of vital importance to timely spot incoming aircraft at long distance. It has the attention of the führer himself."

Now the lieutenant suddenly felt extremely uncomfortable.

"I understand completely. Can I be of any assistance?"

"Yes, you can," answered Chief Engineer Erlmann. "My men have worked the whole morning, and as you must have noticed, it is very cold up here; if you could have one of your men bring us some hot coffee and maybe something to eat, I would appreciate it, and I will mention you to our superiors."

"No problem. I will take care of it. Good day."

When the officer was out of earshot, Robert smiled, and Bob said, "My God, Robert, you have balls."

Fifteen minutes later, two soldiers appeared, one holding a large mess tin with hot coffee and cups, the second one a plate with a pile of dark bread and thickly sliced ham.

But Bob realized that their luck might be running out soon; bluffing usually only worked until someone was smart enough to see through it, and bluffing was the basis of the whole operation.

When the wires were attached to the black box, the coffee consumed, and the tasty bread eaten, they sat down with their backs against the walls, taking shelter against the chilly wind blowing over their heads. One of them stood guard, waiting for the van to return.

It was 1:30 when the van turned a corner and stopped in front of the church. The men descended the tower, found their seats in the van, and were on their way.

It would be the most dangerous performance of their lives.

66

While the team was preparing for the riskiest part of the operation, to bluff themselves into the concentration camp, a meeting called by Hermann Göring took place sixty kilometers north of Berlin, close to the municipality of Friederichwalde, in the center of a one-hundred-thousand-acre forest, Schorfheide.

Göring had commissioned the design of a Swedish-style hunting lodge to architect Werner March, who also designed the Olympic stadium in Berlin. The construction started in 1933 and through many extensions would become an enormous hunting manor, with art galleries to accommodate his stolen art collection. The walls were decorated with Gobelins and old masters, the floors were covered with Persian rugs, and there were priceless art objects, furniture, and statues all over the oversized lodge. The gardens resembled the grounds of a cosmopolitan museum, with famous bronzes and marbles removed from occupied countries. To honor his deceased first wife, the Swedish Carin von Kantzow, the house was called Carinhall.

The corpulent field marshal was dressed in a specially designed master-of-the-hunt outfit, although there was no hunt in his schedule. He was sitting behind a large oak desk with elaborate carvings in his favorite hunting room, decorated with trophies and bronze statues of deer, boars, and naked women.

With him were Alfred Rosenberg, Dr. Binder, Hildebrand Gurlitt, Walter Andreas Hofer, and Hermann Bunjes, all members of his private art advisory council.

Alfred Rosenberg was the person in charge of the project to collect art from Jews in occupied territories and ship it to Germany. It was all looted art, either stolen straight out or paid for with stolen money.

Göring insisted on confidentiality.

In secret, he competed with the führer, Adolf Hitler, to add to his already large collection of art. He aimed to possess a collection of the most precious old masters. He favored Vermeer and Rembrandt.

Hitler dreamed of building an enormous *Kunstmuseum*, art museum, in Linz, the city where he had spent his youth, and he also targeted the most famous paintings of classic masters. He detested modern art. Considering it decadent, Hitler ordered the destruction of it.

Thousands of railcars filled with stolen art had already found their way to Nazi Germany.

Göring started the meeting. "Rosenberg, I feel I paid too much for the Goudstikker collection. Keep your eyes on Miedl.

He may have taken care of that Jew, but if he screws me, I'll take care of him."

"Jawohl, yes, Herr Field Marshal."

"Then what is this nonsense with the Katz brothers buying pieces from Jews that I may want? Are we now competing with some filthy Dutch Jews?"

"Not at all, Field Marshal. We are aware of it. It amounts to peanuts, and much of it is degenerate art—Gauguin, Matisse, Miro, all of that Jewish filth. But it allows my men to pick the great pieces at pennies to the guilder, because of the pressure the Katz brothers put on their fellow Jews."

"The führer has his eyes on the Louvre collection for his Linz Museum. That means certain pieces I would have wanted for Carinhall will be out of reach. What is there that you gentlemen can offer me instead?"

"I know of a Vermeer that was recently discovered, Herr Field Marshal. It is in the hands of one Han van Meegeren in Holland, a non-Jew," offered Dr. Binder.

"Then get it, but I am thinking of something bigger as a centerpiece for the great gallery, something by Rembrandt, Michelangelo, Velasquez. What is the most important painting Rembrandt ever made?"

"That would be *The Night Watch*, which is part of the Rijksmuseum collection in Amsterdam," answered Rosenberg.

"Then make sure it ends up in my collection."

"We will do whatever it takes, Herr Field Marshal. There is one complication."

"Complication?"

"As you know, the führer appointed Seyss-Inquart as *Reichskommisar*, governor in charge of Holland. One of his measures to control cultural groups was the establishment of a Dutch *Kulturkammer*, culture chamber. Within the artist community, resistance was rife. To demonstrate our German respect for art, our troops were instrumental in building shelter for most of Holland's national art treasures.

"That makes it *our* national treasure and mine. I am the man to protect it for future generations of our thousand-year German Reich. Make sure that when the time is right, it will be mine, and I will hold you personally responsible."

"Sebstverstaendlich, Herr Field Marshal," (of course) replied a nervously sweating Rosenberg.

67

It was one of those mornings Krueger hated.

The night before had been one of much food and especially too much booze. The loud voices and doughty songs of his drunken comrades and the vulgar laughter of the whores still resounded in his head. Some poor prisoner might feel the brunt of his hangover. His mind was still clouded by the amount of schnapps he drank.

He had arrived late that morning, which was unusual. He always made sure that every person under his command was busy working at seven sharp.

Now it was almost ten, and he still felt like he did not sleep at all. This was going to be a morning of lots of coffee. He felt sick.

"Cohen, coffee!" he shouted, and Salomon, very much aware of the danger every worker faced that morning, immediately complied.

There was a knock on the door, and the guard who days earlier had brought Salomon's book on aeronautics entered.

He went to the desk where a visibly uncomfortable Major Krueger looked at him through watery eyes.

"Was macht's?" (What is it?)

The guard stood at attention. "A letter for Salomon Cohen, it was still with the censoring department; it was released just now, Herr Major."

"Give it to him."

Krueger would normally read the letter anyway, censor or not, but this morning, he didn't give a damn.

Cohen's heart skipped a beat. This was it, the sign that he had been waiting for. The sachet with the powder was hidden under his clothes. He put his hand on the spot as if to make sure it was still there.

"Cohen, more coffee, Goddamnit!"

Salomon went to Krueger's desk, picked up the cup, turned around, and went to the small table where the major's real coffee was brewed every day.

He put an extra spoon of sugar in the cup and then, with shaking hands, tore open the sachet and poured the powder over the sugar. Then he filled the cup with coffee.

He had to hold the cup with both hands when he brought it to Krueger.

It was maybe fifteen minutes later that Krueger started to sweat.

His already pale face became white. He could hardly avoid vomiting. He felt nausea coming up, and he needed a washroom quickly. Half stumbling, he left barrack 19 to go first to a bathroom and then check himself into the lazaret and see Dr. Holman.

The diagnosis took longer than anticipated. Krueger thought that he would receive some pills and that his problems, his headache, nausea, and diarrhea, would be over in a couple of hours. Dr. Holman's facial expression, however, signaled a concern. After a thorough checkup, he removed the stethoscope from his ears, frowned, and shook his head.

"It has indications that point to cholera, but I don't think it is. I will need to keep you here under constant monitoring for at least three days in isolation. No visitors, no bathroom privileges, and on a strict diet."

"I need to send instructions to barrack 19, Doctor. Can you give me a pencil and paper?"

"Absolutely not Major Krueger. You are in quarantine until I am convinced that we don't face an outbreak of cholera."

68

Almost ten minutes outside Germendorf, on the left side of the road, were the large ruins where they were to meet the cars. The van parked behind them, out of sight from the road.

The team opened the large metal container and changed into their uniforms; after so many rehearsals, it was just routine.

Bob decided that Robert was the better character to be the senior officer. His German was without accent, and his attitude as a military instructor made him the ideal person to act with superiority toward the guards. They were about the same size, so the uniforms fit.

They checked each other's uniform, aligned their watches, and loaded their guns.

Then they waited.

A Kübelwagen soon appeared and behind it a large, open Mercedes, an SS standard attached to the left front fender. Both cars were driven by young SS troopers in uniform.

An SS Oberst, some officers, and men with shouldered guns

walked toward the cars from behind the ruins. The drivers of both cars jumped to attention, clicked their heels, raised their right arms, and loudly greeted them with "Heil Hitler." The officers returned the salute. The Oberst took a seat in the back of the Mercedes together with his second in command. The driver "Heil Hitlered" again, closed the car door, and took a seat behind the wheel, a sergeant next to him.

Then the sergeant and two soldiers with helmets took a seat in the Kübelwagen, and the Oberst indicated it was time to move.

There were two ways to drive to Sachsenhausen: through Oranienburg, the shorter route, and via a secondary road five minutes longer, via the north, avoiding the unwelcome attention of curious eyes in Oranienburg.

Before they left Holland, Vincit received a courier from Harro with additional instructions and papers. The problem was that the camp commander in Sachsenhausen, Hans Loritz, as Oberführer outranked the Oberst that Bob was supposed to be and Robert had become. The solution was to provide a special signed mandate from Heinrich Müller, "Gestapo Müller," to arrest and bring to the headquarters a Jew involved in plans to sabotage the secret activities taking place in barrack 19. Loritz had reasons to fear the Gestapo.

He had been under scrutiny of the SS Verwaltungsamt, the administrative office, for corruption and self-enrichment. The result was that he had been sent to Graz in Austria against his will. He kept trying to return to a post at the concentration camp and finally succeeded in December 1939. He would be very concerned to lose his command due to Gestapo involvement.

The documents now were in the SS-marked folder in Robert's hands.

There was a barrier with two armed sentinels on the road just minutes in front of the concentration camp. When they noticed the Kübelwagen and the Mercedes, they lifted the bar and jumped to attention; the officers saluted.

In front of them, some hundred meters to go, was the forged metal gate with "Arbeit Macht Frei."

69

The Kübelwagen stopped to let the Mercedes pass and be the first car at the infamous entrance. A sentinel opened the gate and jumped to attention.

He turned to the sergeant. "Papieren bitte" (Papers please).

"Gestapo, hurry up!" shouted Robert in his perfect German. "I want to speak to your commander and immediately. Where is barrack 19?"

The sentinel was not going to argue with an Oberst from the Gestapo.

"Straight ahead at the end of the road left." He pointed in the direction.

"Where is your commander? Call him! I want to see him now!"

The intimidated sentinel went to the guardhouse, spoke a few words through the telephone, and then returned.

"Oberführer Loritz awaits you. Please follow the motorcycle, which will take you to his office."

"Danke schön," (thank you) said the Oberst. Then he turned to the sergeant in the Kübelwagen. "You heard; go to barrack 19 now. There should be a Jew by the name of Salomon Cohen. He is a saboteur. Don't kill him. We need his information. No talking. Tie him up and bring him. We need him at the head office."

The Mercedes with Robert and Bob followed the motorcyclist, who stopped in front of an office building, jumped off his machine, and jumped to attention.

The door opened, and a burly man with a small moustache and penetrating blue eyes, his uniform jacket loose over his shoulders, stepped forward and then stopped, his booted legs wide.

"I was not informed about your visit, gentlemen." He greeted them without inviting them in.

"For good reasons, OberFührer, do you want to hear what we have to say here or are you going to invite us in?" Robert held the folder very visibly in front of his body.

The commandant's attitude changed.

"Of course, please come in. Would you like coffee, a drink maybe?" He took a seat at his desk, a large picture of Adolf Hitler looking down at him from the wall behind him.

"Coffee would be fine. Let me show you why we are here."

Robert took one of the papers from the folder for the commandant to read, took off his cap, and set it on the desk.

The word *Gestapo* and especially the signature of "Gestapo Mueller" was enough. The commandant was visibly uncomfortable.

"What can I do for you?"

"Very little actually," answered Bob, not to give the impression that he missed the faculty to speak.

Robert continued, "You may be aware, Commandant Loritz, of top-secret operations in barrack 19, ordered by Himmler on instruction from our Führer ."

Loritz nodded.

"We are here to arrest and transport to the head office a Jew by the name of Salomon Cohen. It has been brought to the attention of the Gestapo that he is taking initiatives to sabotage the operations. We need to know who his coconspirators are."

Now Loritz showed a nervous smile. "Conspiracy? A stinking Jew? Here?"

His hand was on the telephone on the desk in front of him. "I will have his sorry ass here in a second."

"Absolutely not," shouted Robert, putting his hand on the phone, "our men have him already in custody and made sure that there was no time for the Jew to warn his cronies."

The commandant was taken aback.

"We will report that thanks to your full cooperation, the disaster could be avoided and the project could continue unhindered."

When the officers left, Loritz relaxed. His job could have been in danger because of one stinking rotten Jew. What a pity they took him. He would have had a special treatment for that vermin.

The Kübelwagen drove at full speed to barrack 19 and then stopped with screeching brakes. The sergeant, his revolver drawn, and the soldiers jumped out and ran to the door. They kicked it open.

"Was ist ... what the he ..." started a guard who occupied the chair behind Krueger's desk. The soldiers pointed their weapons.

"Maul halten!" shouted the sergeant (Shut up). Addressing the shocked prisoners, caught off guard, he said, "Aufstehen" (Stand up).

The intimidated guard complied as well.

"Who is Salomon Cohen?"

No answer.

"I will ask one more time, and then the first of you will be shot, then the second."

Several heads turned in the direction of Salomon Cohen, who started shivering. *This could not be it,* he thought. Did they find out that something was going on? Would he be executed? Did Krueger die? Uncontrolled tears wetted his face. Would he never see Sarah again, just as he dreamed he would?

Then Salaman Smolianoff stepped forward.

He saw his life passing before his eyes in a flash while standing with the guns pointed at him. He would never see Mother Russia again. Who knew if his family was even alive? This temporary bearable concentration camp subsistence would end in death anyway.

"I am Salamon Cohen," he claimed with an unmistakable Russian accent and the Freudian mistake of saying Salamon instead of Salomon.

The sergeant knew better.

Then Salomon Cohen walked up to the sergeant. "I am Salomon Cohen."

Immediately the two soldiers grabbed him. One hit him hard. He stumbled. The other soldier pushed him in the small of his back with the butt of his weapon.

The Fake Rembrandt

"Mitkommen" (Come).

The sergeant walked up to the Russian, and with pain in his heart the unselfish man would never know of, slapped him hard on the cheek and then turned around and marched out of the building.

They almost threw him into the back of the German car waiting in front of the barrack, the engine running. They blindfolded him and then seated him between the two soldiers. The car drove with great speed toward the gate. Nobody spoke a word. Salomon was silently praying.

The Mercedes was waiting at the gate with both Robert and Bob in the back.

The sentry opened it, and with a last salute, the officers and their prisoner were on their way.

Cohen was still blindfolded, and not a word had been spoken when they reached the ruins behind which the van was parked. The soldiers guided their prisoner to the back of the van and helped him in. Bob took off the man's blindfold. He trembled. There was agony in his eyes.

"Mr. Cohen," Bob said quickly in Dutch, "it is okay. We are here to take you home. Just do what we say, and we may make it. Did you read the book we sent you?"

But there was not a word coming out of the shaking body, only sobs, the emotional release of too much pain, too much uncertainty, too much hope.

The men hurriedly changed back into their coveralls. They

put the uniforms back into the metal case and locked it. When Salomon calmed down, they put him in the extra coveralls brought for the purpose.

The sentries at both roadblocks waved them through, never noticing the extra engineer hardly able to control his emotions.

The high fives the guys were giving each other were an understandable, if premature, elation at the successful conclusion of what could be the most difficult part of the mission, but it was not over yet. They were still in Nazi Germany, and nothing could be taken for granted.

They would soon find out.

The Kübelwagen and the Mercedes had left the moment they reached the ruins where they changed to the van. They would reach the Weinberg estate before the team. They parked both cars in the large shed, changed the license plates, and were removing the standard from the fender when a loud banging with a hard object, like the butt of a gun, startled them.

"Aufmachen!" (Open the door).

70

Earlier, Bob realized that the sooner they were dressed in their civilian clothes, the better chance they would have to be protected by the documents signed by Göring, explaining their involvement in the secret aeronautical project. Instead of driving the van directly to the shed and getting rid of the uniforms, coveralls, and tools, he decided to first go to the houses were they had stayed before. One of the first things to do was get Salomon in the civilian clothing they had brought for him.

When Bob opened the back door of the house he had slept in before, the shutters still closed, he froze, startled by the presence of the old man he had met before.

"Trouble," whispered the man.

"Trouble? What sort of trouble?" asked Bob, taking the old man by his skinny shoulders.

"Two soldiers at the shed" was all the man said, but Bob knew enough.

He called Robert and explained the situation.

"Take one of the men and see what you can do. Be careful."

Robert selected one of the soldiers, a tough-looking character, all sinew and bone; he was a former commando in the elite brigade.

"Bob, if you hear a shot, get the hell out of here; we won't need guns for two German assholes. If you hear a bang, something is wrong. Continue with your mission." He slapped Bob on the shoulder. "It was fun anyway, whatever happens."

The two men, still dressed in their coveralls, did not immediately look suspicious. With sharp fighting knives under their belts, they left in the direction of the shed, partly covered by the slowly forming darkness of the evening.

Approaching stealthily close to the ground, they noticed both large doors were open. Against the sparse yellow light, they spotted two soldiers, guns aimed at Werner and his comrades, who were sitting on the floor, legs crossed and their hands on their necks.

It appeared to Robert that a Waffen SS patrol, the armed section of the SS, just happened to come across something they found suspicious and had not decided yet what was to be done next.

There was evidence of subversive activities inside.

The two soldiers might panic when they found out they had come across a cell of the resistance.

They might put everybody against the wall and shoot them, as they often did.

Flat on his belly, Robert hand signaled to his partner, "You right, me left." Then he made a slicing motion with his hand along his throat.

His partner confirmed.

They crawled closer to the building, moving very slowly so as not to make a sound. When they were less than eight feet behind the soldiers, who kept their eyes and guns on the prisoners, Robert signed one ... two ... three.

They jumped like tigers at the soldiers with their left hands turning their heads back. The Germans dropped their guns, grabbing at the arm that strangled them. Then both men sliced the SS men's throats, hanging on to the convulsing bodies until they no longer moved.

"What took you so long?" said a visibly relieved Werner. "I was shitting my pants. These are some crazy SS bastards. They would have killed us if they had looked a little more at the stuff here instead of at our handsome faces."

Robert and his partner got out of the bloodied coveralls. "That was close, guys. What about the bodies?"

"We'll give them a ceremonial burial, compliments of our comrades in arms they murdered. Don't worry; they'll never find them," answered Werner. "But don't stay an hour longer than needed. When these two don't return from patrol, the shit will hit the fan. We will clean up here and be gone. Thanks, guys, and good luck."

He gave both men a bear hug.

It was finally Friday afternoon again. Johanna Langefeld had taken a bath that morning and sprinkled herself with rosewater. Her hair, which she normally tied in a knot, was hanging down in curls. The night before, she had used curl paper to get some form in the normally straight strands. She wore the tied jacket that made her breasts look bigger and left the top three buttons open.

Willie was late. She became irritated and with malicious pleasure hit one of the women hard with her truncheon without any reason. The left side of the woman's face started to swell.

Then, finally, there was the truck.

It backed up into the building, ready to take that day's load of uniforms.

Willie jumped out, a big smile on his face. Looking over his shoulder, he cried, "Ah, mein Liebchen! I couldn't sleep the whole week. I was so worried that you were fooling around with some guys here."

Johanna laughed, striking her sexiest pose. "Guys ... here?"

Willie turned around facing her.

With both hands, he opened his jacket wide, like an exhibitionist would. In his pants behind his belt and half sticking out was a large bottle of schnapps. He wiggled his hips, presenting the bottle as a phallic object. With a seductive smile, Johanna went down on her knees, closed her lips around the bottleneck, and took a large sip.

With exalted delight, she looked up at Willie, licking her lips.

Sarah turned away from the vulgar scene.

The Fake Rembrandt

Willie removed the bottle from his pants, pretended to take a big quaff but closed the bottle with his tongue, and then handed it to Johanna to challenge her to take as big a swig as he did.

He put his arm around her middle, pulled her close to him, and then whispered in her ear, "I love horny drunk women."

In a low, lascivious voice, the drunk hussy answered, "Then show me, loverboy," and grabbed Willie's crotch.

He pretended to drink again. He held the bottle while she was drinking, not letting go of it. Willie made sure he turned her away from the truck the women were loading.

Franz was on the other side of the truck. He dropped his glasses. Sarah bent down to pick them up, and Franz grabbed the emaciated woman around her waist and threw her into the truck, quickly covering her with the bales. There were two cardboard tubes next to her body.

The Oberaufseherin, (the head guard) was on the floor, totally drunk now. Completely stupefied from alcohol, she was oblivious to what was happening around her. Her jacket was half open, and one of her plump bare breasts was showing. She turned her head sideways and vomited.

A disgusted Willie threw the bottle next to her. He climbed into the cab, and the truck left the concentration camp. It would be the last trip of the Rote Kapelle members Franz and Willie.

The guards waved them through without checking, as they so often did.

About two kilometers away from the camp, the truck stopped

on the side of the road. Franz jumped out as if to check the load. He lifted a bale and made sure that the end of the cardboard tube was unobstructed so Sarah could breathe.

"Are you okay?" he asked with his mouth close to the tube.

The answer sounded like a sob, but then very clearly, she said, "Yes, oh God, yes, I am."

71

So far so good, thought Bob, belittling the incredible stunt they had pulled off, but there they were, dressed again like the aeronautical engineers they were supposed to be. Werner and his men were gone, there were two dead SS soldiers somewhere, and he had a crying Salomon Cohen on his hands.

It had taken some time to explain to the man why he had been kidnapped from the camp, at great risk to the team he met. Bob expected an elated, exalted person, escaped from a netherworld hellhole and ultimate certain death. It was a bit disappointing that he did not show any outward sign of delight, although he expressed his thanks many times.

Bob explained what the purpose of the campaign to liberate Salomon was and how his proficiency in restoration and his knowledge about Rembrandt would be instrumental in saving Holland's most valuable art treasure, *The Night Watch*.

But Cohen was sad.

The coded message he received made him believe that he would somehow be reunited with Sarah. From what he now learned, she was still in Ravensbrück.

What if she was murdered there or simply perished? Salomon knew what concentration camps were like. What would his life be? How could he ever go on living, knowing that his beloved Sarah was a victim of those monsters and never knowing how she suffered or what her last thoughts had been when her hopes crashed.

How could he, Salomon Cohen, be in Amsterdam, the city he loved so much, and paint a Rembrandt while his heart was torn out of his breast; he could not.

Bob and Robert were concerned that the men would take their disappointment out on Cohen. Had they risked their lives for this? For this ungrateful whining asshole?

Both tried to convince Cohen that the chances were good that he would see Sarah again. He explained how Suzan pleaded to also try to bring Sarah back and that the leader of the Rote Kapelle agreed. Freeing her from the work camp for women at Ravensbrück could hardly be more complicated than the operation just behind them.

Finally, Salomon saw the light. From Holland, he would certainly have more chances to do something. If they needed him badly enough to undertake so dangerous an operation, he might convince them that it was impossible to do what they asked of him, without knowing she was safe.

"I am sorry, Bob," he said, offering a handshake. "It was maybe

The Fake Rembrandt

the time spent in hell that prevented me from thinking straight. I am extremely thankful and relieved and will do everything expected from me to show my gratitude."

The men smiled and hugged him. Salomon Cohen, the prisoner, became Cohen, the aeronautical engineer, member of a team.

The problem of how the team of engineers and scientists would get to the central station in Berlin, now that Werner and his men were gone, was resolved quickly.

The same cars that had picked them up upon arrival from Holland appeared in front of the houses. Three to a car, the identical brown briefcases on their laps, they drove unhindered to the station.

As expected, they were asked to show papers, and Bob complied. A bit more self-assured, having passed similar scrutinies several times, Bob handed the Göring-signed document and asked in an authoritative voice, "Show me the station restaurant please. My men and I are hungry, and a long trip to Holland lies ahead."

Instead of just pointing it out, the officer walked them to the first-class restaurant, saluted, and turned back to the entrance hall.

The train to Holland would leave from platform 4 in fifty minutes. On board would be a team of aeronautical professionals, now consisting of seven men instead of six.

72

It was almost dark when the truck arrived at Kleidung Werkstatt Gunter Schneider. Kurt Schmidt was waiting to ensure that nobody touched the load without his instruction.

"How did it go?" he asked Willie, who jumped down from the truck and walked around it to where he knew Sarah was hidden.

"It was easy, Kurt. That SS tart is in a delirium. What a disgusting piece of dirt. Do me a favor, give these kinds of jobs to Franz here. I'll drive."

Franz flipped him the bird.

They helped Sarah climb down from the back of the truck. There was nobody else in the loading dock. Sarah shivered like a frightened deer. Covering her face with both hands, she started to cry softly. With tearful eyes, she went to Kurt and hugged him. Taken aback a moment, Kurt put an arm around her, and then suddenly, heavy sobs shook her body, her knees buckled, and Kurt had to hold her up. Stroking her hair, he whispered, "It's okay, girl. Don't worry; everything will be all right."

The Fake Rembrandt

Franz and Willie felt lumps in their throats. Willie had to blow his nose several times.

When she gradually regained control of herself, wiping her face with the sleeve of her prison uniform, Kurt took her to his office. She was a sorry sight.

On the round iron stove was a large bucket with warm water. On a chair sat a bar of soap and a towel, and on the wooden chair next to it were a dress, a coat, stockings and shoes, a warm shawl, and knitted gloves. The tears rolled freely again.

"Please take your time, we are not in a hurry. The large truck for Holland will be loaded in about three hours. I will give you half an hour, and then I will be back with some food."

Sarah could not talk.

When he returned after forty minutes, a completely transformed Sarah awaited him, a smile on her still skinny face, but her full lips, sparkling blue eyes, and raven-black hair made it obvious that once she was nourished back to health, she would again be the stunning beauty she once was.

He opened the stove door with a poker and stuffed the prisoner's outfit in. Then he opened the door of the ash tray to boost the fire.

From a cupboard, he took a plate, cup, fork, and knife.

He poured some milk into the cup and put two slices of white bread with a thin spread of honey on the plate in front of her.

"Eat slowly, Sarah. The milk is lukewarm. Be careful; your body is not used to food anymore. If you eat the first slice and you can hold it in, wait fifteen minutes, and then eat the second one. You need to build some strength. It will be a tough ride to Holland."

Sarah ate with gusto, fighting the urge to eat the second slice but aware of the danger it could do to her system. When later she had finished her meal, she felt exhausted and emotionally drained. She fell asleep in the chair, half conscious, realizing that she had never asked about Salomon.

"Sarah, wake up!" A soft voice awakened her. For a moment, she panicked, and then she recognized Kurt. "It's time to go, darling."

They went down to the loading dock, where a large truck waited, half loaded with bundles of the uniforms she knew so well and some piles of blankets, boxes, and crates. With wooden pallets, a sort of doghouse was formed in the center of the load. A pile of blankets on the bottom formed a mattress, and a cardboard tube functioned as an air duct for when the space was covered with the rest of the cargo.

"Here is some water and some food if you become too hungry during the trip. God speed, girl."

He helped her up. She crawled to her hiding place, where she made herself comfortable, and then the trusted helpers finished loading. The truck's diesel engine started.

Sarah was on her way home.

That evening, Kurt's wife, Edda, wondered what was wrong with her husband. He usually did not take the problems of his job home, but he looked preoccupied that night. He did not touch the Sauerbraten, normally his favorite.

"What is wrong, darling?" she finally asked.

Kurt told her the story, hardly controlling his emotions.

"What is this world coming to, Edda? What for Christ's sake are we doing to good, innocent people?"

She walked up behind his chair, and with two arms around him, she kissed the side of his head.

"Not you, darling, not you. I am so proud of you." Then she kissed him again when she noticed tears rolling down his cheeks.

73

The train ride back through Germany passed without incident. Most of the men slept, exhausted now that the task they had prepared themselves for seemed to be done.

There were several requests for papers, but every time, the documents they carried seemed to impress, and no questions were asked.

Bob reminisced, half asleep.

The operation went more smoothly than he had ever anticipated. True, there had been fabulous cooperation from the Rote Kapelle. He wondered if his countrymen, given now to hatred of everything German, would ever know how many brave individuals in Germany, opposing Nazism, risked their lives against insuperable odds. Would they ever realize how many Germans perished in Nazi concentration camps—German Jews, homosexuals, Jehovah's witnesses, gypsies, and many members of the resistance?

The Fake Rembrandt

The disguise as members of an aeronautical scientific team, with almost flawlessly forged documents, had been a lifesaver.

The installation of the black box system in the Germendorf tower was genius.

But having Dr. Holman involved to isolate Krueger for at least three days, avoiding any early alarm that a member of the barrack 19 counterfeiting team had disappeared, was nothing short of brilliant. That brute of a camp commander, murdering thousands of Jews, couldn't care less about the one the Gestapo wanted.

Drained from a fatiguing mixture of adventure and fear, exhausted from too few hours of sleep, he completely crashed.

When Bob awoke, the train was entering the station in Muenster. It would only be two hours more and they would be in Enschede, just across the border, back in Holland. But there was a delay; the train was not able to leave the station. After an agonizingly long wait of nearly an hour, knowing they were so close to home, the men became very nervous. Had they been too lucky thus far? Bob decided to take some action. He left the train, taking his briefcase with him. When he noticed a group of officers talking, some gesticulating, he walked up to the highest in rank.

"Excuse me, Obersturmbahnführer." Without being asked, Bob offered his document, which the officer quickly read. "Is there a possibility to let my team know when we may continue?"

The officer appeared to be a friendly person.

"I would like to, sir, but the problem is that the line in front of Gronau has been bombarded. Our best guess is that it will take another three hours. May I suggest you go to the restaurant. There is very little available on the train."

Bob thanked him, and the officer saluted military style, not with Heil Hitler.

The best thing about the restaurant was that the place was warm, which could not be said about the food and the bitter coffee. The travelers, both military and civilian, regarded the group with suspicion. In Nazi Germany, it usually meant trouble. The men were tired of being so close to home. The waiting was nerve-racking. They felt dirty, worried, and irritated.

Finally, someone blew a whistle, and most people left the restaurant and boarded the train. Two hours later, they stopped in Zwolle. They were in Holland and all of them alive. From the compartment, Cohen noticed a sorrowful group of people, mostly men but also women and children. They all wore a yellow star stitched on their clothes. They were driven together by SS guards with dogs on a leash.

Salomon felt as if suddenly a heavy load had fallen from the sky onto his shoulders. He started to sweat, and he felt like his stomach would empty itself.

Salomon was free, or was he?

74

Sarah felt surprisingly comfortable in the dark space created by the pallets.

The layer of blankets below her felt soft, like a real mattress and luxurious compared to the pigsty crib she had had to sleep in, together with three other women. The load of uniforms around her kept the shelter warm, and there was just enough air to breathe. Normally, she might have felt claustrophobic, but what was the difference between this confinement and staring at the bottom of that cursed crib just a foot above her head?

But the enclosure of the cocoon played tricks on her brain.

Sarah felt as if it was all unreal, as if Ravensbrück had never happened but was just a horrible nightmare she had. She saw herself as a young girl again with Mamma and Abba, walking along the Jodenbreestraat, clad in her finest on a sunny Sabbath, Abba with his black moustache and goat beard politely lifting his hat every time he met someone he knew. She felt Abba's strong, warm hand and knew nothing could ever happen to his daughter.

She saw herself with Mamma, walking that first time to the

Talmud Thora school in the Boerhavestraat, and saw the tears again that Mamma had shed.

She felt warm inside when she relived that first kiss. Salomon, oh how she loved him, how she had missed him then, every hour of the day when they were not together. Could there be more happiness than that day under the *chupah*, the wedding canopy? How handsome her *chatan* looked, how painfully long had the week before the wedding been, when she was not allowed to see him. How pretty she felt. She smiled when her new husband lifted his foot high and stamped hard on the glass. Mazel tov.

She still felt the pain when Adonai did not bless her with children, a sadness made bearable by the love and understanding of her dedicated husband.

She realized that she was crying when she felt moisture on her face.

As if Satan insisted on playing his part in her contemplation, she witnessed, powerless again, how that devilish monster Johanna killed and kicked the young Belgian girl, carrying her baby inside her. She saw again the empty places in the cribs when yet another number of women had been worked to death, hanged, or executed.

But now she was free.

Neither Johanna nor any other barbaric Teutonic female could harm her now.

But where was her Salomon?

Was he alive? Would she ever see him again? The odds

were against it. She now knew what the destiny of a Jew in a concentration camp was, extermination.

But the letter, those blessed words she would never forget, claimed that Salomon was still alive, and thus far, all it had said did in fact happen.

What did "When home, ask for Suzan" mean?

She thought it over many times, but she did not know a Suzan.

The truck had been stopped for inspection twice, and both times, the papers of the driver were probably what they were looking for. No one checked the cargo. Through the tubes, Sarah could hear the stern, guttural commands. It was never just a question, but it had ended both times with "In Ordnung, weiter fahren" (Okay, continue).

It must still be dark, thought Sarah when the truck stopped again.

She did not hear any voices this time.

What was wrong? she started to panic.

Then there were sounds as if someone was doing some mechanical work on the left side of the truck. She relaxed when a familiar voice came to her through the tube. "Sanitary stop, Sarah. We'll get you out for a moment."

It was not a moment too early; she badly needed to pee.

Although it was still dark, it had been much darker in her doghouse, so she was aware of her surroundings when they helped her out.

On the ground next to the truck was a spare tire and a jack, but there was no flat tire. She understood.

There were thick bushes on the side.

The whole stoppage did not take more than ten minutes, and she was back in her cocoon. The truck continued. Feeling relieved, she fell asleep.

75

Sarah woke up, alarmed, when the truck stopped again. She could hear the slamming of both doors, and then a voice said, "Sarah, we're here."

"Sarah, we're here"—three simple words, the most hoped for, prayed for, blessed sentence she had ever heard.

She was back in Holland.

They helped her out of her hiding spot and off the truck. She felt stiff, she needed to exercise her limbs a bit.

"This is it, Sarah. We can't take you any further, ahead of us is Enschede where we will need to deliver the cargo." They had stopped on a side road with thick forest on both sides. "Hide yourself here till dark, and then follow this country road till you see a farmhouse with the name 'Weltevreden' on the entrance gate. Be careful."

She gave both men a quick hug and then disappeared among the hazel brushes and oak trees. Far enough inside, she sat down on a fallen tree, her heart beating fast.

Now what?

It would be a long and lonesome day before she could try to find that farmhouse, Weltevreden, which meant "acquiescence." What if she could not find it? She shook off her concerns. What could be worse than Ravensbrück. She was in Holland, and one way or another, she would find her way home. Sarah ate the bread she had saved, but there was nothing to drink. That would have to wait until tonight. A sound behind her startled her, but she smiled when it turned out to be a deer. She realized that maybe she was too close to the road when she heard cars passing. She should go further into the forest, but how would she find her way back? She broke a small twig from each tree she passed, a roadmap visible only to someone who knew, until she was far enough into the forest not to hear anything. There was a small, open space with ferns and mosses. She made a bed of dried oak leaves on the edge of it. Tired now, she bedded down and fell asleep. The trip, the excitement, the emotions, and the fear took a toll on her.

She realized how long she had been sleeping when, cold and stiff, she tried to stand up, and every muscle in her body ached. She brushed the leaves off her body, then noticed that it was getting dark. She had to hurry; if it got too dark, she would never see those broken twigs and might get lost in a forest that went all the way to Germany. She walked as fast as she could until she could hear sounds of the country road again. To stay out of sight, she followed the path until the forest opened. The road turned to the left, and on the right side were open fields. At the far end, she noticed a farmhouse, a haystack, and some sheds. Out of sight of the road now, she walked to the gate. A chained dog started barking. On the gate, she could read the word "Weltevreden."

Alerted by the barking, a farmer in his blue jacket, wooden clogs, and black cap approached the gate.

"Yes?"

Sarah did not know what to say. She stammered, "Somebody gave me this name. I am Sarah." Immediately, she realized her mistake. Sarah—a more Jewish name was hardly imaginable. What if this was the wrong address? Many Dutch people had no qualms betraying their Jewish country folk.

The farmer waited for what felt like eternity, all the while observing the woman in front of his gate.

"Come in," he said, short but not unfriendly. He opened the gate. Sarah followed him to the farmhouse. The dog barked even louder.

He opened the door and invited her in. She walked into the half-dark room. Two men in long coats stepped forward.

"Sarah Cohen?"

She almost fainted and wetted herself.

76

The two men were not prepared for the scene that followed.

Sarah fell to her knees, completely falling apart. She sobbed and screamed, totally losing control of herself.

"Oh my God!" stammered one of the men. "What does she think?"

He knelt next to her, putting his arm around her shoulders.

"It is okay, Sarah. I am so sorry, we are here to help you."

It took quite a while before they could reach her. The farmer's wife quickly took charge and led Sarah, still on wobbly legs, to a chair. "Here, child, drink something." She held a glass of water against Sarah's trembling lips.

"That was some stupid performance, I thought you guys were smarter than that," she scolded the abashed men, who looked perplexedly at the woman they had unintentionally terrified.

Knowing approximately when Sarah would arrive, Roger had sent two of his men to meet her in Enschede. Crossing the country to Amsterdam with police collaborators and German

The Fake Rembrandt

Gruene Polizei all over and a Jewess on board would be virtually impossible. The resistance did not have a picture of Sarah that could be used for a forged *Ausweis* in the name of a non-Jewish woman. The Ausweis was an identity paper introduced by the Germans that every person was forced to carry; it was stamped with a large J for Jews.

The solution Roger came up with was that the two men would act as plainclothes policemen who had arrested a Jew they were taking to the Euterpestraat in Amsterdam, the feared Gestapo headquarters. They carried the necessary documents in case they were stopped.

The DKW car with license number L 39941 was parked behind the haystack.

How could a woman, any woman, especially one who had survived the most unimaginably inhumane existence, keep her sanity when she went from hell to heaven and back again. Sarah was drained. She had no reserves anymore. She had no tears to shed anymore. She was just sitting there dazed, staring apathetically at nothing, feeling nothing, caring no more.

The farmer's wife tried to make her eat some of the warm porridge she had cooked for her, feeding her with a spoon, like a baby. Sarah just slowly shook her head, with a sadness in her eyes that brought the poor woman to tears. She put the plate and spoon on the table, and then the voluptuous woman lifted the emaciated girl from the chair, sat on it herself, and put the young woman on her lap. She began rocking her softly, while stroking her hair. Burned out, Sarah fell asleep again.

When she awoke, the farmer and the two men were sitting around the table, no long coats anymore. When one of them noticed that she, somewhat embarrassed, was awake again and now sitting in the chair instead of on a lap, he came closer, knelt next to her, took her hand, and in a soft voice, said, "Sarah, Salomon is alive. He is in Amsterdam. You will see him soon."

For a split second, it did not seem to dawn on her, and then suddenly, she came to life. Salomon, her Salomon was alive! She looked at the faces of the others, all smiles now, and then she hugged the man and held on to him like she would never let go of God's angel who had brought her the message.

Salomon home in Amsterdam.

Now she ate the porridge and drank the warm milk in a hurry; she wanted to go, to run, or to fly. She kissed the kind farmer and his wife and then followed the men to the car. One of them sat with her in the back. He explained, "Sarah, you have no papers. The only way we could take you to Amsterdam was by acting as plainclothes police who arrested a betrayed Jew. Sorry but there was no other way, so play the role when necessary and take our acted abuse for what it is."

Now Sarah smiled. "I just mastered in taking abuse; don't worry."

"By the way, who is Suzan?" she asked.

The men looked at each other. How did she know.

"She is waiting for you in Amsterdam," the man behind the wheel answered over his shoulder.

77

The picture of that pitiful group of innocent, doomed people stayed with Salomon throughout the train ride to Amsterdam. How could he ever enjoy being free when this horror continued unhampered? Why should he, Salomon Cohen, be the chosen one?

Cohen, victim himself, wrestled with an uncomfortable, undefined feeling of guilt.

Bob intuitively felt that he needed to stop Salomon's musing.

"We are almost there, Salomon. Act normal. Even in Holland, you are a member of this engineering team. Someone is waiting at the station with transportation, and you will be taken to a safe house. Do not panic. Act natural. The people who will pick you up can be trusted. I will walk you to the car."

Salomon started to feel better.

The central station in Amsterdam was busy. Salomon felt uncomfortable when they walked through the great hall. There were Germans all over the place, but as just one within the group, nobody paid specific attention.

The car waiting for him was an old Ford pickup truck. Bob exchanged a few words with the driver, a man with a weathered face, a big white nicotine-stained moustache, and a cap deep over his forehead.

"Hop in, Anton," he told Salomon.

The moment Salomon sat in the worn-out car seat, the truck left the station,

The man, who introduced himself as Frank, handed him an envelope. "Read this."

Salomon became Anton Bakker, born in Amstelveen. He was a clerk at the Dutch Cheese Factory in Bovenkerk, where Frank was employed. His Ausweis, with his picture, signature, and the swastika stamp, was a so-called *Facharbeiter Ausweis*, (professional worker's ID), indicating that the bearer's work was of value to the occupying forces.

"Welcome to the club, Anton." Frank smiled. "I hope you like cheese, because you are going to smell a lot of it."

"No problem if it is kosher," answered Anton, and they both laughed.

Frank turned out to be a jovial, cordial guy. He explained the special position of a company like the one he worked for. All factories producing products that benefitted the Germans were kept running—hence the papers signed by Seyss-Inquart, the German governor himself, protecting the bearer.

They rode through Amsterdam South, passing the Olympic stadium, and then through the village of Amstelveen to Bovenkerk.

It was a small hamlet with a church and houses on both sides of the road, only accessible via small bridges across the gully in front.

At the end of the road was a large plant with a wide driveway. Trucks were backed up against the loading docks of a main building. On the roof was an enormous, probably metal yellow painted cheese with the letters "DCF." They had arrived at the Dutch Cheese Factory.

Frank drove the truck to the back of the building. Separated from it was a two-story office building.

"Follow me."

They climbed the wooden stairs in front of the office and walked through the hallway until they stood in front of a double door marked "Direktie" (management).

Frank knocked. They were invited in immediately.

"Mister De Boer, this is Anton."

A middle-aged man with friendly eyes behind gold-rimmed glasses in a three-piece gray-striped suit with a red-striped necktie stepped from behind his loaded desk to shake Salomon's hand.

"Please sit down, Anton, and welcome back. Frank, I'll see you later."

When the two were alone, Mr. De Boer picked up the phone and ordered coffee.

"I am well informed about your story, Anton. I hope you like that name; it has been quite an adventure, I hear. Brave men, I say. For the time being, you will be safe here. Behind this building, if you follow the gravel path, is a small cabin that I sometimes use.

My friends stay there when they wanted to go fishing in the Poel." De Boer paused when a woman brought in two cups of coffee. "The Poel is the name of a small lake above our village, popular among local sport and professional fishermen.

"You are completely safe there. Do not attract unnecessary attention. Keep a low profile, and hang on to your papers. Frank will be your contact man."

The little cabin was not that little at all. It was a cozy, well-furnished man's den, with trophies and pictures of big fish and broadly smiling friends. There was a small kitchen, one bedroom, a bathroom with toilet and a shower.

Salomon took off his shoes and went to the bed, fully dressed.

On his back, hands behind his head, he kept staring at the ceiling until he fell asleep.

78

In the back of the small German-made DKW car, Sarah felt surprisingly at ease sitting next to the man who earlier had given her that harrowing scare. The trip would take more than two hours, but she was comfortable and the apprehension she initially felt was gone.

Salomon was in Amsterdam.

Could it really be true?

How many nights did she fall asleep crying inside, with his name the last thing in her thoughts? How many prayers did she say in silence while working and fearing, afraid she would die without ever seeing him again?

How worried had she been that no one would say Kaddish if the unspeakable happened to him?

Thank you, Adonai. Y'hei sh'mei Rabbi m'varach l'alam ul'almei almaya. (May God's great name be blessed forever and through an infinity of worlds and eternities), she prayed in her heart. Only a few more hours and she would be in his arms.

The first test came just outside the city of Ermelo.

A military car was parked on the side of the road. A man in a military uniform gestured for the DKW to stop. He signaled that they all had to step out, so they did.

A second man walked around the car, his gun at the ready.

"Papieren." (Papers) A German, these guys were Gruene Polizei, green police, a dangerous corps of German special police active in Holland.

He carefully checked the identity and papers of both men and then handed them back without comment.

"Who is she?"

"A Jew who thought she could hide in a barn. We are taking her to the Gestapo in Amsterdam to find out about the network. Then as far as I am concerned, they can give her to the dogs."

Sarah started to shake and cry convincingly. The lowlifes laughed.

"Weiter gehen" (Continue).

The second stop was just east of the city of Amersfoort.

This time, two *Schalkhaarders*, Dutch police collaborators trained by the Germans, wearing helmets and carrying carbines, walked up to the car.

The papers were not enough. They insisted that the Jew should come out of the car and be interrogated. Sarah did not have to pretend; her terror was genuine.

The driver now jumped out of the car and with his full six-foot-two-inch frame confronted the policeman.

"Absolutely not! We are under strict orders of the Gestapo that she is to talk to no one. I advise you to immediately step aside and let us pass. If you have any doubts, feel free to call Aus der Fuenten, and I will have a few words to say to him too." The bluff worked.

Without further questions, the puppets stepped aside.

They arrived in Amsterdam and drove straight to the Ruysdaelkade. They parked the car in front of a stately three-story house. After checking the surroundings, one of the men pulled the brass doorbell handle. The lacquered dark green door opened immediately. A housemaid stepped aside. Sarah and the second man went quickly inside. She noticed the Persian carpets on the black-and-white checkered marble floor and the large, shiny brass chandeliers. A large pendulum clock chimed just when a pretty young woman appeared from the salon. After welcoming the men, she went with open arms to Sarah.

"Welcome home, my dear. I am Suzan."

Seated in the salon, stylishly furnished with golden-framed classic paintings on the walls, Suzan explained to Sarah that just that day she had received word from the resistance. A similar operation to the one that had liberated Sarah had been successfully concluded and brought Salomon home.

"Where is he?" Sarah could not help herself.

"You will soon meet him, dear, but you have to understand that moving Jewish people around, especially those not wearing the yellow star, is punishable by death. In spite of that, there are many brave people whose consciences do not allow them to negate the terrible injustice our Jewish citizens are suffering. All I can tell you now is that Salomon is safe. As soon as I receive the green light, we will take you to him."

79

Bob was not prepared for the emotional welcome when he came to see Suzan. He filled her in about the operation, but she intuitively felt that Bob's life had been at risk. She literally jumped into his arms and hung on to him like she would never let go.

She wanted to know every little detail, and he took his time.

"What about Salomon, Bob? Is he okay?"

"He could not be better under the circumstances. He is in a safe house and surrounded by people we trust, but he of course is very eager to see with his own eyes that Sarah is fine. By the way, how is Sarah? I heard horrible things about Ravensbrück."

"She is hanging in there, Bob, but very frail. I know they want to see each other as soon as possible, but I wish I could nurse her back a bit first."

"There will be time for that later, Suzan. They both will need to slowly get used to normal food and gain some weight. Not much is left of the man Salomon must have been once, and I assume it is the same with Sarah."

"When can we take them to Bovenkerk?" Suzan wanted to know.

"Tomorrow afternoon, Suze, there will be a truck delivering cheese at a warehouse on the Achtergracht. After delivering the load, the truck will meet the DKW around the corner, and Sarah will jump over. There is a white cotton coat with the logo of the Dutch Cheese Factory for her to wear. Nobody will bother her."

"Who takes care of her at that plant? It is going to be an emotional reunion."

"You and me. The DKW will pick us up, and we should be there before the truck arrives."

Salomon stood in the room of the cabin overlooking the lake. It was a very quiet late afternoon except for the call of a cuckoo and the chiming of a church bell in a village nearby. This was the second day he had been there, and he had hoped to see Sarah. He started to doubt that she was in Holland. Would it not have been the logical thing to immediately reunite him with his wife if she were free?

But then again, was it fair to doubt the people who had risked so much to bring him back? Could he do something? Maybe ask Frank if he could take him to wherever Sarah was or at least let him know when he would see her?

He kept staring at the surface of the lake. He could do nothing. He was free, but what sort of freedom? The picture of the poor people huddled together came back. Would he end up like that, betrayed maybe and sent back to Sachsenhausen?

He turned around when he heard the door softly open.

There in the door opening, not able to take another step, not able to control her emotions, stood Sarah.

Salomon ran to her, embraced her, kissed her, smelled her, and felt her—his Sarah, who now cried her heart out. She just kept repeating between sobs, "Sally, oh God, Sally." All the pain, all the misery, all the despair was now shared between the two in a wordless, long embrace.

Suzan wiped away her tears, and Bob swallowed a few times. Then both hugged the couple, the four just standing there, not able to move or talk.

When some bright smiles appeared on the faces of the reunited couple, Suzan handed Sarah a box with groceries and some other necessities, which she accepted with gratitude. Salomon showed Sarah the cabin that would be their home, and for the first time since what seemed to be a lifetime, they both felt the dawning of happiness.

80

In the Dutch windmill outside of Amsterdam, Bolkestein, Sandberg, Roell, and Trip were discussing what needed to be done next, now that Cohen was in Holland and reunited with his wife.

"A remarkable success indeed," offered Bolkestein. "When this horrible war is behind us, these brave men deserve to be recognized."

They all agreed.

"Willem, please fill us in on where we stand today and how to proceed."

"Of course. The first and most important thing is that the couple is safe and the location guarantees that nobody will touch them. De Boer is extremely well organized and made sure that everybody working for him is loyal to our cause. His cheese production is important to the Germans, for consumption here and for the weekly transports to Germany. He will be left alone."

"But I assume that there is no way he can work there on a large painting such as *The Night Watch*," Trip commented.

The Fake Rembrandt

"Indeed not, but we were able to find an ideal solution. As you know, just a bit beyond the village of Bovenkerk, we have the flower city, Aalsmeer. There is no export market presently, and many of the greenhouses are empty. One, on the bank of the same lake that Salomon's cabin is on, is available to him, compliments of a supporter. It is whitewashed with chalk on the outside, so nobody can look inside if ever somebody would be interested to walk there. But it would be ideal as a studio. There is a roomy brick building attached to it for heating, tools, water supply, et cetera. In a corner of that building is a wooden doghouse that functions as a trapdoor for the hiding place below it. If ever there would be danger, Salomon could hide there in seconds."

"Brilliant, but there is still the danger of getting there every day, Willem," suggested Bolkestein.

"Every morning, when it is still dark, a fisherman rows his boat along the edge of the lake to check his eel nets. He will pick up Salomon and drop him off at the greenhouse. He does the same at the end of the day, so he can take him home."

"Can he be trusted?" Trip wanted to know.

"His only brother, twenty-three years old, was executed. Oh yes, he can be trusted."

The owner of the windmill joined the meeting.

"Gentlemen," Bolkestein continued, "I asked our host to join us. He will update you on what transpired here over the past few days."

The miller put a piece of wood on the table, a few feet long and three by one inch.

"I had this cut from the old wood as you requested, Mr. Sandberg. As you can see, it is still strong but looks as old as it is."

The men all inspected the piece of wood.

"Gentlemen, as you can see, building the frame won't be a problem. This wood is as old as *The Night Watch*. And here are the nails." The miller threw a handful of old rusty nails on the table. "They are upholstery tacks that I put in a tin of horse piss. As you can see, they are rusty enough to look very old." The nails indeed looked like they were as old as they needed to be.

"So, gentlemen, the frame is there. The next problem, of course, was where were we going to find a canvas that size?" He left the question unanswered for a while, and then he continued, "Gentlemen, the sails that we need to cover the wings of our mill with, in our times, are obtained from a few professional sailmakers. In my great-grandfather's day, they had to cut and hand stitch them from a large roll of linen canvas themselves. Below, in the shed, there is still some left, which must be more than a hundred years old. I cut a piece off it. Here look." He threw a square piece of weathered but still strong canvas on the table.

"What do you think?" asked Sandberg.

Roell tested the strength of the piece, held it against the light, and then rubbed it with his thumbnail. "Looks surprisingly good. After the necessary preparation, it will take more than superficial inspection to determine the exact age. I am sure it will do."

The miller had another surprise.

One of his colleagues owned a paint mill, De Kat, where the powders needed to make paint were milled. There, on the wooden shelves, hundreds of different pigments were stored.

Salomon would use manufactured oil paint for some effects; however, the meticulous restaurateur might insist on making his own. But the painting was supposed to be nearly four hundred years old. To achieve that effect, a lot more than powdered pigment was needed.

81

The four men were still at the windmill, where they continued their discussion.

"How will we be able to get everything Cohen may need together within the short time available?" Roell wanted to know.

"We sent Ernst Jan and two assistants to help Salomon with whatever he may need," replied Sandberg. "Ernst Jan is a fine furniture carpenter and restorer. He will build the frame and stretch the canvas. He will also build a sort of an easel, long and strong enough to provide solid support for the canvas. He will work in the greenhouse, so Cohen will have input."

"I can see everything brought together in that building, Willem, but what I cannot see is how we will be able to have one or more of Rembrandt's paintings in there. Then what about the photographs and all the details from Besnyoe? Are we able to get that to Cohen? I assume that is a condition sine qua non," suggested Leo Trip.

"Indeed, Leo, the photographs and all the detailed prints are already in our possession and will be taken to Cohen as soon as possible. As for the Rembrandts, when we told him that we thought he might need to study Rembrandt's hand with the help of some paintings, he laughed. His comment was, 'The only person knowing more than me about Rembrandt's methods and style of painting, his brushwork and paint application, is Rembrandt,' so we don't have that concern."

"What bothers me though," said Bolkestein, "is what if a German patrol or some police fanatics happen to come across Cohen working on a Rembrandt? And secondly, what is the scenario when he is done and we are in the possession of his *Night Watch*? What do we do next?"

"It is quite a distance from the entrance of the flower nursery to the last greenhouse," Sandberg answered, "the entrance gate is always closed and even a patrol would have to ring the bell to be let in. There would be ample time for the family living in the main house to activate the warning system and for Cohen to go into hiding."

"As for your question 'What do we do next?' sometimes fate offers a helping hand."

"I was approached by a representative of the Cinetone studios. It appears that Dr. Joseph Goebbels, the Nazi propagandist, wants a movie about the life of Rembrandt. The massive production receives virtually unlimited funds from Germany. The films should prove how Rembrandt's downfall was caused by Jewish swindlers. Nazi Germany admires Rembrandt but also Tromp and de Ruyter, our naval heroes, as Germanic examples of excellence or bravery.

"The director will be Hans Steinhoff, who produced Nazi propaganda movies before. Most of the production will be filmed here in Amsterdam in the Jodenbreestraat. My intention is to transport Cohen's *Night Watch* as a film prop for Steinhof's production, and nobody will bother us. It will be crated and marked with 'Set prop Rembrandt.'"

"Great, Willem," remarked Trip enthusiastically, "but is the intention not to ensure that Cohen's *Night Watch* enters the hands of the Nazis, while the real one is hidden somewhere?"

"Indeed, and let me present for discussion the following thoughts. Rembrandt's *Night Watch* is still safely stored away in the bunker in Heemskerk, taken off the frame and rolled up in a carpet. But soon, it will have to move again to Limburg and will be stored in the art cellars specially constructed deep in Mount St. Pieter. We will move Cohen's painting to Heemskerk and will make sure that the papers are made aware of the hiding place of this 'real' *Night Watch*. We are almost convinced that somehow this news will reach Göring, who we know has his eyes on the *Night Watch*. We are also convinced that if it ends up in Carinhall, Göring will keep quiet about it so as not to upset Hitler."

"What do you think?"

Everybody kept quiet, and then Bolkestein spoke. "Gentlemen, I do not think that anyone of us could come up with a more feasible plan, so I propose that this is indeed the scenario we should follow."

82

It was still dark.

In his Manchester pants, warm sweater, jacket, tainted clogs, and woolen cap, Salomon could have been a helper of the fisherman who just tied his wooden boat to a stake at the edge of the water. Salomon climbed in, helped by the man who almost crushed his hand, "Bart" was all he said, and it would have to do for the whole trip to the greenhouse. With his back to the direction they were moving, the man lifted the oars in a slow, rhythmic movement, just enough so the oars never made a sound when he dipped them through the surface of the water. In the early morning, the lake was as smooth as a mirror. Bart strained his back and pulled the boat straight to the next net, never once looking over his shoulder.

He stopped a few times to inspect and empty his nets, attached to a long pole and placed with the open side close to shore. In the bin in front of Salomon, a wriggling mass of fat eel grew. They soon would be thrown into salt water at the fisherman's cabin and then smoked to a golden brown, a centuries-old delicacy for Dutch people.

There was a short wooden landing behind the greenhouse. The boat bounced against it, and Salomon jumped out.

He thanked Bart, who signaled that it was okay. "About seven" was all he said, and Salomon understood that would be the return pickup.

When he entered the greenhouse, it was still half dark. A voice startled him. "Good morning, Mr. Cohen, my name is Ernst Jan. This here is Chris, and that is Judi. We were sent to find out how we can help you."

Salomon was taken aback. What should he say? How did he know this was not a trap? He instinctively looked behind him, but the rowboat was already gone.

Ernst Jan noticed Cohen's concern. "It is okay, sir. Don't worry. Frank will be here anytime, and he will vouch for us. You will need quite a lot of products and material before you can start working. Each one of us will scout for whatever is needed, and Frank will pick it up."

Salomon felt better.

There was already a long wooden table at the far end with some folding chairs, and the four sat down.

"Maybe the best thing is to just list everything you may need, Mr. Cohen, as if there was no war going on. We may still be able to get a lot of it together."

Salomon thought for a moment. "Would you be able to get me some of the things that are in my house? That would make it a lot easier."

The three looked at each other, and then, clearly abashed, Ernst Jan answered, "Mr. Cohen, just a few days after you were arrested, the company of Abraham Puls, a traitor and collaborator, went into your house and took everything in it. It is what they do to virtually all the houses from which Jewish people are deported. I am so sorry."

Salomon swallowed. What did he think, that his house would be waiting for him?

"What are they doing to it?"

"Most of it is shipped to Germany; some of it is sold on the local market."

Who would buy someone's misery? Salomon thought.

Tragically, the honest answer would be many more people than one might think.

"Then let's see what we will need." Salomon sighed. "You have something to write with?"

At that moment, Frank came in. He was carrying a basket with a canister of hot coffee and some cheese sandwiches. Invited by Salomon, he took a seat and then greeted the others.

"Let me start with the very first things needed," said Salomon.

83

"I will need a strong easel, large enough for the canvas, and a solid footing."

"That will be my job, Mr. Cohen. I am the carpenter here," offered Ernst Jan.

"Great, but please call me Salomon."

"Then the next most important thing is the canvas. Are there any thoughts about that?"

"Yes, Salomon. Mr. Sandberg took care of that. There are enough pieces of very old wood that I will cut to size here. Then a large piece of old linen canvas is available, which I understand comes from the same windmill. There are enough aged tacks that I can use to tighten the canvas to the frame. You just have to tell me how you want it done, and I'll do it."

"What about brushes, paint, and the oils and liquids I will need?"

"That's my department, Mr. Cohen, eh ... I mean Salomon," answered Judi.

"Just give me an exact specification and I will get it."

"Everything? In these times?" Salomon remarked with some doubt.

"Almost everything. I have a special contact in Van Beek Art Supplies at the Stadhouderskade. Except for some pigments you may request, they told me that everything would be available."

Chris added, "We have a supplier for whatever pigment you may need. A paint mill that has a stock of hundreds can supply whatever you wish."

"Fantastic. I will also need a thick sheet of glass and spatulas and two dozen fresh eggs."

"Eggs?" Ernst Jan asked, surprised. "Are you going to work with tempera?"

"No," answered Salomon, "but Sarah and I love omelets."

They all laughed.

"While you work on the painting, Salomon, I will work on the crate that will be needed to transport the fresh painting to where they want it. I need to make sure that nothing can touch the wet paint."

Now Salomon smiled.

"There is a difference between a painter and a professional art restorer, Ernst Jan. When my Rembrandt is finished, it will be for all intents and purposes four centuries old. What about the light? As you can see, it is already getting dark and it is not even six o'clock."

To demonstrate that his presence was not just to feed the group sandwiches and coffee, Frank answered, "We thought of that, and

Alfred Balm

for the duration of your work here, the only solution is that we build a second easel and put it in the brick house. There are no windows, and we can add as many lights as you need. If you need to work late, I will just help you to move the painting there. A bit of a hassle, but we can't ignore the blackout rules."

"Then that's it, I guess," said Cohen. "I thank you all for your great assistance. I assume that everything may not be as simple as you make it sound. I really appreciate your help."

"There is one more thing, Mr. Cohen," continued Frank. "You may not like this, and I am sorry, but it is necessary to establish the exact time between the warning signal and your disappearance. That phone over there will only ring in case of danger. Don't use it for outside calls. So I will blow a whistle in a bit, and you take that for the ringing. Then as fast as you can, get to the doghouse, lift it, jump in, and lower it over your head. We will time how long it takes, but be fast; your life may depend on it."

Those last words sounded familiar to Salomon Cohen, and he did not need any further encouragement.

Frank blew on the whistle he took from his pocket.

As if hit by an electric shock, Salomon jumped up, ran to the brick building, pulled the doghouse back, jumped in the hole, and pulled the doghouse back over his head.

They checked their watches, fifty-five seconds. That should be fast enough. Nobody would be able to walk from the entrance to this greenhouse in less than ten minutes. They shook hands when Salomon surfaced and each went his or her own way.

The oak rowing boat bumped against the landing. The fisherman's calloused hand helped Salomon on board, almost crushing his hand again. He never realized how close his handshake came to jeopardizing a most complicated operation.

84

That morning, the boat ride to his new studio was a different experience for Salomon. He woke up before daylight, filled with anticipation, not used to it yet but delighted by the familiar so recently missed intimacy of Sarah's warm presence. He kissed her softly on the cheek, careful not to wake her. He quickly dressed in the clothes the artist would be wearing for so many weeks, opened the back door without making noise, and then took a deep breath of the fresh morning air.

The sounds of the early morning before daybreak, the wake-up call of a rooster in the distance, the twittering of birds, and the splashing of waterfowl, it all meant one thing to Salomon—freedom.

This time, he took the wrist of Bart the fisherman before his hand could end up in the vise of his grip and happily took his seat on the wooden board, knowing this would become his morning routine. The strong, rhythmic pulls on the oars, the certainty of direction on the dark water, and the stoic presence the man exuded had a comforting effect on Salomon.

He was more aware of his surroundings than he was that

very first morning, now several days ago—the lakeshore in the distance, absorbing the very first shimmers of light; the contours of the village behind the distant shore; the church tower protruding dark gray from a yet undetermined auburn mass that soon would dissolve into individual houses; the reflection of it in the tinted mirror of the undisturbed lake. Salomon experienced the illusion of rowing into the reality of a Rembrandt landscape.

"Can I give you a hand?" he offered when Bart lifted his first net, blissfully loaded with wriggling eel. There was no immediate reply. Bart emptied the heavy net into the bin. With a thin smile on his unshaven face and a twinkle in his eyes, after first spitting a dollop of chewing tobacco spittle overboard, he said, "You do the painting; I do the fishing."

It was the longest sentence from Bart's mouth thus far. It amused Salomon, who understood that the man was better informed than he had thought.

When he entered his improvised studio, Ernst Jan was already there. The scent of freshly brewed coffee made him realize how hungry he was, and he dove into the cheese sandwiches on the table.

"Morning, Salomon. Test the easel. I finished it last night."

Salomon did. The structure was as solid as a rock.

"What do you think of the frame? Is this what you meant?"

Salomon inspected the large frame that would become his canvas; it was solid and appeared to be very old. Ernst Jan used old hand-forged rusted nails he must have found somewhere.

"Looks great. Where did you find those nails?"

"Some restoration work I did years ago in the Warmoesstraat. I kept them as a curiosity, never knowing they would come in handy one day."

Both men now worked for several hours to tightly attach the canvas to the frame, but first Salomon explained something to Ernst Jan.

"*The Night Watch* has been reframed several times. It was also cut in 1715 on the top and both sides to fit a spot in the royal palace on the Dam square. Before we tighten the canvas, we should make several tack holes on all sides of the frame, which I will fill with dirt."

Ernst Jan hammered tacks on the back of the frame and then pulled them all out. Salomon rubbed dirt, which he simply picked up off the floor, into the tack holes.

They attached the canvas to the frame, spanning it tightly, and hammered all the tacks in it again. Then they stretched the canvas until Salomon was satisfied. After scooping up dirt and dust from the floor again, Salomon rubbed it in on the back of the canvas. Once dried, most of it brushed off. It would give an extra appearance of age, although the many years it had been stored in a shed at the mill and the influence of moisture made it already appear very old.

They lifted the large frame onto the easel.

Cohen was ready to prepare the canvas for painting.

85

The shopping list had been quite extensive, and it would take Chris and Judi many days to get most of it together. They expressed their concern to Cohen, who then attached priorities to certain items on the list.

The first thing Chris supplied was a cardboard box with twelve tubes of lead white and then a bag of course silica sand, a fine sieve, and several bottles of a quick-drying oil and a tin of linseed oil and turpentine. Quick-drying oil did not exist in Rembrandt's time, but Cohen would need it to be able to finish the painting in time. In Rembrandt's years, lead would be used to enhance the drying process of linseed oil, but Cohen would use siccatives of manganese, zirconium, and cobalt.

While Salomon was passing the silica sand through the fine sieve, Judi arrived with a large variety of brushes, most of them round pig-bristle brushes. She also brought several pallets and an old suitcase loaded with large-size tubes of paint, almost too heavy for one woman to carry.

The thick glass sheet now on the table and the number of

tins, glass bowls, bottles, brushes, and canisters, along with the spicy smell, added to the impression of a real artist's studio, with at the center the very large canvas. The light, slightly tempered by the whitewash on the outside of the glass house, was ideal for the painter.

In a small copper bucket that Salomon found in the building, he prepared a mixture of boiled linseed oil to which he added some siccative, the fine silica sand, and then a small amount of lead white. He stirred it until it became a creamy ivory-colored substance, added a small amount of brown ochre, stirred it again, and then applied it with a wide brush to the canvas. He covered the whole surface in one layer. When dry the next day, the surface would feel like fine sandpaper.

In the meantime, Ernst Jan was building his second easel, which they would be using in the brick building. Next to it, he built a table large enough to lay the canvas down on it. Above it, he installed a battery of grow lights from an incubator section of the plant nursery. It was Cohen's solution to simulate aging; in combination with special varnishes and just the right amount of craquelure, the fresh painting would look old enough for nonscientific inspection.

Ernst Jan made sure that no light would be escaping from the windowless brick building by adding strips of wood to the doorframe.

The Fake Rembrandt

The evening before, Salomon and Sarah had received visitors, Willem Sandberg, Bob, and Suzan. Sandberg brought a large portfolio with Besnyoe's photographs of *The Night Watch*; Bob and Suzan carried baskets of groceries. It had been one of those evenings that brought back memories of prewar years when they would be receiving friends, enjoying life, and being happy in the city where they were born.

Amsterdam, their city; the Jodenbreestraat, where Rembrandt's house still stood unchanged, the weathered dark red bricks still exuding his presence; the flea market called Waterloo Square across from the Moses and Aaron Church, where the throwaways of one family became the treasures of another; the lime trees mirrored in the water of the canals encircling the center; the call of the Jewish peddlers, "Oranges ... sweet as honey! Haddock ... fresh haddock! Pickles ... five cents, my pickles!" an army of hopeful hawkers, pushing their carts along the canals; a street organ playing; children dancing; "Limping Sally" with rolled-up sleeves, turning the heavy wheel in flawless rhythm, his old father politely lifting his cap for small change thrown from the open windows on the second or third floor of the stately merchant houses—the sounds and smells of the streets of Amsterdam, all gone now.

But that evening brought something back—warm feelings of friendship, of mutual respect, something Salomon and Sarah used to take for granted until that disastrous loud knocking on the door one cursed early morning.

"We never asked ..." Bob looked at Sandberg. "How would a

man like Salomon feel about producing a forgery, even sanctioned apparently by influential people and a minister of our prewar government?"

"May I answer that question?" Salomon said. "I do not look at my copy as a forgery, rather as an acceptable way to protect one of our country's most precious art objects. Nobody within our sphere of influence will derive any material benefit from it. What happens when it ends up in the hands of Nazi culture barbarians is completely irrelevant. I will do my utmost to paint a copy that will withstand all but scientific scrutiny, which I believe is all that may be expected under the circumstances. I realize that brave people risked their lives, and Sarah and I are most grateful to have a second chance, so many we have known never will. In Sachsenhausen, I was forced to work at forgeries, false currencies produced to create economic devastation in foreign countries.

"If all my training, my hard work, my experience was meant to lead to this moment, then it was not in vain. Let it be a blessing for future generations. Let us hope that whatever we together are accomplishing today will help save our national cultural heritage for posterity."

"Hear, hear!" said Suzan, and everybody agreed.

Sarah kissed her husband.

86

Ernst Jan followed in silent wonder the progress the painter made. He knew that Cohen did not want to be disturbed while he was working, so from time to time, he would watch the process from the other side of the building. Not completely ignorant about old masters, he used to think that those paintings must have taken the artists years and years to finish. To see how, in front of his very eyes, a Rembrandt grew filled him with admiration for so skilled a human being.

Salomon did not draw a grid to transfer the composition from Besnyoe's magnificent photographs onto the canvas; he just started to paint the central figures—Captain Frans Banning Cocq with his aristocratic appearance and Lieutenant Willem Ruytenburch, pointing his tasseled spear—and then worked his way to both sides, left and right, adding the soldiers, the girl with the rooster, and all the other details. What surprised Ernst Jan the most was that the whole painting seemed to be finished in just days, but in only one brownish shade, with light and dark accents Cohen would probably add color later he thought, or maybe he did not have enough paint?

When drinking coffee and enjoying lunch, he asked.

Salomon laughed. "No, that is not because I don't have enough paint, Ernst Jan. It is called underpainting. Classical painters first painted the whole composition in one tint, sometimes light, sometimes dark, depending on the artist and the painting. Then the real painting starts, and often there are still changes or additions, because the artist likes it better. In extreme cases, the result is completely different from the underpainting. Often, the artist would discuss the finished underpainting with those who commissioned it, to be assured of their acceptance and payment when it would be finished. Rembrandt was, in many respects, an innovator; sometimes he made an underpainting, and sometimes he worked directly in color. When working on a copy, as I am, where every detail needs to be meticulously correct, I prefer to make the underpainting first, as precise as possible. I am using lead white, adding some turpentine and raw umber to make the paint mixture dry quickly."

That night, they moved the canvas to the table in the brick building so the next morning it would be dry and Salomon could start painting in color.

Ernst Jan had more questions. It was almost an hour before the time that Salomon would be picked up, so they sat down and Cohen explained, enjoying the sincere interest of the young craftsman.

"No, there is no way to tell how long it may take me but definitely less than Rembrandt took; of course, that has nothing to do with skill. I simply have a different goal and different means at my disposal. For one thing, the aging chamber you built to quickly dry the paint and then the oil paint in tubes I use. It saves time, but it also confronts me with a problem. All these oil paints in tubes are solid, fully saturated colors. Rembrandt had to make his own paints from linseed oil and pigments. That was a laborious process, but it allowed him also to determine the mixture he favored. He could make the paint somewhat transparent and use several layers, one on top of the other, either with the same or different pigments, some opaque to achieve the effect he wanted, or he would saturate the paint with pigment to give it more body. Rembrandt favored earthy colors—ochres, vermillion, sienna, smalt, umbers, lead white, and bone black—but also red, orange, and yellow. Lead white would be used, adding small amounts of pigment, for example in flesh tones or the lace collars. He would typically work up a painting, applying thick layers of translucent dark colors from back to front, using texture and thickness, so-called impasto, to achieve depth, and use cool half tones between light parts and shaded areas.

"Rembrandt preferred that his paintings were viewed from a certain distance. He used bold, dynamic brushstrokes, achieving the effects he wanted through his painterly techniques, working most of the time with round pig-bristle brushes.

"I will copy his methods as much as possible but necessarily have to work with ready-made paints. Sometimes, however, I will make my own. That is why I asked for the glass sheet and for the pigments the miller could supply. There is so much more to tell, Ernst Jan, but why not do that while my work is progressing?"

Both men were so engaged in the discussion that they forgot about the time.

With a shock, Salomon realized his pickup, so meticulously on time every day, had not arrived. Where was Bart? What could have happened to him?

87

Something was wrong.

Bart could sense it, and he was not the only one.

Rufus, his shepherd dog, usually friendly and wagging his tail when clients arrived to buy eel, pulled up his lips, growled, and stayed back to hide behind Bart.

It was almost dark. The light from brass petroleum lamps in the fisherman's cabin throwing dark shadows in the corners added to the vibes of danger radiating from the two men. Bart was just taking a rod from the smoker, emptying the impaled fish from it, and sorting the golden-brown smoked eel in a flat wooden crate when two men suddenly appeared behind him.

Observing the intruders for a moment from under his greasy cap and taking his time to walk on his wooden clogs to the smoker and close it to avoid further fumes filling the place, he turned around and asked, "Can I help you?"

They were between thirty and thirty-five years old, dressed in long coats and gray fedora hats, and the way they behaved suggested they were not there on a grocery-shopping mission.

"Yes, I would like to buy a pound of smoked eel," answered one of them, pointing at the flat crate. Meanwhile, the second one was not at all interested in the delicacy but observed shamelessly every visible detail of the cabin, without saying a word.

Bart took a bundle of the still-warm eels, put it on the scale, and then added two and wrapped them in a newspaper.

"Two guilder fifty."

The man handed over the money. Without so much as a "Thank you," he turned around, and both men left.

Appearing unperturbed and in control, finishing the work he started, Bart felt his heart hammering in his chest. These bastards reminded him too much of the wretches who came for his young brother.

When Bart walked to the back of his cabin where his boat was tied to the small dock, he looked stealthily around him to check if the creeps were still watching him, but he did not see them.

He got into the boat, as he did every day, untied her, and then pulling hard on the oars, disappeared into the growing darkness of the evening. But ten minutes out, instead of going left toward his nets and Cohen's pickup place, he turned toward the right shore. He tied his boat to the landing of his friend, a fisherman who worked that side of the lake. As fast as he could walk, he went to the back door of the low cabin, its reed roof sloping down to a man's height, knocked on the Dutch door, and then went in without waiting. Klaas was still there, thank God.

His friend immediately realized that there was a good reason for this unannounced visit.

"Morning, Klaas. I need your phone, urgent" was all Bart needed to say.

Bart dialed the number he was made to remember by heart.

"Dr. De Bruyn's office, how can I help you?"

"Orange alert," replied Bart and put the phone down.

"Trouble?" Klaas wanted to know.

"Probably. Keep your eyes open, buddy. There are two creeps sniffing around and not because they like smoked eel."

"Got it. Want some coffee?"

"No, thank you. I have to finish something." Bart went back to his cabin.

88

Roger picked up the phone.

"Orange alert" was all the girl on the phone said before hanging up.

Roger dialed a number. It took a nerve-racking twelve rings before it was picked up and a dark voice answered, "De Boer."

Roger passed on the same coded message to the owner of the cheese factory and then called Bob, who jumped to action immediately.

In the meantime, Mr. De Boer sent Frank on his way to pick up a frightened Cohen. It startled both Ernst Jan and Salomon when suddenly the door opened.

"Come with me, right now" was all Frank needed to say.

While in the truck, he asked, "You have your papers with you?"

Oh my God, Salomon thought. *Did I get used to the normality of routine that quickly? Could I be that stupid?*

The carefully forged papers identifying Salomon Cohen as Anton Bakker were in his bedside table drawer but should have been in his pocket.

Frank did not say anything, but the expression on his face, very visible in the dim light from the truck cabin's dashboard, said enough.

"I am sorry," Salomon whispered timidly, "but what is the emergency?"

"Just a warning, but we cannot be careful enough. Don't worry too much; we are well prepared for such things, as you may see soon."

The truck turned around at the back of the cheese factory. With the engine still running, Frank helped Salomon out. "Go to your cabin. Stay inside. Tell Sarah to be quiet and no lights at all. Everything will be fine. You will hear from me later."

Frank ran back to the truck and left in a hurry.

Salomon and Sarah were not aware that, on either side of the cabin, well hidden among the reeds and bushes alongside the lake, two armed men from the fighting brigade of the resistance were guarding the cabin.

They would stay there until dawn.

But nothing happened that night.

The next morning, long before daybreak, Frank knocked the agreed number of times on the cabin door. Salomon opened it as if he had been waiting behind it. It must have been a sleepless night.

"Everything is under control, Salomon, but stay in the cabin today. Go to bed and get some rest. You'll hear from me later." And he was gone again.

About an hour later, just before morning light, a fisherman

rowed his boat along the lakeshore, inspecting and emptying his nets, never even paying attention to the greenhouses he passed each morning.

In one of them, closest to the shore, there was some activity only apparent to those who knew or to anyone for some reason interested in it.

To the last category belonged two men in long coats and gray fedoras, now ringing the bell at the entrance gate. The owner took his time and then slowly walked up to the gate.

"Yes?"

The shady figures showed some IDs.

"We would like to inspect one of your greenhouses."

"For what? They are empty."

"We'll see about that. Open the gate."

"Why not? But you are not gonna like this." And the gate opened.

They walked hastily to the back of the long row of buildings. It was daylight now. They opened the door, stepped in, and with the authority of those who assume their audience will cower at their presence, shouted, "What is going on here?"

Bob was behind the easel, a palette with blotches of paint in his left hand, a brush against the canvas. He was wearing a blue farmer's tunic, all smeared with paint. Suzan, in a large skirt also stained in many colors, was mixing some colored powder with thick oil on a glass sheet at the end of the table.

Bob looked surprised.

The Fake Rembrandt

He walked up to the table, put his palette and brush down, and then turning to the intruders, obviously disturbed and annoyed, bellowed, "Who the hell are you?"

The two seemed taken aback, not used to confrontation, but regained their authoritative composure.

"You may find that out soon enough. Now again, what is going on here?"

Bob walked to the telephone, dialed a number, spoke a few words into the phone, and then, addressing the tallest of the two, said, "Here is somebody who would like to explain to you exactly what is happening here."

The man walked toward Bob and took the phone from his outstretched hand.

"Who is this?" was all he said.

The voice on the other side of the phone was so loud and so meticulously articulating that everyone in the greenhouse could listen in. It was a voice the two collaborators knew so well from the propaganda radio broadcasts.

"Who is this? ... Who is this, you minnow?" shouted the person on the other end.

"This is Mussert, ignorant fool. You just intruded ... But, eh ... I didn't know, Kamerad," tried the panicking minnow.

"Shut up! Don't you interrupt me! You just intruded in a film project starting in Amsterdam on direct orders of Dr. Goebbels. He apparently forgot to inform the two biggest fools in my command. Get the hell out of there *now*, and don't you ever speak a word about it to anyone. No one, you hear? Or I will personally rip the insignia off your disgraceful collars. *Now go!*"

His face flushed and sweaty, the trembling man held the phone for a moment and then put it down, almost with respect.

He turned to Bob. "I, eh ... I am sorry. We didn't know, sir." He gestured for his friend to follow him and left faster than they came.

Anton Mussert was head of the large wartime NSB organization in Holland. Collaborating with the Nazis, he was a would-be Hitler or Mussolini, taking himself more seriously than the occupying German forces ever did.

From his hiding place in Brabant, it had been one of Albert van Dalsum's most convincing voice imitations, an example of the great actor's sublime talent and abilities.

89

The events now more than a week ago were soon forgotten, but the first thing Salomon did from that day on was make sure he pocketed his papers before he left the cabin.

The painting was progressing, and the entire underpainting had disappeared. Salomon now added stand oil, which is linseed oil boiled in the absence of air, and siccative to the oil paint from tubes to achieve a fast-drying, somewhat darkened transparent mixture. It produced the opaque paint that he applied in impasto layers, one on top of the other. Aging, in general, tends to fade the brightness of colors, and over time, a layer of dust, smoke, and other impurities contaminating the environment to which a painting is exposed forms a film of dirt that diminishes the colors. The open wood and coal fires of old times and the heavy smoking still quite common then were notorious polluters.

To achieve the proper shade, Cohen toned down the colors by adding small amounts of brown ochre or umber, using especially dark oils.

The result mesmerized Ernst Jan, who often just sat quietly on a chair on the opposite side of the painter. He watched in amazement how a Rembrandt grew in only weeks, and as far as he was concerned, it was even nicer than the original he once saw in the Rijksmuseum. But the painting was far from finished.

Experienced scholars might soon discover a fake, were it not for the cornucopia of tricks forgers can draw on. There is a fine line between professional restorers and forgers, called ethics, but the methods and techniques applied are often the same.

Before he started working on aging, Salomon signed the painting, on the curb just under the girl with the rooster, "Rembrandt F 1642" ("Rembrandt Fecit" or "made by Rembrandt").

Fresh varnish and paint are easily detected by rubbing a bit of alcohol on a small spot. To avoid that, Salomon applied a thin layer of size over the paint after it dried enough in the aging room. Size is a gelatinous solution, basically a glue. After the size completely dried, the first layer of a varnish, which Salomon mixed himself and to which he added small amounts of phenol formaldehyde, could be applied. It would harden enough under the heat of the grow lights to create the correct amount of craquelure. Cohen preferred this method over the varnishes from the French manufacturer Lefranc et Bourgeois, specially formulated to simulate age and craquelure and often used by art forgers.

The almost finished painting now needed time in the improvised bakery. A temperature of 200 to 250 degrees Fahrenheit would have been ideal but was not achievable even when they stoked the oven that used to heat the greenhouse. But the brick house became extremely hot nevertheless, and it would have the intended effect in days. By the end of the week, Cohen was satisfied and the aged *Night Watch* placed back on the table in the greenhouse. A network of fine craquelure covered the entire picture frame. Salomon knew that late afternoon his work would be scrutinized by the men responsible for the whole operation.

He gathered dust from the floor, sieved it so only the finest particles remained, added just a small amount of fine charcoal powder, and then dried it under the lamps. With a fine brush, he worked the powder into the craquelure, brushing it off where necessary. He finally took a three-inch block of wood and rubbed it on all sides of the fresh painting. He then took a fine brush and added a very thin layer of varnish over the areas he had rubbed the wooden block on.

"Why is that?" Ernst Jan was used now to asking every time something puzzled him.

"Look over the painting, and you will see just a little difference between the whole area and the sides I just worked on. When *The Night Watch* was still in the Rijksmuseum, it was framed. Those three inches on all sides would have been protected from the influence of light, dust, and so on. They should be looking just a bit fresher, so to speak, when the painting is taken from the frame."

They lifted the canvas on the easel and then took a chair while enjoying a coffee about twenty yards away from it, Ernst Jan gazing in awe. Salomon was critical but satisfied.

It would take real connoisseurs to determine it was a forgery.

90

"Darn!" exclaimed Trip in utter amazement. "That is incredible, unbelievable."

"My God," said Bolkestein, "that is dangerously perfect. Except for the size, how would one ever distinguish between this and the real thing?"

Sandberg smiled. "Only after some serious studying and testing, but I agree, it is even better than we could ever hope for. My compliments, Salomon."

"I am still in awe that a work like that can be produced in less than a month, and I assume not in the most ideal circumstances." added Roell. "Is it now ready for transportation?"

The group stood at the distance Salomon advised them to to view the painting. The compliments, he accepted with reservation; he was not a forger but a highly skilled restorer of classical paintings. Nevertheless, it filled him with satisfaction that he could have done something to show his gratitude for having regained his, all be it conditional, freedom.

The Fake Rembrandt

"No, Mr. Roell, not yet. Let me show you. Ernst Jan, can you give me a hand?"

He did but not without an element of difficulty. The painting was not exactly as large as the original but still large enough to be awkward to handle by both men, who lifted the painting from the easel, turned it around, and with the back toward the viewers, put it back on.

"Gentlemen, as you can see, the back of the painting appears convincingly old, thanks to the old wood and canvas you supplied. As you know, every scholar would inspect the back as much as the front to determine age. *The Night Watch* received its name much later, because its original name *The Company of Captain Frans Banning Cocq and Lieutenant Willem van Ruytenburch Preparing to March* is of course an impractical name. The painting was and is the property of the city of Amsterdam. It has been in the Doelen, the palace on Dam square, and in the Rijksmuseum. All that information should appear somehow on the back."

It was silent for a moment.

"Then how would you go about that?" asked Sandberg.

"Well, I need your help. Against my will, I have recently obtained experience in forging documents, but I would need a few pieces of very old paper; any book from the seventeenth century would do."

"I can provide that," answered Roell. "You'll have it tomorrow."

The next day, an often-used copy of *Chorographia Sacra*

Brabantiae, dated 1659, arrived, with a note that Salomon could do with it what he wanted.

He felt apprehensive but with a sharp knife cut the endpaper out.

He fixed the paper to the glass plate, now clean of the paint residue, turned it upside down, and with a little size, let it dry.

He then prepared a mixture of Indian ink and water and with a thin marten-hair brush, wrote "Rembrandt F. 1642" directly on the side of the frame. It appeared faded enough to be believable.

Now he drew the coat of arms of the city of Amsterdam—three Xs above each other on a shield—on a strip of the old paper and wrote in the calligraphic curly letters of the seventeen hundreds, "Property of the City of Amsterdam."

With some thick glue, he attached it to the frame.

The last thing he added was a strip of the same paper, which he had bleached and then dried to make it look old, but not too old. He wrote on it in more contemporary lettering, "Rijksmuseum Amsterdam. Rembrandt Harmenszoon van Rijn, De Nachtwacht 1642 Cat. Nr. 40.221," glued it to the frame as well, and then stood back and smiled.

Now, Salomon thought, *the company of Captain Banning Cocq is ready for inspection.*

91

"As we discussed before," Sandberg opened the meeting, held again in the windmill strategically so well situated for the purpose. "As we discussed before, the best scenario is to have the painting crated, clearly marked on the outside, and transported with controlled publicity."

"What do you mean, Willem, 'with controlled publicity'?" Bolkestein wanted to know.

"Our aim is that the news ends up in the hands of Göring; that's all. Too much noise makes the whole transport suspicious. We may want to involve one or two newspapers and Polygoon news for the cinemas, but more won't be necessary, I suppose."

"That seems hardly possible, Willem," Trip suggested. "Both are heavily censured; why would the Germans advertise that they are removing our art?"

"Because it can be presented to them as something actually in their favor."

"Oh come on, Willem; is that not wishful thinking?"

"Not at all. Think of it. Bad Allied forces bombing and

destroying our poor country's treasured art, and those true art-loving Germans protecting it."

They all laughed.

"Good God, Willem, you have a nasty brain!" Trip complimented Sandberg. "Never thought of it that way, but I guess you are right."

"So do I," added Roell. "But one thing bothers me; we are all convinced that Cohen has done an extraordinary job. We are all focused on what is next with the painting, but what about the painter? How can we be sure, and I mean really sure that he and Sarah Cohen will stay out of the hands of these Teutonic murderers? We, and for that matter maybe our nation, owe them that for their role in saving *The Night Watch*."

A bit embarrassed that it might appear as if that issue did not concern them, Willem answered, "You are right, David, and it is maybe because we did think of it that I did not address it. I will ask Bob to fill us in next meeting. Is that okay with you?"

It was.

The next issue on the agenda was the transport from the greenhouse to the bunker in Heemskerk.

"Any suggestions?" asked Bolkestein.

"Yes, I think I have one," answered Roell. "I know that the company Van Gend en Loos has a special truck combination they transport large pieces with. You must have seen how glass sheets are transported; it is something similar but of very large size, and there are racks on either side of the trailer that go down to a foot and a half off the road. They transport props and decor for theater shows with it and can cover those with large tarps."

"And we just send that vehicle to pick up our crate?"

"Not that simple, but yes, we could," offered Willem. "This is what I propose."

Sandberg took his time to introduce his plan on how to transport the painting from the greenhouse in Aalsmeer all the way to the bunker in Heemskerk. It would be a bit more complicated though. For one thing, why would *The Night Watch* be in Aalsmeer? After much deliberation, the solution all agreed on was that a large piece of thin plywood with the text, "Movie props. Rembrandt. Cinetone Studios" would be screwed on to the crate.

The crate would then travel to Amsterdam and be parked under the underpass of the Rijksmuseum, the cargo covered with the tarp. Late that evening, the plywood signage would be replaced with another sheet, bearing the words "De Nachtwacht, Rembrandt. Rijksmuseum Amsterdam." The next morning, press representatives would be invited to follow the trip from the museum to the bunker. The German authorities would be cooperative, grasping the propaganda possibilities, and it would certainly not miss the attention of Reichsmarschall Hermann Göring.

92

Making the crate was not the only problem. There was enough material, and with the help of Salomon, experienced carpenter Ernst Jan only took a couple of days. There was paper enough in the greenhouses and foam in the plant hatchery to safely wrap and pack the painting. But the crate was, of course, way too large to go through the door—a problem they could have faced at the bunker too. Luckily, the bunker was built for the sole purpose of storing art, and the steel sliding doors would be large enough.

The front of the greenhouse needed to be taken apart; that and bringing it back to its original state took more time than building the crate did.

In the meantime, Cohen painted both plywood signs in large black letters and screwed the one with "Movie Props" on it with the text visible and the one with "Nachtwacht, Rijksmuseum" with the text toward the crate so only a plain sheet was showing.

When the truck and trailer arrived with two muscular workers, it took all the strength of four men to move the crate, lift it on the rack, and secure it with the tie-downs.

When the combination left the grounds, both Salomon and Ernst Jan just stood there, following it in silence until it left the gate. Both had an empty feeling; a friendship had developed during the weeks of working together, along with a great admiration for each other's different skills.

Salomon subconsciously felt attached to the painting he created, not as an expression of his proficiency, but it gave him a feeling of safety and belonging.

What would happen to him, to Sarah, when his services were no longer needed?

The answer to that question came sooner than he anticipated.

He was surprised to find Sarah dressed up in something he had never seen before. She had done her hair and looked younger than ever now that she had gained weight. She welcomed him with a secretive smile.

"Wow, what is all this? Is it my birthday and I forgot? Then let me unwrap my gift." He grabbed her around her waist, she pretended to resist, and they both laughed.

"Bob and Suzan will be here around four. They want to take us somewhere. She was a bit secretive about it. She said it was absolutely safe but warned that we should carry our papers."

"In that case, I better get dressed. Do you think white tie will do?"

Sarah laughed. "Just get those paint spots off your body, Sally. You look like an impressionistic version of the man I married."

There was that strange feeling again when Salomon shed his painter's clothes, as if he had stepped out of something comfortable into the nakedness of the unknown. But he cleaned up nicely, and when he showed himself to Sarah, in a suit and tie he had found in his closet, she shamelessly wolf-whistled him.

Bob and Suzan were still secretive and answered Salomon's questions with a smile, but they both were dressed just a bit more festively than usual, and a faint scent of Soir de Paris indicated that this might not be an evening of hard work.

The black Citroen car stopped in front of a stately home on the Heerengracht in Amsterdam. Bob gallantly opened the door for Suzan and Sarah and then asked all three to follow him. After climbing the granite entrance stairs to the large, glossy dark green door, Bob pulled the brass handle. A bell sounded inside, and the door opened. The young woman welcoming them was dressed in traditional Volendam costume but was wearing black leather slippers instead of clogs.

"Please follow me," she invited and then turned and walked in front of them through the long, empty corridor. On either side were whitewashed walls, brass chandeliers, and gold-framed classical oil paintings. Black-and-white checkered marble tiles covered the floor, until they reached a double door at the end. Sarah and Salomon were apprehensive, but the young girl, Bob, and Suzan were all smiles.

They waited to let Sarah and Salomon go first, and then the door opened.

93

The thick damask curtains in the large salon were drawn. Crystal chandeliers illuminated the room, and a group of ladies and gentlemen, all finely dressed, faced the arriving couple.

They were all smiling and applauding.

Both Sarah and Salomon were perplexed, shy, not immediately comprehending the situation. Then a gentleman stepped forward, extending his hand. "Welcome Mrs. and Mr. Cohen. My name is Bolkestein. On behalf of all of us here and also on behalf of all our art-loving country folk, of all our loyal citizens praying for better times, we thank you for what you have done. May one day this nightmare be behind us, and may you again live the life you are entitled to."

They shook hands.

Then Sandberg stepped forward. "Thank you again, Salomon, and you too, Mrs. Cohen. This whole project hinged on one thing, a credible copy of Rembrandt's *Night Watch*. I know you would be most defensive if I would say you equaled the master, but in our eyes, you did."

While he was talking, two servants went around with silver trays, skillfully balancing tall flutes of champagne. Sarah and Salomon accepted with both hands to hide the trembling.

A handsome young man, between thirty-five and forty, approached, a glass of champagne in his hand.

"Mrs. Cohen, Mr. Cohen, my name is Walraven van Hall, but please call me Wally. It is my pleasure to host this little event to express our gratitude to you. As you know, many brave men and women are involved in a dangerous and complicated operation like this one. But it could not even have been proposed were it not for your ability to provide us with that fantastic painting. Many of the faces here you will recognize, others not, but rest assured, they are all friends.

"You may have thought that this was the end of your involvement, of your contact with the people you came to know." Noticing the surprise on Cohen's face, he quickly added, "No ... no, we don't need more Rembrandts." Many guests laughed. "I just want you to know that we may have a surprise for you later," and then to all present, raising his glass, he said, "Ladies and gentlemen, friends, may I propose a toast to Mr. and Mrs. Cohen."

They all toasted and then stepped forward to shake hands. *Like a reception*, thought Sarah.

They were all there—Minister Bolkestein, the banker, Sandberg, Roell, and their ladies, but also Mr. De Boer, Klaas, Ernst Jan, Judi, Chris, and even Bart, not immediately recognizable without his cap and in a black jacket he may have bought for a wedding forty years earlier. Then there were several ladies and gentlemen they had never met or heard of but who seemed to be involved one way or another. Sarah and Salomon now were at ease, happy, and feeling a bit surreal whenever flashes of that terrible recent past surfaced as it daily did. They wrestled with a strange feeling of guilt, something they never talked about, not even among themselves. And now here they were, as if they had done something heroic.

It had been a wonderful event, but there was still a curfew, which was hard to believe in the surroundings they were in. Sandberg tapped his glass for attention.

"Ladies and gentlemen, as Wally promised, we have a little surprise. Salomon and Sarah, can you come here please? I may seem a bit empty-handed for the one selected to present you with a surprise." Salomon smiled. "We never talked about remuneration, but when we did, a financial buff among us started to translate Rembrandt's payment into today's guilders, until we all violently wrestled him to the ground."

All laughed.

"But I am proud to say, that among us, your future safety was as much a concern as the protection of our national treasure. With the help of many of us, not in the least Bolkestein and his contacts in London, we are pleased to tell you that we have all the paperwork in place and all the logistics organized to provide you with safe travel and a place to live in England."

A loud applause smothered Sarah's sobs, tears welled in

Salomon's eyes, and many a male guest blew his nose while the ladies touched their eyes with a lace handkerchief.

"You may have many questions, but Bob and Sarah will fill you in while taking you home for now. Ladies and gentlemen, thank you very much for coming. Please be safe when going home."

After taking leave from everybody in a daze and thanking the host for his kind reception, Sarah and Salomon stood, flabbergasted, outside. They were breathing the fresh air of the canal and admiring the trees along the banks as if they were seeing them for the first time. The spice traders' step-gabled houses, the lanterns without light now, the brick streets and narrow sidewalks—they absorbed it all, printing it in their memories, etching it on their souls.

Amsterdam.

And now they would be going to England. They would be safe there, safer than in wartime Holland, where the Nazis and Dutch collaborators treated Jews worse than cattle.

Then why would the shadow of nostalgia temper the feeling of euphoria, even before they had left?

That night, they held on to each other, seeking consolation and assurance in each other's arms.

"It will all be all right, Sarah. It will all be all right," he whispered, stroking her hair until she fell asleep.

94

"Kendal," explained Bob, while they were driving back to the cabin. "It is a small town in the South Lakeland district of Cumbria, with a history going back to Roman times, as witnessed by a ruined fort known locally as Watercrook. It has a small population of less than twenty thousand and a west coast marine climate—mild winters and moderately warm summers.

"The Kendal Museum is one of the oldest in the country, and there are several art galleries mounting important exhibitions. The locals are somewhat reserved but friendly once they know you. Their dialect is basically a Cumbrian variant, but you won't have a problem understanding.

"There is a small, charming house along the River Kent, a shop with an apartment above it. George Romney, the well-known British painter, used to have his studio there in the mid-eighteenth century. The house is bought and available to you. An account has been opened at the local bank and a deposit made, which is described as the inheritance you received from your wealthy aunt in Holland. It will be enough to last for many years, and there should be enough left when this terrible war is over and you decide to return to Amsterdam."

Both Sarah and Salomon were speechless.

"All the documents needed are here in this envelope—the birth certificates for both of you, IDs, and a certificate of good standing from the police. A birth certificate in the name of Anton Bakker and Anne Marie De Vries. So, Mr. and Mrs. Bakker, get used to that and start calling each other by those names."

"What are we going to do there?" Salomon wanted to know, starting to get used to the idea, even welcoming it.

"They also thought of that, and by the way, 'they' are officials of the Dutch government in hiding in London, not in the least Queen Wilhelmina. Your fame as restorer of classical paintings has been forwarded to a thankful Kendal Museum, and we suggest that you establish a studio in the ground-floor shop. Sarah, sorry, I mean Anne Marie, could offer her service as *modiste* or dressmaker, which would make her quite popular in the village."

They had arrived at the cabin, and Sarah invited them in.

Suzan looked around her and remarked, "Anne Marie, you made this place so quickly a cozy home, I am convinced you'll do the same over there."

"It won't be too difficult with Anton here close to me, but I will miss you all, I will miss Amsterdam, the life we used to live here before the apocalypse. But I am extremely thankful for everything done for us. By the way, whom do we thank?"

"No thanks due. We are still in debt to both of you."

"Bob, how will we get there?" Anton wanted to know.

"That is why they wanted Suzan and me to fill you in. We will accompany you to Antwerp. You will be traveling under your new identity. There is no ship sailing from Holland anymore after the *Bodegraven* left. But there will be a fishing boat picking you up and taking you to Liverpool. Once there, a car will be waiting to drive you to Kendal. The harbor authorities are aware of your arrival and will escort you through customs."

It was getting late. Bob and Suzan needed to leave.

Before they did, Anne Marie and Anton received a warm hug.

Afterward, it felt like the Bakkers were already on their way to a new life.

95

The Van Gend en Loos truck and trailer with a tarp now covering the crate entered the city of Amsterdam, passed the Olympic Square, drove down Lairesse Street and the Ruysdaelkade, and parked at the far side of the underpass of the Rijksmuseum. The guards were made aware of its arrival. Both had ties to the underground organization the Free Artist.

Later that night, they partly removed the tarp, changed the Cinetone signage for the Rembrandt signage, and put the tarp back.

The phone call that woke the night editor of Polygoon Profilti up was short and anonymous. "Tomorrow at noon, Rembrandt's *Night Watch* will leave the Rijksmuseum." That was all.

But it was enough for him to jump into action. The first thing he did was call his friend at De *Telegraaf* newspaper. The men exchanged hot tips, and both benefitted from it.

The next thing was sending a message boy to Bart, the cameraman, to have a team together at ten, and then he had to send a reporter to interview whoever would be in charge. To depend on Polygoon had been a smart decision. There was a close cooperation with the

German news channels under direct supervision of Propaganda Minister Dr. Goebbels. Made aware of the publicity value of the Germans safeguarding Dutch masters from the destructive policies of the Allied enemies guaranteed coverage in Germany.

Finally, he made a blank space reservation for the item, to appear the next day in the newsreel of all cinemas.

It was long before noon when several news reporters, photographers, and a Polygoon film crew gathered in front of the museum. There was even a German reporter and photographer. Twenty to twelve, a spokesman of the museum was available to be interviewed. To the questions about what was going to happen to *The Night Watch*, where it was going, and why, the answers were simply that it was no longer safe, with increasing Allied bombardments, to keep it in the unprotected museum building. It would be driven to Heemskerk and stored in a specially constructed bunker vault, together with other masterpieces.

When the driver and a helper climbed into the truck, they were bombarded with questions, but they just smiled, shrugged their shoulders, and waved at the cameras.

When the truck left, loudly blowing its horn, two policemen on motorcycles with sidecars, carrying passengers armed with automatic weapons, drove in front.

A short caravan of cars followed all the way to the west coast, those inside hoping to witness the placement of a national treasure in the bunker.

The Polygoon Filmnews report appeared two days later, after

the proposed text was scrutinized and altered by Germany. The cameraman first showed a previous shot of *The Night Watch* and then the Rijksmuseum and the departing truck, zooming in on the crate and the text "DE NACHTWACHT. REMBRANDT. RIJKSMUSEUM," followed by a shot of the truck arriving at the bunker site and eight men manually carrying the crate through large metal doors into the vault.

The voice of the announcer, sounding like he was announcing the departure of a train from the station, explained, "With the increasing bombardments of enemy planes targeted at Dutch cities and killing thousands of civilians, Holland's art treasures are in extreme danger. The masterwork of the Aryan Germanic painter Rembrandt van Rijn is on its way to join other masterworks, to be protected from barbarian destruction, in the air-safe building German troops constructed in the coast city of Heemskerk."

"That should do it!" exclaimed Sandberg with a sigh, addressing Roell and Bolkestein, while Trip poured small glasses of Dutch Genever. They had just returned from the Tivoli Theater, where they went to watch the Polygoon Journal and suffered through one of Leni Riefenstahl's propaganda films. Handing one glass to each of them, he raised his. "Gentlemen, from here, it is in the hands of the one mightier than all of us. May He bless the outcome of this operation."

"Proost!" (cheers) they all answered, emptying the strong liquor in one swig in a centuries-old tradition.

96

Field Marshal Göring was dressed in a light blue uniform of his own design, with large white lapels and covered with decorations. His facial expression grim, he marched through the long art wing of Carinhall.

Rosenberg followed at a respectable five paces ... terrified.

Göring stopped in front of a large, empty space on the wall. To the left and right of it were a Vermeer, Velasquez, Pieter Lastman, and Frans Hals.

Pointing with his bejeweled marshal baton, he shouted, "What do you see there?"

Rosenberg almost fainted and then stammered, "N-nothing, Herr Field Marshal."

"Exactly ... exactly, and why is that, you little cockroach?"

This time, Rosenberg just stared at the empty wall. He could feel his heartbeat behind his eyes. He started shaking.

"Let me tell *you*, you twitchy little maggot. It is because there should by now have been a very large painting, and instead, when

I receive guests, they will walk by this embarrassing empty space. Now guess who is embarrassing me, maggot?"

The furious marshal kept silent for a moment and then, in a very slow movement, pointed the baton at Rosenberg, who was close to crying and wetting himself.

"Me, Herr Field Marshal?" he whispered, hardly audible.

"Aha, indeed, you, and which painting do you think this valuable space is reserved for?" He now lifted Rosenberg's chin with the baton, so the terror-stricken man had to look him in the eyes. "Well, my cheating, self-enriching personal art adviser, which famous painting should be there?"

"*The N-Night Watch*, Herr Field Marshal, Rembrandt's *Night Watch*."

"Ah, lieber Gott, the maggot has brains, and where is my painting, smartass?"

"Still in the Rijksmuseum in Amsterdam, Herr Field Marshal, and Seyss-Inquart—"

"Maul halten ... Seyss-Inquart, Seyss-Inquart, am I now the subordinate of a measly governor of a tiny part of our Grosz Deutsches Reich, our German Empire?"

"No, Herr Field Marshal, but—"

"Listen, good Rosenberg." Göring pretended to have cooled down a bit, the whole charade had been theater, and he always enjoyed the impact it had on people. "Let *me* tell *you* where *The Night Watch* is; it is nicely stored away in a bunker in a small coastal town called Heemskerk in Holland, with the kind assistance of

The Fake Rembrandt

our troops there. So now you know where it is and where it should be, what will you do about it?"

Sensing that his execution might still be postponed, the man, his jacket wet now from perspiration, stammered, "I-I will get it, Herr Field Marshal."

"Ach so, you will get it. Now I even start to believe you, and how, may I ask, do you think you would accomplish that miracle?"

Rosenberg slowly regained his composure; a plan started to form in his distressed brain.

"I will need your written authorization, Herr Field Marshal."

"You will have no such thing. You will have to use the authority I bestowed on you as my art adviser—is that clear?"

"Of course, Herr Field Marshal. May I ask if the field marshal thinks of transporting it to Germany on his private train?"

"Nein, you will have to arrange transportation yourself, using our military vehicles. You will bring it to Carinhall as a gift of the thankful Dutch nation. Once it hangs where it belongs, right there ..." He pointed with his baton to the empty wall again. " ... the führer may be willing to let me have it; however, if he demands it, I will not refuse, but at least it does not appear that I took possession of it to interfere with Hitler's wishes. Understood?"

Rosenberg understood and quickly grasped the cunning strategy.

"One last word, Rosenberg, if within the next two weeks, the painting does not hang on my wall, I will donate you to my most loyal Gestapo friends, and may God then have your failing soul."

97

The two German guards at the entrance of the bunker were bored to death.

Okay, standing watch at a bunker with some large iron doors that no one could open anyway without the key he, as the sergeant, kept in his pocket was better than being at the front but still ... They put you in this uniform for something different from just standing there, watching the two low-down Dutch policemen at the gate feeling very important. They hardly spoke a word of German, so it was no use trying to communicate with them. All the better. They walked a few times around the bunker every day, but other than that, there was not a damn thing to do.

A week earlier, he had shot a deer, which was a welcome addition to the tasteless military food. These cooks should be court-martialed. The big brass should be made to subsist on that crap for just one week; it would result in drastic improvements.

And two weeks earlier, suddenly, after dark, when he had the night patrol, a whole regiment of important people, German officers and Dutch guys, had showed up. After he handed them the key, one of them showed some kind of authorization but hey, the responsibility was with the highest-ranking officer anyway. They carried an enormous roll out, something like a huge carpet, loaded it onto a large truck, and disappeared in the night.

And then a couple of days ago, in the afternoon, another circus arrived. They talked to the policemen at the gate, who jumped to attention like real soldiers, and then two motorcycles with sidecars approached, grim-looking assholes like the ones at the gate, holding a weapon like it was an umbrella. "The key?" asked one of them, probably not interested in a discussion.

"On whose authority?"

The police officer produced a document signed by some colonel with sufficient seals and signatures to open the central bank of Germany, so he complied. Then a truck and trailer backed up to the front. Two guys jumped out and started to remove a tarp from a large crate on the trailer. A German press photographer approached and told the guards, "This is a news reel ordered directly by Dr. Goebbels. Please put your gun away and help those men bring the crate inside."

They did. The crate was heavy, but they managed, especially when the two police gate rodents, seeing the cameras, offered to help. Photographers took pictures from all sides.

It took less than an hour. He received the key back, checked if the doors were properly locked, and then continued his daily routine.

Just before dawn, a loud explosion startled them.

It came from the area clearly marked "Trespassing forbidden, minefield." Did a deer step on a mine?

But the blood-curdling cries that followed were clearly human. The sergeant walked to the barbed wire. About one hundred yards into the field, he noticed a heap of what once had been a human being, screaming for help, not able to move without legs. His cries for help turned into sobs.

A local poacher, who was used to snaring rabbits in that field, thought his prey worth risking his life for. He had no chance of survival; neither could he be approached. The sergeant felt sorry for the poor bastard and with one shot, stopped his suffering.

He went back to the bunker, leaned against a wall, and with trembling hands, lit a cigarette.

To lose your life over a Goddamn rabbit, he thought.

98

Rosenberg sat down on the chair in front of the large oak desk that the senior officer behind it offered.

"What can I do for you this time, Rosenberg?" asked SS Lieutenant Colonel Bachmeier. "Coffee?"

"Yes, please, I need one badly."

Rosenberg and Bachmeier knew each other well. The assistance of the senior officer had been of great help in assuring that Miedl would sell most of the Goudstikker collection to Göring through Rosenberg, for less than a tenth of the market value. That Rosenberg doubled the price without Göring being aware of it benefitted both him and an appreciative Bachmeier. It took the SS officer's convincing persuasion to ensure that Miedl would not talk. In addition, Rosenberg delivered an original Duerer and a Holbein to Bachmeier's villa outside Heilbronn in Baden-Wurttemberg.

"I thought Fatso was going to kill me," Rosenberg lamented.

The corpulent field marshal was secretly known as "Der Dicke," the fat one.

"He summoned me to Carinhall, and the moment I arrived,

I could tell from the way he looked at me that he might have me hanged."

"What did you do, steal his nail polish?"

"I wish ... No, I am in deep shit, Bachmeier. The self-styled art collector and connoisseur has his eyes on *The Night Watch*. The Rembrandts he already has are apparently not enough to suit his exquisite taste."

"Carinhall looks like a bloody Louvre, and it is never enough. Somebody showed him a Polygoon Profilti film journal that appeared in Germany, moving *The Night Watch* to that bunker in Heemskerk. Now all I have to do is go get it and deliver it to Carinhall, compliments of a thankful Dutch population."

"Why is that?"

"Oh, Fatso is smart enough. He knows very well that a painting like Milo's *Venus*, the *Mona Lisa*, or Rembrandt's *Night Watch* are on Hitler's list for the Volks Museum in Germania, the führer's Fata-Morgana capital of Grosz Deutschland that Albert Speer is designing for him. If he finds out that Fatso is becoming too greedy, the shit hits the fan. So he came up with this brilliant idea that the people donated it; then if Hitler finds out, he can always just have it sent to him."

Bachmeier laughed. "That scheming son of a bitch. So now you just want me to get you Holland's most precious national art treasure?" he asked sarcastically.

"No, Bachmeier, but I will need your help. I believe I have enough authority here—everybody thinks I work for Göring—to

The Fake Rembrandt

take possession of it. But I will need your presence there when I do and a large military truck to take the crate to Carinhall."

"That should not be too difficult, then what?"

"Well, nothing really other than I may be saving my neck, and of course, I will explain to Göring that it cost me dearly to pull it off. I will make a stop on my way back at Heilbronn and hand Mrs. Bachmeier a thick envelope with your compliments."

"Is friendship not a nice, profitable thing, Rosenberg? Just let me know when."

The officer rose from his chair, walked around the desk, and then shook hands. When his visitor had left, he leaned back in his chair, boots on the desk, cut the tip of a fine Dutch cigar, lit it, and blew smoke rings toward the ceiling. Then he took a sip of the Courvoisier cognac in the crystal tumbler on the side table.

"War," he contemplated, "can be a profitable thing indeed."

99

By then, the guards at the art bunker in Heemskerk were used to surprise visits, so when the large military truck arrived, together with an escort of soldiers and an SS staff car, the gates opened before anybody asked.

Lieutenant Colonel Bachmeier ordered them to open the metal doors; he and a civilian man entered, switched on the lights, and went to look for a crate marked "Rembrandt." They soon found what they were looking for, but Rosenberg was puzzled. A crook he might be, but he was not a stupid one, and what he found here could hardly contain *The Night Watch* he knew so well.

"I need to see it," he said to Bachmeier.

Pointing at the soldiers waiting outside in front of the building, he shouted, "Du, aufmachen!" (Open the crate!).

It took a nerve-racking twenty minutes to unscrew the lid and to lift the brown-paper-wrapped painting out of its hiding. When the paper was taken off, Rosenberg was both flabbergasted and terrified.

The painting, although quite big, was smaller than it should be.

A closer inspection showed that nothing was cut off the sides, as had been done ages ago. But there seemed to be no mistake—this was a Rembrandt.

"I need to check the painting, to make sure that no damage was done," he lied to Bachmeier. "That will take some time. Do you mind?"

"Not at all. Go ahead. That painting never ceases to amaze me. I have seen it several times but never can get enough of it."

Rosenberg checked the back of the painting, sniffed the wood, scratched it, and checked the nails and the canvas; he could not find anything wrong with it.

He took a magnifying glass from his pocket and looked closely at every part of the painting. He then uncorked a small bottle of pure alcohol he had brought with him, doused a piece of cotton wool, and rubbed it on the lower corner, a tiny spot, but nothing indicated that the paint was not very old. He zoomed in on the craquelure and found it just the way he expected.

Rosenberg had seen enough forgeries.

There was no doubt; this was a real Rembrandt.

But how could it be? Paintings didn't just shrink a foot on all sides.

The only possibility was that this was a study, a painting Rembrandt made to assure himself that the nontraditional composition would work.

But why was it never published?

Ah, but there was an easy answer: *The Night Watch*, property of the city of Amsterdam, would draw crowds in the hundreds of thousands, maybe in the millions, and why would the city or the

Rijksmuseum jeopardize such a lucrative interest in fine art by admitting there were two *Night Watches*?

His first apprehension mitigated, he realized that Bachmeier, not really an art simpleton, never thought something was wrong.

Then why would the field marshal?

In the euphoric excitement of owning the painting, Göring would not realize that the smaller size should tell him something. It was still large, still a real Rembrandt as far as Rosenberg could tell, and it would fill the terrifying empty spot in the art wing of Carinhall.

"Thank you for your patience, Bachmeier. Everything is fine, no damage at all, but we have to be very careful rewrapping it and putting the foam back around it."

The crate was closed and loaded on the large military vehicle. Rosenberg jumped in; he would not let the crate out of his sight until it turned into the gate of the field marshal's estate.

The military truck, carrying the crate safely secured, strapped down, and resting on a bed of rubber foam, crossed the German border at Glanerbrug, east of Enschede, without too much trouble.

The Kübelwagen Bachmeier had sent to escort the truck to the border needed to return, so only the driver and Rosenberg remained. The curious guards at the border wanted them to open the crate, so they could convince themselves that there was indeed a painting in the crate and nothing else, weapons for example. But Rosenberg insisted, and after he showed them documents that he was a Göring-appointed art consultant, they reluctantly let them through, writing names and numbers down.

The Fake Rembrandt

Rosenberg started to be concerned that without an escort, a lot of trouble might still lie ahead before he would be able to deliver the painting to Carinhall.

He stopped at the old hotel Hermanns Hoehe in Steinfurt, some twenty-three miles from Enschede. While instructing the driver to stay in the truck, he went inside, asked for a table, ordered lunch and a lager beer, and then went to the phone booth.

He dialed the number that he knew should only be used in extreme urgencies, but since his life was at stake, he thought it was.

Two telephone operators and a secretary later, a familiar voice shouted, "Yes, what is it?"

"Rosenberg, Herr Field Marshal, I have the package you are waiting for; however, I am alone with a driver and afraid that something might happen on my way to your estate."

"Where are you?"

"In Steinfurt at the Landes Hotel Hermanns Hoehe."

"Are you trying to be funny, minnow?"

"Oh no, absolutely not, Herr Field Marshal. It is the first stop I could think of from where I could ask for an escort and keep my eyes on the truck."

"Stay there until I send some of my men. They will ask for my package. I will be at Carinhall when you arrive." The phone went silent.

When he returned from his phone call, he noticed that he was the only person in the restaurant. *So much for ordering a table*, he thought.

Rosenberg took a big swig from the cool lager beer served in a large stoneware mug and then bit into the rye bread with speck.

He was still worried. With the help of several of his colleagues, he had provided Göring with a list of the most important paintings, sculptures, tapestries, books, silverware, and porcelain from museums and known private collections in occupied countries.

The Night Watch was certainly on that list with a photograph, but if there was more than that, the name and date of the artist plus the location of the painting, Rosenberg did not remember. If the exact measurements were in the book and the Fat One checked, Rosenberg would be toast. Just the thought of it made his heart beat faster again.

Where would the escort come from? Not from Berlin, way too far.

The closest unit of Göring's special forces, men unquestioningly loyal to his person, was outside of Muenster. It might take them twenty minutes to ready themselves and then close to an hour before they could be there.

He sent a large coffee and slices of black bread with speck to the driver, went to the washroom and then back into the empty dusky restaurant, stretched out on a couch in the far corner, and fell asleep.

He never noticed that the waiter, who had overheard Rosenberg's phone conversation with Göring from the switchboard in reception, picked up the phone and whispered, "Grey Wolf, thirty minutes."

100

Rosenberg was still asleep when a motorcycle arrived. It took a right behind the truck to the back of the building so no one would spot the two men entering the restaurant through the kitchen in the back. They were in their late twenties or early thirties. They walked self-assuredly straight to the provision cellar. The man who had made the phone call joined them.

"What is it, Bernhardt?" asked the tallest of the two.

"Not sure, but I overheard a phone call between that person sleeping in the restaurant and Göring. There seems to be a very important package he is instructed to deliver to Carinhall; it must be in that truck outside. I thought the organization needed to know, especially because Göring is sending an escort; it should be something big."

The two men looked at each other. "Good job, Bernhardt. Thanks. We're off," one of them said. Then they disappeared as quickly as they had arrived, remembering the license plate of the truck, noticing there was only a driver in it and a large crate.

The two men drove at top speed to the impressive administrative building of the Friedrich Wilhelms University in Muenster. They parked the motorcycle in front of the entrance, walked as quickly as they could without suggesting panic through the large entrance hall, and then knocked on a door with the sign "Konrektor" (vice president).

Vice President Rudolf Winkler was among the many in wartime Germany's academic circles who despised the vulgar Nazi politics. He was forced to witness the disastrous and inhumane discrimination against many of his brilliant Jewish colleagues, who for decennia had contributed to the excellent reputation of the academy they were forcibly removed from to make the university "Judenfrei," or free of Jews. Winkler was a secret leader in the regional organized resistance, with ties to the Rote Kapelle.

He listened to the briefing from the young foot soldiers, asked a few pointed questions, and then thanked them. The men left.

Winkler picked up the phone and called two of his colleagues, inviting them to come to his office right away. Both were members of the same underground movement.

Professor Brehmann was a gifted physicist with the rare ability to make complicated theorems like Feynman's diagrams understandable to even the least capable of his students. He used to theorize with his Jewish colleagues about yet undiscovered fields in quantum theory.

Professor Buchholz was a somewhat eccentric mathematician,

resembling a painter or a sculptor more than a scientist. According to his peers, he might one day be up for a Nobel prize.

"What do you think?" asked Winkler after giving as much detail as the two young men provided him with.

"Damned strange, Rudolf. Why would Göring, who must have assembled hundreds, if not more, valuable paintings in his vulgar castle, ship just one by truck while all others traveled first class on his private train?"

"Good point, Heinrich. It must be something very secret and for his eyes only. Why, otherwise, would he send his SS goons from that murderous unit in Muenster? No art, I am convinced of that. He would never go through the trouble and would just leave it up to others to deliver the crate to his doorstep."

All agreed and remained silent for quite a while.

The only sound in the room, which was daily checked for possible hidden microphones, was the ticking of a large ornamental cuckoo clock. Brehmann ended the silence.

"It may be far-fetched, but I have an idea."

101

"What is less known in the public domain," Brehmann continued, "is the animosity between Hitler and Göring. Göring's star shone bright before 1940; the ace pilot of the First World War calculated his chances with Hitler. Although in his soul despising the Austrian corporal who floated to the surface, he decided to bet on him, ostensibly with success. But then the disastrous outcome for Germany of the Battle of Britain changed Hitler's admiration for Göring's Luftwaffe. Too many German planes were lost, and the planned invasion of Britain indefinitely postponed.

"But the field marshal was not satisfied with his air force in a secondary, supportive role to the tanks and artillery in the blitzkrieg and lent a willing ear to opportunistic scientists. They explained the potential of Otto Hahn's discovery of nuclear fission, taking place in Germany in December 1938. What was called an *Uranmaschine*, a nuclear reactor, was already under construction, as were heavy water production and an isotope separator.

"It was enough for Göring to pull the activities close to home and move the center of activities to Oranienburg. It is all still in its infancy, but among scientists, the potential of a source of energy unknown to mankind is certain. I, for one, am in agreement with that.

"The project is hampered in its development as a result of all our Jewish colleagues being kicked out of the diverse disciplines. Hitler's interests are far from science, and he rather supports bigger and better canons and tanks and his Speer-designed Fata Morganas.

"It has been rumored that Göring makes large amounts of money available to the project, under certain conditions. He aspires to one day be the number-one in Germany, based on the fearsome potential of nuclear energy."

"What are those certain conditions, Hans?"

"Well, that is what worries me most. One can think of the benefits of unlimited energy at our disposal. I received a coded report from Lise Meitner, Otto Hahn's colleague and friend, who fled to Holland. She is very informed about the process. She confided in me that scientists involved with the developments in Germany are concerned about Göring's ambitious intentions and are worried that he will direct them to focus on a nuclear weapon.

"Some of the science essential in the complicated processes has left Germany with the scientists who were part of the team. Without that information—the calculations, the mathematics, their individual contributions to the physics and science of quantum theory, the drawings—it is doubtful that Göring will ever have the nuclear-based weapon arsenal that he is dreaming of, before this destructive war ends.

"My concern is, friends, that the crate could contain exactly that kind of treasure and not some painting, which the field marshal needs to add to his vast collection."

"My God, you may be right, Hans. that could be disastrous. Now what do we do?" uttered Winkler.

"That may be a problem for others to deal with." Rudolf suggested.

102

The others Rudolf Winkler referred to consisted of a section of the resistance in North-Rhine-Westphalia involved in sabotage and espionage. The members represented all levels and professions of society and even included senior officers of the army, opposing the Nazification of the forces. The organization was, in good German tradition, layered with three men in charge of actions and taking ultimate responsibility, then units involved with intelligence, communication, infiltration, finance, execution, and sabotage. Although there were lines to other underground organizations, each sector operated rather independently.

The trio in charge now concentrated on the information that had arrived by courier thirty minutes earlier in a blank envelope marked, "Urgent."

It concerned the possible interception of an escorted truck-transport with instructions to deliver the truck and cargo to a given shelter.

"Where are they presently?" the person leading the trio asked.

"I just contacted Gray Wolf; two Kubelwagens with eight of Göring's elite troops arrived. They could be on their way anytime soon. It is a long trip, so Grey Wolf offered them lunch to give us time, which they accepted. They are heavily armed; the truck driver apparently is not. Grey Wolf brought him some lunch earlier and checked him out."

"Good. Then let's have a look at the map. We may assume that there will be one car in front and the other one in the back."

"We must take them before Osnabrück. What about Lotte? We have several men from our team in Osnabrück who could be there in time. They can wait in the Teutoburg Forest, west of the city, and take them there. Easiest to get rid of the Kubelwagens and the contents."

"Where should they take the truck with whatever is in the crate?"

"To Ibbenbueren. There are some dilapidated buildings from the old iron mine often used by our men; they want the truck in one of them."

"What about those men though, eight in the Kubels and two in the truck?"

"The eight are, each one of them, volunteers of Göring's SS Sonderkommandos. They are murderers by choice, selected for dirty work. I would kill them gladly with my own hands if I had the opportunity. The two should be taken prisoner."

"How do we get the necessary men together?"

"Only one way, you take my car. Leave now. Assuming one

hour for them to depart after taking lunch, you have about two hours ahead of them. Stop at Café Zum Oxen, ask for Dieter, and follow him; he'll take it from there."

The man giving the instructions picked up the phone and dialed a number.

"Hermann's Höhe, how can I help you?"

"My name is Wertheim. I am supposed to have lunch with eight of my friends, but I was held up. If they have arrived before me, please feed them well. Give them whatever they want to drink. I may still need some time."

Grey Wolf understood.

The lunch was pork knuckle with sauerkraut, peeled potatoes, sausages and fat gravy, Rhine wine compliments of the house, and a large ceramic jug of Bockbier, the strong, dark German lager. None of them wanted to bow to his comrades. They all drank whatever was served. The lunch took an hour and a half, and the men were all a bit intoxicated.

They then climbed into the Kubelwagens after shouting at Rosenberg, "Mach Schnell, du Schweinhund" (Hurry up, asshole). The car in front indicated for the driver to follow him, adjusting the speed to the much slower truck. The second car followed.

103

"Is Dieter available?"

The man behind the bar counter dropped the jug he was cleaning with a dirty rag. "Follow me."

They went to a small room in the back of the alehouse Bierstuebe Zum Oxen.

It took less than ten minutes to verify each other's legitimacy and explain to Dieter what was expected of him and his men. Understanding that time was of the essence, both went on their way.

Lining up his men and instructing them where to meet in the forest outside of Lotte took thirty-five minutes. Dieter was the first to arrive. Within ten minutes, a dozen of his men arrived, taking strategic positions on both sides of the road, well hidden among the bushes. Two of their cars were parked in the middle of the road, as if an accident had occurred, one car with an open hood and passenger door askew against the side of another, completely blocking the road.

They waited. All in all, it had taken more than an hour.

About a mile back, at a fork in the road, two workers closed one stretch and guided the traffic—actually only three cars passed—to the right. As soon as the convoy was in sight, they closed off the right and directed it to the left where a roadblock awaited them.

Then everything happened quickly.

The first Kübelwagen driver stepped on the brakes just in time, the truck hitting its back. The second car skidded off the road, where the four were shot before they knew what had happened. The four SS fanatics in the front car tried to get to their weapons, but three of them were shot. The third, before he too died, was able to fire a round, wounding one of the resistance fighters.

The driver and Rosenberg jumped out of the truck, white as sheets, shouting, "Nicht schiessen! Nicht schiessen!" (Don't shoot! Don't shoot!)

Two men quickly tied both, blindfolded them, and put them in the back of the truck.

Clearing the road, they moved the truck a few hundred yards ahead.

After taking the weapons, watches, and billfolds—everything of value—from the bodies, they drove both Kubelwagens with the corpses in them in opposite directions a spread of a few hundred yards. They started the cars, put a rock on the accelerator, and then with a stick, pushed them into gear and jumped to the sides of the road. The cars collided with an enormous bang.

They doused the wreckage with gasoline and then threw a match at it.

Dieter and a second man jumped into the truck and the others into their cars. The whole operation had taken less than fifteen minutes.

The papers would only talk about an accident, the high brass being told that it was an ordinary case of drunken troopers. The innkeeper would attest that the group departed drunk. It was a policy of Dr. Goebbels not to let the public know about sabotage activities against the regime; it simply did not happen in Hitler's Reich.

One member of the group took his wounded comrade back to town; the wound in his side was painful but not critical. The others and the truck with two men blindfolded and handcuffed in the back, fearing for their lives, drove to Ibbenbueren.

104

Nobody paid any special attention when the large military truck turned into the town and then continued to the old mining side. The doors of the large central building opened, and the truck drove in. The doors immediately closed again.

The team members had arrived earlier and taken strategic positions around the building and from behind the remnants of other structures on the periphery.

Dieter and his comrade jumped out of the truck and greeted Dr. Winkler, Professor Brehmann, his colleague Professor Buchholz, and two other official-looking men they did not know.

"Thank you, Dieter. I assume all went well?"

"As well as could be expected, sir. Nothing serious."

"What about the escort?"

"Their services to the Reich for lethal interference are no longer available, sir."

"And the cars?"

"A regrettable accident, sir. Ran into each other and then caught fire."

"Well, good job, I guess. Now, please give us a hand and open that crate in the truck. I hope you brought the tools I requested."

"Indeed, sir. Will take just a sec."

A long sec, the large crate was very well built and screwed together. At least eighty large screws needed to be undone. Dieter and his helper worked from the bottom to the sides and then from the center of the top to both sides, until only two screws held the cover, with the marking "DE NACHTWACHT. REMBRANDT. RIJKSMUSEUM."

With a man on each side, holding the cover, Dieter unscrewed the last two screws, and the cover was off.

There was a large package inside. It was nearly as large as the crate, except for some foam strips around it. The parcel was wrapped in paper sheets taped to each other. It resembled a giant birthday present. They lifted it from the crate.

Professor Brehman started to carefully remove the wrapping, handing it to Professor Buchholz. "Please hang on to this, Heinrich. We may want to check this later."

What appeared was a large oil painting, old, as one could easily tell from the paint and the craquelure.

Winkler gasped. "Rembrandt," he said reverently. "*The Night Watch*? Good God, no wonder the secrecy surrounding the transportation. That damned Göring stole Rembrandt's masterpiece from Holland."

Both professors were silent.

"So nothing important." Dieter wanted to know, not believing

The Fake Rembrandt

this whole operation was to intercept the delivery of a bloody painting.

"Not in the way we thought, Dieter, but unimportant, no. How important exactly, we may all one day understand, hopefully in better times, in a more civilized society."

After they had inspected the paper for possible secret messages, it was soon clear this had nothing to do with science, only with robbery.

"Take those two men from the truck, Dieter, will you?"

Addressing a sweating, trembling, half-sick remnant of the once cocky Rosenberg, Winkler asked shortly, "Who are you?"

The terrified man, who could not overhear the discussions while in the back of the truck, not knowing who these people were or why they would ambush the truck and kill eight heavily armed elite SS troopers, forgot his own name for a moment.

"Rosenberg," he stammered at last.

"And that man?"

"Just a driver."

Addressing Dieter, Winkler said, "Shoot them."

Both men fell on their knees, crying and begging for mercy, Dieter and his comrade took them by the arm, raised them up, and started to walk.

"Hold it," ordered Winkler. "Bring them here."

Changing his normally civilized use of language to the local vernacular, Winkler looked both men straight in the eyes, first the driver and then Rosenberg.

He then instructed his men to put the driver back in the truck.

Alone now with a devastated, crying Rosenberg, he said, "What the hell was you suppose to do with a damn painting?"

"Orders of Field Marshal Göring, sir. I have nothing to do with it. I was only instructed to make sure it got to him or I would be killed."

"So now I should kill you anyway, shouldn't I?"

"I did nothing wrong, sir. Please, sir, I have nothing to do with it."

"I don't give a shit about yourself or a painting. We were thinking there was a load of gold or something. I won't kill you or the other guy, not yet anyway." To Dieter, he said, "Put him in the truck too."

Then, alone with Dieter, he said, "Make them believe this was a robbery, assuming there was treasure in the truck. Do you have a place to hide the truck for the time being and lock up those two until we know what to do next?"

"No problem, sir."

"Then please do. Don't harm the poor men. I put the fear of God into them for a reason. Make sure nobody comes even close to that painting or the crate."

"Won't happen, sir"

After the painting was wrapped carefully again and the crate closed, Dieter and his friend left with the truck.

Winkler and both professors left for Muenster, and the rest of the men each went their own way.

105

Back in his office the next day, Winkler picked up the phone and dialed a number in Berlin. When it was answered after ringing only three times, he said, "I would like to speak to Marga."

"Sorry, you must have dialed the wrong number," answered Harro.

Winkler locked his office door.

He moved a painting from the wall, put it on the ground, opened the small door in the space behind it with a key from his pocket watch chain, and then picked up the microphone of the short-wave sender and receiver. He soon had contact.

"We intercepted a truck with a Rembrandt painting destined for Carinhall, two men. What do we do? Over."

Silence on Harro's end.

"Was it *The Night Watch*? Over."

"Positive. Over."

"Utmost importance, send truck with painting to destination. Repeat, send painting to destination. Confirm. Over."

"Will send painting to destination. Over and out."

He locked the door, puzzled, and then put the painting back on the wall.

So there must have been a reason after all to treat this consignment differently than all the other stolen art decorating Ali Baba's robber's cave. The direct response from Rote Kapelle, however, indicated they were in the loop, so he would not question the decision and would send the truck on its way.

But first, he'd have a little talk with those two on board.

He met them again in a small cottage outside town, under the gun of Dieter.

"Our leader decided to let you go," Winkler said, pretending not to be too happy about it. "But we know who you are and where you are at all times. You say one word about this thing, and we'll have you ripped apart. Do you understand?"

Both men nodded fervently.

"I said, 'Do you understand?'"

Now both confirmed loudly, "Yes, sir, we do. Not a word, sir."

"Dieter, take them to the truck and send them on their way. Let our people keep an eye on them until they arrive."

"Will be done, sir."

Not until they arrived at Brunswick did Rosenberg gather the courage to stop, against the protests of the driver, and phone Göring from a road tavern.

The field marshal was livid.

"Where Goddamn it have you been, you vermin? Who do you

think you are to let me send an escort and then make me wait? Give me one of my men, now."

Rosenberg was shaking like a French poodle. Hardly able to control his voice, he answered, "Dead, sir."

Then the unbelievable happened; the field marshal laughed. He *roared*. Then, finally, he said, "What do you mean, dead? You killed them all, Little Tom Thumb? Put them on the phone."

"We were ambushed, Herr Field Marshal. Some street vagabonds held us up, killed everybody."

Now there was an eerie silence on the other end of the line.

Then, he asked, "What about the painting?"

"Still in the crate on the truck, Herr Field Marshal."

"Where are you now?"

"Brunswick, Herr Field Marshal."

"Then I give you three hours to be here, or my dogs will have your nuts for breakfast ... you understand?"

"Yes, Herr Field Marshal." He added, "And screw you, fat son of a bitch," but that was after he put the phone down.

106

It was a cocktail party like Carinhall had seldom seen before. Once the truck arrived, the crate was taken into one of the side buildings, and the painting appeared undamaged in excellent condition. Göring was delighted. Still calling Rosenberg names, he nevertheless gave him a large bonus in addition to the sum Rosenberg claimed he needed to bribe the people in Holland. As promised, he later brought a thick envelope to Bachmeier's spouse.

Göring cared little about the killed men. If the suckers could not win a skirmish with a bunch of vagabonds, they deserved to be eliminated.

Everybody who wanted to be invited, needed to be invited, or could not avoid being invited was present. Decorations on mess kits from land, sea, and air forces shone brighter than stars on a wintery night. Ladies glittered in diamonds and pearls with cleavages like in a posh brothel.

The host was dressed in a newly designed evening uniform, extravagant and pompous, like France's King Louis XIV.

Waiters dressed in livery served sumptuous hors d'oeuvres

from large silver plates held in white-gloved hands—caviar from Russia, foie gras from France, white truffles from Italy, salmon from Denmark, a cornucopia of delicacies in unlimited supply.

Exquisite vintage wines were served and cigars from Holland offered.

Like a peacock, Göring marched the guests through the art wing, pointing to paintings, statues, and tapestries, giving shallow information as the connoisseur he considered himself to be.

Not conscious of the vulgarity of extraordinary opulence, he bragged about his art collection. His twisted way of thinking considered masterpieces, paid for far below market value with stolen money or confiscated from Jews transported to camps, as legally acquired. He presented himself to the melee of guests, many well educated, some of old noble families, in bombastic language as the custodian of true Germanic art, which only he valued and would protect for posterity.

Many suffered in silence at the destiny of so many great art pieces in the hands of an ignorant, dangerous fool but kept silent.

The purpose of the cocktail event was to impress the audience with Rembrandt's masterpiece, now hanging on the wall in the art wing, with a Han van Meegeren's Vermeers on either side, like the crucified Jesus and the two criminals.

One of the guests, an obviously aristocratic high officer, gazed long minutes at *The Night Watch*, absorbing every detail. He stepped away from it and then took a monocle from his inside pocket and moved close to the painting to better judge.

Göring stood there, inflated like a frog, proud as if he had painted the masterpiece himself, waiting for praise.

"Extraordinary, absolutely magnificent," commented Baron Oberst Weinberg zu Falkenhause.

107

Göring's *Night Watch* remained the centerpiece of his extensive, criminally acquired collection until the end of the war. Visitors were systematically marched through the art wing and made to listen to the field marshal's boasting about Rembrandt's masterpiece. He never bothered to ask an opinion from experts; one just does not ask for a certificate of originality when it concerns so famous a painting. He rearranged that section of his exhibition when Miedl sold him *Christ with the Adulteress*, a Vermeer painted by Dutch art forger Han van Meegeren and a second Vermeer by the same hand.

With the inevitable end of the war in favor of the Allied forces in sight, he moved most of his collection to an Austrian salt mine, along with almost seven thousand art pieces looted by the Nazis. On May 17, 1945, American Captain Harry Anderson made the sensational discovery that would inspire Robert Edsel to write *The Monuments Men*, which was turned into a movie under the same title—a few pieces, among them *The Night Watch*, were missing.

Before Göring ordered a Luftwaffe air force demolition squad to blow up Carinhall on April 28, 1945, the last of his art collection, his favorites, were evacuated to Berchtesgaden.

It was chaos in Berchtesgaden those final weeks of the war. As if there was still a future for the crumbling Reich, thousands of workers continued to work at what was supposed to become Hitler's headquarters outside of Berlin. The influx of supplies by train caused congestion, as about fifteen thousand freighters arrived in less than a month. Inspite of the mayhem, Göring was still able to send three trainloads of loot; however, he still needed more capacity, so several motorcades of loaded trucks were sent as well.

One of the eight trucks in a motorcade contained a large crate marked "Rembrandt—*Night Watch*" and contained several other masterworks of mainly seventeenth-century Flemish painters. There were four men in the vehicle, the driver and his longtime army buddy in the front and two SS subalterns in the back. The driver maneuvered the truck to be last in the chain. It would take the motorcade close to twelve hours, passing through obliterated parts of the country, to reach its destination, Berchtesgaden. The two men in the back were fast asleep. After drinking the coffee from a thermos bottle the driver offered, they would never wake up again.

About five hours into the ride, the last truck had engine trouble. It stopped on the side of the road. The motorcade continued, but two SS officers following the motorcade in a Kübelwagen stopped.

"Was ist los?" (What's the matter?)

"Don't know yet," answered the driver, his head under the hood. "It just stopped. May take some time to find out."

"Well, hurry up; we need to catch up with them."

The two officers lit a cigarette, walked to the side of the road, and urinated.

The driver and his buddy shot them in the neck.

They hastily dragged the two poisoned bodies from the truck, put them in the back of the Kübelwagen, and then lifted the corpses of the SS officers and put them in the front of the car. They started the Kübelwagen and then drove it off the side of the road against a tree. They emptied a bottle of schnapps over the driver's body and then poured a can of gasoline over the car and set it on fire.

The driver closed the hood. They got back in the car, started it, and continued in the direction of Switzerland.

Aware of the danger from fanatic young SS men ignorant of the demise of their dream and trigger-happy Hitler Jugend, armed young boys shooting everyone they suspected of being a deserter, the two had taken the automatic weapons of the men they had just murdered.

At the border city of Schaffhausen, they intended to surrender and claim they wanted to bring these important masterworks to the safety of neutral Switzerland.

They were immediately arrested.

Swiss authorities took possession of the truckload, and the

paintings ended up in the safe of a bank in Basel, where some of them remained until today.

But not *The Night Watch*.

Once the war was over and people could freely travel again, numerous experts flocked to Basel to inspect what was claimed as an unknown version of *The Night Watch* by Rembrandt. Most of them considered it a wartime forgery but not all of them.

Famous Swiss art critic and Rembrandt connoisseur Dr. Stroebel insisted that this was a genuine Rembrandt, painted by the master himself and not by one of his pupils, as was also suggested.

Then a letter arrived from a Mr. Salomon Cohen, living in Amsterdam, claiming that he was the artist who made the painting early in the war, at the special request of high authorities and not for egocentric financial purposes. The details he provided did not leave any room for doubt.

It spelled the end of the history of a fake Rembrandt—until that phone call.

AUTHOR'S NOTE

It was a beautiful day of spring in 2002. I was doing some work in my library at our villa at the Lac in Cologne Bellerive, between Geneva and the French border.

There was a knock on my door, and our manservant entered. "Sir, there is a gentleman on the phone who insists he wants to talk to you."

I do not like to be disturbed when working, so I asked, "Who is it, Giovanni?"

"He did not give his name, sir, but he said it is important."

A bit irritated, I picked up the phone. "Yes?"

A Swiss German voice, no name yet. "Sir, I know you are from Holland and an art collector. I have something for sale that may really interest you. Could I have half an hour of your time?"

"What is it that may interest me, Mister ..." He then mentioned a name that could very well be an alias.

"A Rembrandt, sir."

I was dumbfounded.

"Are you still there, sir?"

"Oh yes, I am. I was just thinking, when was the last time I bought a Rembrandt over the phone from an unknown person?"

"I understand. I apologize, sir. Of course it is not a real Rembrandt, and it is not so much the painting as the story behind it."

Against my better judgment, he now had my attention. I could certainly spare half an hour to satisfy my curiosity.

"Okay, half an hour, tomorrow morning, ten thirty. Would that suit you?"

"Certainly, sir. I will be there."

When I put the phone down, I realized that I'd never given him the address, but then again, if he knew my name and phone number, I was convinced he would have done his homework. He arrived exactly on time.

When he showed me a photograph from a pile of documents pulled out of his briefcase, I was disappointed. *The Night Watch*—what else?

Then he started talking, not half an hour, half a day. I asked him to come back the following morning. Two days later, I wrote a check for the large copy that now hangs in our home. It often impresses those who have never visited the Rijksmuseum. After trying to verify his story and studying the documents that came with the transaction, I knew that one day I would write this book.

―――

Nobody knew what happened to Cohen's *The Night Watch* during the nearly seventy years after the war or who owned it. While it may have been in Switzerland, some claim it went to Russia before it returned to Switzerland.

The Cohens lived a good life in England but soon after the war returned to Amsterdam, where Salomon continued his old profession and Sarah started a new sewing shop. She made no uniforms anymore.

Bob and Suzan married and became the happy parents of a son and two daughters; they emigrated to Canada in the sixties.

Many of the brave men and woman, both in Holland and in Nazi Germany, mentioned in my book, risking their lives for something they believed in, did not see the end of the war and were executed or perished in concentration camps—some with victory in sight.

Too many perpetrators of the atrocities were never punished.

Geneva—Calgary
September 2016

CPSIA information can be obtained
at www.ICGtesting.com
Printed in the USA
LVHW090220270219
608828LV00001BA/1/P

9 781532 021008